Praise for Catherine Bybee

Wife by Wednesday

"A fun and sizzling romance, great characters that trade verbal spars like fist punches, and the dream of your own royal wedding!"
—Sizzling Hot Book Reviews, 5 Stars

"A good holiday, fireside or bedtime story."
—Manic Reviews, 4½ Stars

"A great story that I hope is the start of a new series."
—The Romance Studio, 4½ Hearts

Married by Monday

"If I hadn't already added Ms. Catherine Bybee to my list of favorite authors, after reading this book I would have been compelled to. This is a book *nobody* should miss, because the magic it contains is awesome."
—Booked Up Reviews, 5 Stars

"Ms. Bybee writes authentic situations and expresses the good and the bad in such an equal way . . . Keeps the reader on the edge of her seat."
—Reading Between the Wines, 5 Stars

"*Married by Monday* was a refreshing read and one I couldn't possibly put down."
—The Romance Studio, 4½ Hearts

Fiancé by Friday

"Bybee knows exactly how to keep readers happy . . . A thrilling pursuit and enough passion to stuff in your back pocket to last for the next few lifetimes . . . The hero and heroine come to life with each flip of the page and will linger long after readers cross the finish line."
—*RT Book Reviews*, 4½ Stars, Top Pick (Hot)

"A tale full of danger and sexual tension . . . the intriguing characters add emotional depth, ensuring readers will race to the perfectly fitting finish."
—*Publishers Weekly*

"Suspense, survival, and chemistry mix in this scintillating read."
—*Booklist*

"Hot romance, a mystery assassin, British royalty, and an alpha Marine . . . this story has it all!"
—Harlequin Junkie

Single by Saturday

"Captures readers' hearts and keeps them glued to the pages until the fascinating finish . . . romance lovers will feel the sparks fly . . . almost instantaneously."
—*RT Book Reviews*, 4½ Stars, Top Pick

"[A] wonderfully exciting plot, lots of desire, and some sassy attitude thrown in for good measure!"
—Harlequin Junkie

"Bybee concludes her popular Weekday Brides series in a gratifying way with a passionate, troubled couple who may find a happy future if they can just survive and then learn to trust each other. A compelling and entertaining mix of sexy, complicated romance and menacing suspense."

—*Kirkus Reviews*

Not Quite Dating

"It's refreshing to read about a man who isn't afraid to fall in love . . . [Jack and Jessie] fit together as a couple and as a family."

—*RT Book Reviews*, 3 Stars (Hot)

"*Not Quite Dating* offers a sweet and satisfying Cinderella fantasy that will keep you smiling long after you've finished reading."

—Kathy Altman, *USA Today*, "Happy Ever After"

"The perfect rags to riches romance . . . The dialogue is inventive and witty, the characters are well drawn out. The storyline is superb and really shines . . . I highly recommend this stand out romance! Catherine Bybee is an automatic buy for me."

—Harlequin Junkie, 4½ Hearts

Not Quite Enough

"Bybee's gift for creating unforgettable romances cannot be ignored. The third book in the Not Quite series will sweep readers away to a paradise, and they will be intrigued by the thrilling story that accompanies their literary vacation."

—*RT Book Reviews*, 4½ Stars, Top Pick

Taken by Tuesday

"[Bybee] knows exactly how to get bookworms sucked into the perfect storyline; then she casts her spell upon them so they don't escape until they reach the 'Holy Cow!' ending."

—*RT Book Reviews*, 4½ Stars, Top Pick

Seduced by Sunday

"You simply can't miss [this novel]. It contains everything a romance reader loves—clever dialogue, three-dimensional characters, and just the right amount of steam to go with that heartwarming love story."

—Brenda Novak, *New York Times* bestselling author

"Bybee hits the mark . . . providing readers with a smart, sophisticated romance between a spirited heroine and a prim hero . . . Passionate and intelligent characters [are] at the heart of this entertaining read."

—*Publishers Weekly*

Treasured by Thursday

"The Weekday Brides never disappoint and this final installment is by far Bybee's best work to date."

—*RT Book Reviews*, 4½ Stars, Top Pick

"An exquisitely written and complex story brimming with pride, passion, and pulse-pounding danger . . . Readers will gladly make time to savor this winning finale to a wonderful series."

—*Publishers Weekly*, Starred Review

Not Quite Forever

"Full of classic Bybee humor, steamy romance, and enough plot twists and turns to keep readers entertained all the way to the very last page."
—Tracy Brogan, bestselling author of the Bell Harbor series

"Magnetic . . . The love scenes are sizzling and the multi-dimensional characters make this a page-turner. Readers will look for earlier installments and eagerly anticipate new ones."
—*Publishers Weekly*

Not Quite Perfect

"This novel flows extremely well and readers will find themselves consuming the witty dialogue and strong imagery in one sitting."
—*RT Book Reviews*

"Don't let the title fool you. *Not Quite Perfect* was actually the perfect story to sweep you away and take you on a pleasant adventure. So sit back, relax, maybe pour a glass of wine, and let Catherine Bybee entertain you with Glen and Mary's playful East Coast–West Coast romance. You won't regret it for a moment."
—Harlequin Junkie, 4½ Stars

Not Quite Crazy

"This fast-paced story features credible characters whose appealing relationship is built upon friendship, mutual respect, and sizzling chemistry."
—*Publishers Weekly*

"The plot is filled with twists and turns, but instead of feeling like a never-ending roller coaster, the story maintains a quiet flow. The slow buildup of a romance allows readers to get to know the main characters as individuals and makes the romantic element more organic."

—*RT Book Reviews*

Doing It Over

"The romance between fiercely independent Melanie and charming Wyatt heats up even as outsiders threaten to derail their newfound happiness. This novel will hook readers with its warm, inviting characters and the promise for similar future installments."

—*Publishers Weekly*

"This brand-new trilogy, Most Likely To, based on yearbook superlatives, kicks off with a novel that will encourage you to root for the incredibly likable Melanie. Her friends are hilarious and readers will swoon over Wyatt, who is charming and strong. Even Melanie's daughter, Hope, is a hoot! This romance is jam-packed with animated characters, and Bybee displays her creative writing talent wonderfully."

—*RT Book Reviews*, 4 Stars

"With a dialogue full of energy and depth, and a twisting storyline that captured my attention, I would say that *Doing It Over* was a great way to start off a new series. (And look at that gorgeous book cover!) I can't wait to visit River Bend again and see who else gets to find their HEA."

—Harlequin Junkie, 4½ Stars

Staying For Good

"Bybee's skillfully crafted second Most Likely To contemporary (after *Doing It Over*) brings together former sweethearts who have not forgotten each other in the 11 years since high school. A cast of multidimensional characters brings the story to life and promises enticing future installments."

—*Publishers Weekly*

"Romance fans will be sure to cheer on former high school sweethearts Zoe and Luke right away in *Staying For Good*. Just wait until you see what passion, laughter, reconciliations, and mischief (can you say Vegas?) awaits readers this time around. Highly recommended."

—Harlequin Junkie, 4½ Stars

Making It Right

"Intense suspense heightens the scorching romance at the heart of Bybee's outstanding third Most Likely To contemporary (after *Staying For Good*). Sizzling sensual scenes are coupled with scary suspense in this winning novel."

—*Publishers Weekly*, Starred Review

Fool Me Once

"A marvelous portrait of friendship among women who have been bonded by fire."

—*Library Journal*, Best of the Year 2017

"Bybee still delivers a story that her die-hard readers will enjoy."

—*Publishers Weekly*

Half Empty

"Wade and Trina here in *Half Empty* just might be one of my favorite couples Catherine Bybee has gifted us fans with so far. Captivating, engaging, lively and dreamy, I simply could not get enough of this book."

—Harlequin Junkie, 5 stars

"Part rock star romance, part romantic thriller, I really enjoyed this book."

—Romance Reader

FAKING
Forever

Also by Catherine Bybee

Contemporary Romance

Weekday Brides Series

Wife by Wednesday
Married by Monday
Fiancé by Friday
Single by Saturday
Taken by Tuesday
Seduced by Sunday
Treasured by Thursday

Not Quite Series

Not Quite Dating
Not Quite Mine
Not Quite Enough
Not Quite Forever
Not Quite Perfect
Not Quite Crazy

Most Likely To Series

Doing It Over
Staying For Good
Making It Right

First Wives Series

Fool Me Once
Half Empty
Chasing Shadows

Paranormal Romance

MacCoinnich Time Travels

Binding Vows
Silent Vows
Redeeming Vows
Highland Shifter
Highland Protector

The Ritter Werewolves Series

Before the Moon Rises
Embracing the Wolf

Novellas

Soul Mate
Possessive

Erotica

Kilt Worthy
Kilt-A-Licious

CATHERINE BYBEE

FAKING *Forever*

BOOK FOUR IN THE FIRST WIVES SERIES

Published by Montlake Romance, Seattle

www.apub.com

Amazon, the Amazon logo, and Montlake Romance are trademarks of Amazon.com, Inc., or its affiliates.

ISBN-13: 9781503905221
ISBN-10: 1503905225

Cover design by Letitia Hasser

Cover photography by The Belief Agency

Printed in the United States of America

To Kayce and Libby
Tulum will never be the same

Chapter One

"I'm going to have a baby." Stunned silence met Shannon's announcement.

The First Wives, as they called their tiny club, consisted of four women, three of which were now married for the second time, and Shannon.

"You're pregnant?" Avery, the hostess, asked.

Shannon quickly shook her head and set her wine aside. "Not yet. But I made my decision. I'm giving myself six months to do this the natural way. If that doesn't work, I'll schedule an appointment with a fertility clinic."

Shannon had hinted at her desire to become a mother several months before, but with Avery and Trina still in the honeymoon stages of their marriages, Shannon didn't want to take away from their recent marital bliss and put the spotlight on herself. In fact, it wasn't in Shannon's nature to stand in the spotlight at all.

Lori, the lady lawyer who had founded the group of First Wives, regarded her with a narrowing of the eyes. "Do we have a baby daddy in mind?"

Shannon offered a placating smile. "If there was someone, you'd all know about it."

"You're going to have sex with a stranger." It wasn't a question.

Shannon glanced down at her slim frame. The last time she'd had sex, it was with her ex-husband . . . and he ended up being the biggest stranger of all. "We've all had sex with someone we didn't know at one time in our lives or another."

Avery sat taller. "I might need something stronger than wine for this conversation."

Shannon waved Avery off before she broke out the hard liquor. "I'm only telling you guys so you're not surprised when it happens. I want a baby. I'm not getting any younger. I have the means to support another person . . ." Her list of reasons to go through with her plan sounded off from her lips like a chant.

"When was the last time you kissed someone?" Avery was the free thinker of the group, but even she was surprisingly against Shannon's idea of conceiving a child from a one-night stand.

Shannon considered her question and knew that her answer would open a negative stream of conversation. "I know how to kiss, Avery."

Three sets of eyes questioned her.

"It's been a long time," she finally admitted.

"And when are you planning on getting knocked up?" Avery asked.

"I've been monitoring my ovulation—"

"This is a stupid idea!" Avery jumped up and moved to her kitchen.

Shannon watched as her friend found the tequila she'd threatened to break out.

"I think what Avery is trying to say is . . . Have you thought this out completely?" Trina asked with a smile.

"I've thought about getting pregnant more than I ever thought about *not* getting pregnant." She turned her stare away from Avery. "I don't want to miss out on the experience of being a mom, with all the good and the bad that comes with it, just because I don't have a man in my life."

"Why not see a fertility doctor? Wouldn't that be safer?" Trina slid a little closer on the couch.

"Probably. It would also be sterile. Reading sperm donor profiles and picking a father for my child by a list of attributes or checking boxes on an application makes me cringe."

"You'd at least know if the guy behind the sperm is healthy or smart." Avery stood pouring tequila into tiny shot glasses.

"What self-respecting college kid, and that's probably who ends up in sperm banks, is going to say he's struggling through his first year of general education? Not to mention choosing a daddy from a height, weight, and eye color chart makes me feel like I'm picking a breeder for a puppy."

"Still safer." Avery walked over with the shots.

"I want the father of my baby to be kind and witty enough to make me want to sleep with him. I know you don't approve, Avery, but try and see this from my perspective. I could go to a clinic and get pregnant next month . . . or at least attempt to. Or I can find a perfectly willing candidate and have a night to remember. Don't tell me for a minute that you'd pick the former."

All eyes moved to the youngest member of their club. Before Avery settled down, she was the one always talking about her endless prowess.

Avery's scowl softened. "When do you plan on finding this baby daddy?"

"I'm shooting a wedding next month in Tulum. The bride's family is putting me up in a hotel for a couple of days, and then after that's over, I'm moving up the beach to continue my stay. According to my calculations, I should be ovulating by the following weekend."

"Plenty of time to scout out the right guy," Lori said.

"That's what I thought. It's away from here; chances are no one will recognize me. The wedding guests will all be long gone. There are a lot of expats living in that part of Mexico. Flirting bartenders."

"Bartenders are a good choice," Trina said.

Shannon leaned forward. "I almost went there in Colorado at the Peterson wedding. The guy I met was working the bar. Way too young, but that didn't seem to stop him from hitting on me."

"What happened?" Trina asked.

"I chickened out." There was no other way to explain it. "But I considered it. I took it as a sign and extended my stay in Tulum. Even if it doesn't work out, I'm making steps in the right direction to move forward with my plan."

"I think someone working a beach bar in a foreign country is ideal," Lori said. "Every bartender I've known plays around a lot. Most don't want more than a night or two. You can talk to them without commitment, make sure they're not batshit crazy. Keep your real name out of it."

"Of course. I can't have anyone looking for me later." Not that she worried that they would.

"And if you don't find someone in Mexico to fit the profile?" Trina asked.

"I'll plan monthly trips to other places."

"Girls' trips," Avery announced.

Shannon narrowed her eyes. "I don't need a backup team." Especially if that team had a player that wasn't into the game . . . like Avery.

"You told me you'd take me with you when you went daddy hunting. I'm taking you up on this."

"Aren't you newly married and have better things to do than finding my next date?"

Avery shook her head. "Nope."

Lori laughed.

"I think Avery's right. One of us should come along and make sure you're seeing the good and the bad in the guy you plan on sleeping with."

"That's ridiculous."

"Not really," Lori chimed in. "If you were in a relationship and considering a permanent step, you'd ask us what we thought. Just like we all did at one time or another before we got married. This isn't any different."

Shannon sipped her wine and considered what they were saying. "I can't ask you guys to drop your life to come with me."

Avery raised her hand. "I volunteered for Tulum. If no one fits the daddy bill there, we plan the next month and make sure one of us can come."

"Or all of us," Trina said.

Lori lifted her glass. "Or all of us."

Avery picked up a shot of tequila. "Let me go on record and say I really don't like this idea, but I feel better knowing we're with you."

"I'm going to be fine."

Shannon Wentworth wore a plastic smile as she witnessed her clients bickering.

Corrie Harkin sat with her back rod-straight, hands folded in her lap, while her mother did most of the talking. Mrs. Harkin, Shannon had met with before. Corrie, the bride to be, was in Shannon's studio for the first time.

"He's late," Corrie said, watching the front door.

"He's a busy man, honey. I'm sure he's on his way."

Shannon liked to meet with the bride and groom before the actual wedding in order to ensure that she captured the images they wanted on their wedding day. Mrs. Harkin had hired Shannon based solely on her name. Being the ex-wife of the former governor of California was a status the mother of the bride couldn't pass up. From what Shannon could tell, Corrie was marrying up. And Mommy couldn't be happier for it. The bank accounts of Shannon's clients, or the budgets for their weddings, weren't something she bothered to find out. Her fees were steep, which already put her outside the range of many couples' resources. Mrs. Harkin didn't blink an eye. It helped that the groom was footing the bill; at least, that's what the deposit check suggested.

"We can get started without him," Shannon said.

Corrie glanced at her mother and forced a smile.

"We probably should."

Shannon pulled up the images of the venue they were using for the ceremony. The pristine white sands and turquoise waters of the Yucatán Peninsula were picture-perfect by themselves. "I've been working with the coordinator at the hotel. This is about where the sun will be during the ceremony. There is always a chance of a few clouds, but that will simply make the pictures better."

"It better not rain," Corrie said, her tone flat.

"It wouldn't dare," her mother assured her. "Don't worry, Shannon."

She wasn't, but from the way Corrie was twisting the ring on her finger, the bride was.

Shannon had learned that brides came in a few categories. Bridezillas . . . much like the TV show. Excitedly nervous. Or passively quiet when in the presence of their overcontrolling mothers.

Corrie was the latter.

"How many people are in the wedding party?" Shannon asked.

"Six. Three on each side."

"Since your fiancé isn't here, can you describe your dress?"

Mrs. Harkin quickly pulled out her phone. "It's beautiful."

Shannon caught Corrie's tight smile. For a brief moment, Shannon thought she'd be seeing a dress three decades too old. One her mother held on to so her daughter could wear it.

The second Shannon saw miles of billowing tulle, she faked a smile. The dress would be a nightmare at a beach wedding. Even a slight breeze would make this dress dance. Heaven forbid there was an updraft of any kind. The layers would catch. Shannon made a note to bring double-sided clothing tape to attempt to hold the tulle down.

"She'll look like a princess," Shannon said despite the doom in her mind.

"It's beautiful."

"What about your bridesmaids' dresses?" *Please don't say tulle.*

"The same, only in a soft gray and shorter."

All Shannon could see were pictures with women holding skirts to their legs for fear of showing the world their Spanx.

More tape, she wrote on her notepad.

"Where is he?" Corrie removed her phone from her purse.

"Don't bug him, darling. If he can't make it, we'll plan this without him."

Mrs. Harkin placed a hand over Corrie's phone to keep her from texting her fiancé.

"Ideally, I like to take pictures of you and your bridesmaids while you're getting ready, if you're open to it. Then once you're all perfect, we'll take several preceremony pictures to avoid making your guests wait for hours after the ceremony and before the reception."

"We're having a cocktail hour set up for pictures," Mrs. Harkin told her. "Corrie's fiancé and the groomsmen are all staying at the neighboring resort so there won't be a threat of him seeing Corrie before she walks down the aisle."

"Did you nail down a guest count?"

Corrie opened her mouth to answer, and her mother cut her off. "A hundred and twenty-six. So many people weren't willing to fly to Mexico for a wedding."

"Which is what we wanted. A small wedding." Corrie offered a strangled smile.

For several minutes, Mrs. Harkin expressed her great knowledge as to why larger weddings were better. Corrie sat back and listened.

Nearly twenty minutes later, Corrie's cell phone rang, and she excused herself to answer it.

"Where are you? Did you forget?" Shannon heard the tightness in the bride's voice.

Mrs. Harkin directed Shannon's attention back to her. "We're so pleased you could squeeze us into your busy schedule. I hope it's not too inconvenient to fly all the way to Tulum for us."

"It's my pleasure. I plan on taking a couple more days while I'm there to soak up some local color." Not to mention fine-tuning her flirting skills with eligible bartenders.

"I'd be happy to extend your days at your resort."

"That won't be necessary. I've already booked another location after the wedding." If she did find a baby daddy, the last thing she needed was the Harkin family getting in the way of being anonymous.

"He's not coming," Corrie announced when she sat back down. Moisture gathered in the corners of her eyes. "He's stuck in a meeting and asked me to handle this."

"You're marrying a wealthy man, Corrie. He didn't get that way talking to photographers." Mrs. Harkin stopped herself, smiled. "No offense."

"None taken."

"I'm sure he has every confidence in your ability to manage the wedding."

Considering Corrie was all of twenty-five years old and still lived with her parents, Shannon doubted her ability to plan much of anything.

"We're just about done here, anyway," Shannon told them.

Corrie blinked several times without comment.

Shannon asked a few more questions, which Mrs. Harkin answered, and then drew their meeting to a close. When Mrs. Harkin excused herself to the restroom, Shannon took the opportunity to talk quietly to Corrie.

"My mother was a lot like yours when I was your age," Shannon said under her breath.

Corrie tightened her jaw. "It's unbearable. She steamrolls over everything. I don't have a chance to think, let alone make any decisions on my own. I don't know a third of the people coming to the wedding."

"That happens sometimes," Shannon said, trying to be optimistic.

"You would think she's the bride and not me. I'm not even sure I want to get married."

That was not what Shannon thought she'd hear. "So why are you?"

"Oh, I don't know . . . because I won't do any better?" Corrie shook her head. "Never mind. I'm tired. Pissed off my fiancé can't be bothered to show up. Angry that my mom is making this all about her."

Mrs. Harkin walked back into the room.

Corrie closed her mouth and faked a smile. "Normal bride nerves . . . right?"

Nope. Not right at all.

Mrs. Harkin pushed her purse up to the middle of her forearm and held her hands together like the queen. "We will see you in three weeks."

Shannon couldn't help but think the wedding would be called off before she had a chance to board a plane.

Chapter Two

Shannon checked her phone one last time before switching it over to airplane mode and slipping into her first-class seat. The flight attendant offered a preflight cocktail while the other passengers boarded.

Shannon happily sipped a mimosa and leaned back for the five-hour flight into Cancun. From there she would take an hour and a half drive to her resort destination in Tulum.

The weather in LA had been unusually wet all winter, even the spring managed to get off to a damp start, so the white sand and sunshine were calling her name. She'd work for all of two days, barely making back what she would spend on her upgraded plane ticket and the postwedding accommodations. Her accountant would scoff at her again this year. She didn't photograph weddings because she needed the money. No, her divorce from Paul had set her up with six million in the bank. All of which she bundled in investments that trickled out a sum of well over twenty thousand a month. Plenty to live her life, especially considering her home was paid for free and clear. Even the taxes on the home were taken care of by her ex for as long as she lived there.

Wedding photography kept her from boredom.

This week, it would pay for a much-needed vacation in a destination where she'd never been before.

As what appeared to be the last passengers filed into the plane, Shannon glanced at the empty aisle seat next to her. Not a normal occurrence in first class. Most of the time someone in the back attempted to upgrade their ticket for a fraction of what it cost her to guarantee a seat with more legroom and free drinks.

She opened the shade on the window after the attendant took her empty glass.

"I told you, I'll be there on Tuesday."

Shannon glanced up to find a man in a three-piece suit shoving a carry-on bag into the compartment above their heads while talking on his cell phone.

"No, no. I'll take care of it."

Trying not to stare, Shannon turned back to the window. All the while hearing every word the man said. As everyone within ten rows probably could.

Rude.

A briefcase landed on the seat beside her, making her glance over.

Tall, dark hair . . . probably close to her age, if not a little older. She didn't make out his features as he shifted his phone and wiggled out of his jacket.

The flight attendant was right there, taking it from him and hanging it up in a forward closet.

Mr. Phone didn't even thank the woman.

"Ladies and gentlemen. The cabin doors have been closed, and we're asking for all of your electronic devices to be placed in airplane mode and all larger electronic devices to be stowed for takeoff."

Several sets of eyes turned toward the man who flopped into the seat beside her.

She looked again and was met with a hand, a phone, and a partial profile.

"I'll take care of it. Just make sure the contracts are on my desk Tuesday morning."

"Sir?" The flight attendant approached Mr. Phone as the plane started to back away from the terminal.

"What?" he paused long enough to ask.

Someone in the seats in front of them said, "Oh, please."

The attendant faked a smile.

That's when Shannon spoke up. "Tell your Tuesday appointment you'll call him when you land."

Mr. Phone slowly turned his head toward Shannon.

Golden brown eyes narrowed against his tanned complexion. Strong jaw and a full mouth that opened ever so slightly. He was beautiful.

"I've got to go," he said to whomever he was speaking with, and promptly hung up.

Shannon blinked several times and the attendant walked away.

"How did you know I had a Tuesday appointment?"

"Everyone on the plane knows."

Mr. Phone looked around while the nearby passengers skirted their attention away from him.

"Was I loud?"

And clueless!

She considered softening her response. Then decided to be herself and not the perfectly polished version she'd spent most of her life showing the world. "Yes. You were."

He was working his seat belt when his phone rang, startling everyone around them.

For a second, she thought he was going to answer it.

"Airplane mode. You know, the image of a plane in your settings," she said as if he were three. No, scratch that, three-year-olds probably knew where that was on a cell phone these days.

The phone kept ringing. "Right. But this is—"

"Sir?" The flight attendant returned, her smile gone.

"Right." He silenced his phone, played with it for a few seconds, and then set it on the armrest separating the two of them.

Faking Forever

Once again, Shannon focused her attention out the window and pulled in a deep breath. She paused, tilted her head slightly, and purposely breathed through her nose.

What was that?

Not cologne.

She sniffed again.

Definitely not man perfume. No, this was something completely different.

She shifted in her seat, crossed her legs in the other direction, and took the opportunity to turn her head toward the flight attendant as she demonstrated all the safety features of the airplane. When she did, she caught Mr. Phone tilting his head back and closing his eyes.

Shannon leaned in, just a hair, and silently sniffed the air.

This was going to drive her crazy. She ruled out food scents. No, he didn't smell like he'd just had a succulent meal that had no choice but to filter through his pores. Not earthy . . . like musk or pine.

She sniffed again and Mr. Phone shot his eyes open.

She sat back quickly, not that she was very close, but still.

"Are you sick?" Mr. Phone asked.

Mortified, Shannon narrowed her eyes. "No."

"You sure?"

"Yes."

"Good. The last thing I need is some bug right now." He closed his eyes again.

"Well, you won't get one from me."

"Good to know." And just like that, Mr. Phone fell asleep. The plane hadn't even lifted off the ground and he was out.

Thirty minutes later, Shannon had a second mimosa in her system . . . which was uncharacteristic, considering the time of day. But something happens when you board a jet and someone starts pouring liquor into tiny glasses. It didn't help that most of the passengers in first class were filling up on Bloody Marys, mimosas, wine, and cocktails. The destination

13

almost mandated that you start the party early. With the exception of Mr. Phone—who still slept—and her, the other passengers were all wearing casual clothing and appeared to be on their way to beach vacations without a care in the world.

She'd start her vacation after the doomed marriage of Corrie and . . . what was his name again? Brooks. His first name escaped her. Attending the festivities during the rehearsal was her way of learning the family dynamics and demands. Corrie could have an equally demanding grandmother that would attempt to boss Shannon around, or a drunken uncle that she'd need to rally the wedding planner to help with. Weddings took a village, and Shannon considered herself one of the town leaders. So when the flight attendant asked if she wanted more wine with the lunch provided, Shannon hesitated.

The rehearsal was eight hours away.

The book she packed for the vacation portion of her time in Mexico was packed in her checked bag.

Mr. Phone was sound asleep. No conversation there.

"Yes, that would be nice," she told the attendant.

Before her meal arrived, Shannon took the opportunity to wiggle out of her seat without waking her neighbor to use the restroom. Somewhere in the five minutes she was up, Mr. Phone woke up long enough to lean his seat all the way back, legs stretched out, and once again was sound asleep.

Note to self: always take an aisle seat!

She cleared her throat.

He didn't move.

Option one: wake him up.

Option two: climb over his stretched out legs. She was tall—she could do it.

The passengers around her were either deep in conversation or had on the headphones the airline provided and their eyes glued to the in-flight entertainment.

A second clearing of her throat.

Nothing.

Okay . . . did she climb over facing him, or away?

Away. That way she could hold on to the seats in front of them and keep her balance.

With her decision made, she pulled her shoulders back and lifted one leg over. Thank God she'd never carried too many extra pounds or touching the stranger would have been a given.

Halfway there . . .

She shifted her weight, lifted her remaining limb up . . .

The plane decided that was the perfect moment to hit a pocket of unstable air. Shannon tried to correct her weight, grabbed for the back of the seat in front of her. A second shift in the airplane and someone's glass rolled on the floor. Shannon lost it.

"What the . . ."

Her ass landed in Mr. Phone's lap.

His hands on her hips.

Humiliation boiled in her veins.

Victor was dreaming.

Or at least he was before his eyes popped open to the stunning woman next to him who now sat in his lap.

Or more to the point, was scrambling off his lap.

"What in the . . . ?"

"I'm so sorry."

Victor reached for the button to lower his leg rest and somehow caught his seatmate a second time . . . or maybe the way the plane tilted had her losing her balance again.

He couldn't stop his hands from moving to help her off of him any more than he could stop his pulse from jumping in his chest.

She grabbed ahold of the seats in front of her.

Someone close by started laughing.

The woman scrambled and fell into her seat. When she turned his way, the crimson color on her cheeks gave away her embarrassment.

"That was awkward," he said, trying to make light of what happened.

She lifted her chin a little higher and tucked a strand of long, dark hair behind her ear.

"You could have waited to stretch out until after I returned. It isn't like I could have gone far."

"So it's my fault."

"Well, you certainly didn't consider how I might get back into my seat."

How rich was that? She fell in his lap and blamed him. *Story of my life.* "My apologies, Miss . . ."

"Annoyed." She turned to look out the window.

Victor bit back a laugh. Chuckling *at* her might not be the best way to spend the duration of the flight. "I'm sorry, Miss Annoyed. I didn't realize that you'd gotten up."

She huffed out a breath and waved at the flight attendant. "I'll have that glass of wine now, please."

The attendant snickered. "I'll keep your glass full."

Victor glanced around at the other passengers, many of which were trying not to watch him and his annoyed companion.

He stopped the attendant from running off. "Excuse me."

The attendant turned, her lips pinched.

Okay . . . apparently he was doing a good job of frustrating more than one female today. "Gin and tonic?" he asked.

She hesitated.

"Please," Miss Annoyed said for him.

"Sorry. Please."

The flight attendant flashed a smile. "Of course."

He checked his watch. "I slept for an hour?" He couldn't remember the last time he'd fallen asleep on an airplane.

"Excuse me?" Miss Annoyed was still unhappy with him.

He pointed to his watch. "Did I really sleep for an hour?"

She turned to give him the full face of her disapproval. "You did."

Miss Annoyed was model beautiful. High cheekbones, full lips . . . the depth of her eyes seemed to take everything in around her. She was what Victor would label conceited, privileged, and out of his league.

The flight attendant arrived with their drinks, and he took the opportunity to glance at her left hand.

No wedding ring.

He wasn't surprised. She didn't seem to have a warm bone to spare.

Not that he was interested.

He thanked the woman handing him his drink and attempted to calm his fidgeting fingers. Flying wasn't one of his strong suits. Years of hearing his father talk about the airplane parts he'd machined in his career, and insinuate his lack of trust in a chunk of steel defying gravity, made it hard to relax. It didn't matter that Victor flew all over the world, several times a year. It still bothered him and made him more chatty than he cared to admit.

Only his seatmate didn't seem all that interested in conversation.

Not that her scowl kept him from trying. "What takes you to Cancun?"

She regarded him out of the corner of her eye. For a minute, he didn't think she'd answer. She opened her mouth to respond, and hesitated.

"You don't look like you're on vacation." She wore slacks and a button up shirt. Something he would expect his assistant to show up to work in.

She looked down at herself, then back at him.

"Neither do you," she told him.

Victor loosened the tie her comment reminded him he was wearing. Truth was, he'd dressed that morning on autopilot. If it wasn't for the packed bag at the door leading into his garage, he might have jumped in his car and driven to work. His life had somehow taken on a routine, and anything outside the norm was quickly overlooked.

"I live in a suit," he told her.

She attempted a smile. "That might be uncomfortable on a beach."

He thought about the clothes he'd packed. "Hotels always have gift stores, which I'm sure I'll need to use."

"And if not, I'm told there are nude beaches on the Yucatán."

Victor blinked several times, somewhat surprised those words had come out of Miss Annoyed's mouth. "Maybe when I was twenty. I'd be a little concerned about certain parts getting too much sun."

He was pretty sure she smiled. But the moment passed, and she turned back to the view out the window.

A full minute flew by.

Yeah, she wasn't going to talk. He set his drink aside and reached for his briefcase under the seat in front of him to remove his laptop. He might as well get a few things done, since conversation obviously wasn't going to happen without a struggle.

He quickly found his head deep in an article that spelled out why he should be buying more junkyards full of destroyed cars while the prices were low. He removed a notepad and wrote a few highlights of what to check on when he returned to his office.

When the flight attendant arrived with Miss Annoyed's lunch, he passed on food and asked for another drink. He was two sips in when his seatmate spoke.

"I don't think you have to worry."

He tore his eyes from his computer. "Worry about what?"

She looked down. "The sun burning certain parts of your body. Your laptop will serve as great sunscreen."

He followed her gaze. "I don't think my girlfriend would appreciate me taking this on the beach."

Her eyes opened wider. "You're meeting a girlfriend in Cancun?"

Why did she sound surprised? "I am."

"You didn't fly with her?"

He shook his head. "That was the plan, but I had a last-minute meeting." With his acquisitions manager. Not that it could be helped.

"My condolences to your girlfriend."

Victor frowned. "Why do you say that?"

She looked at him as if he were a few cards short of a full deck. "You're here on vacation, right?"

"Yes." *For all intents and purposes.*

"You're wearing a suit, didn't pack clothes for the environment, brought your work with you, and ditched your girl on the flight over." She shook her head. "I don't care who your girlfriend is, she deserves better."

Victor opened his mouth to respond, closed it, and opened it again. "Come again?"

"Women don't like coming in second, third, or fourth. If you were *my* boyfriend, I'd find the first cabana boy I could and ditch you at the door." She reached for the earphones the airline provided and turned on the small screen in front of her, effectively telling him that their conversation was over.

What the hell?

Chapter Three

Shannon wasn't sure what personality had invaded her, but she liked it. The remainder of the flight was silent between her and Mr. Phone. When they landed, he offered a final glance over his shoulder and muttered his goodbye. He seemed to be in quite the hurry to leave her behind as he hastily made his way up the ramp to the terminal.

She couldn't help but think she'd made him uncomfortable. Good. Men like him who took their girlfriends for granted didn't deserve to have them. Yet somehow it seemed the good-looking men were never alone on a Saturday night. Or in his case, a weekend in Cancun.

The humidity smacked down hard as she worked her way through the long line at immigration. By the time her passport was stamped, the silk shirt that had been comfortable to fly in was sticking to her body. She weaved her way through the crush of people outside the secure portion of the terminal, passed the many taxi drivers waving at her in an attempt to drive her to her destination, and searched the signs bearing the names of passengers that had prearranged transportation.

Her married name was scribbled in black ink on a plain white piece of paper. She approached the driver and smiled. "I'm Ms. Wentworth."

The driver lowered the clipboard that held her name and flipped up the paper. "Welcome to Cancun," he said, smiling.

"Thank you." Shannon's gaze moved to the cloudy sky above.

"You're going to Tulum, yes?"

Shannon glanced down at his paper. "Yes. Casa Kai."

"Sí, sí . . . I have it." He smiled and reached for her bag. "Only you, yes?" His thick accent had her concentrating hard on his words.

"Only me."

"Good. Come. I park over here."

She followed him to the SUV and took the back seat he offered while he loaded her bag. She hoisted her camera equipment into the seat next to her and waited for him to close the door.

He slid behind the wheel, turned over the engine, and turned the air on high. "I have Corona or water in the cooler if you like."

"Thank you."

He nodded a few times and backed out of the parking space sandwiched between dozens of other drivers, all picking up passengers. Unlike most of the airports Shannon had been to in her life, this one was primarily filled with tourists rushing in and out. Most people traveled in pairs, if not groups of four or more.

"My English is not so good," he told her.

"Your English is better than my Spanish," she said with a slight laugh.

He grinned and nodded. Although she wasn't sure he understood.

Shannon removed her phone from her purse and pulled up the group text she shared with the First Wives. I made it. She added a palm tree emoji and pressed send.

Almost instantly, Trina returned her text and told her to have fun. A few seconds later, Lori's text told her to take a picture of the potential daddies she came across and share.

Avery's text came in last. I will see you on Monday. Don't shack up until I get there.

Shannon giggled. I'll try my best.

She tossed the phone in her purse and turned her attention out the window. The side of the main highway looked more like a back road outside of Los Angeles. Only this road had men piled in the backs of pickup trucks, drivers of motorcycles that didn't bother with helmets, and kids sitting in laps in the passing cars. The safety laws of the States had obviously not filtered south. Except for maybe the speed limit, which her driver stayed surprisingly close to. She didn't question it and watched the landscape as they slipped farther out of the city of Cancun and down the highway to the south.

The first few drops of rain that hit the windshield didn't surprise her, but the bolt of lightning that came from nowhere did.

She looked out the back window and noticed a large mass of black clouds closing in. "Oh, wow."

The driver switched on the wipers and slowed down. "Lots of rain this week," he told her.

"Just here in the city?"

He looked at her briefly through the rearview mirror and smiled. "All over."

Shannon lost her smile and took a longer look at the country moving by. Deep puddles of standing water were evident everywhere she looked. The jungle, just a few yards from the highway, was dense and as lush as any. Right as the thought that rain forests needed rain entered her mind, the sky opened and the clouds dumped.

Her driver slowed down and hit the flashers on the dash, while others did the same in surrounding cars.

Shannon noticed a band of drenched men huddling under a single tarp in the back of a truck and counted her blessings.

"How long will this last?" she asked.

He shook his head.

Again, she was pretty sure he didn't understand her question.

Poor Corrie, she thought. No bride wanted the threat of rain on her day.

An hour into the drive it seemed the weather wanted to relax, but once they turned onto the long, narrow road leading to all the boutique hotels that made up the resort location of Tulum, the clouds seemed to pull in tighter and join forces. For what seemed like hours, they dodged past people running out of the rain and skirted around the locals walking calmly along the side of the road.

Once at their destination, the driver jumped out of the car and ran around as an attendant of the hotel moved forward with a massive umbrella. Not that it mattered. Once the door was open and Shannon stepped out, she stood in an inch of water with the rain hitting her sideways.

She tucked her camera equipment close and hurried to the shelter of the registration desk. As she did, an onslaught of water started to cascade down a meandering path to the right of the desk. "This is crazy."

The woman behind the desk shrugged. "It just started to come down here."

Shannon jumped as the sound of thunder roared overhead. "How long will it last?"

"Thirty minutes, three hours? Hard to tell. It's spring. Sometimes the weather is unpredictable. Most of the time the rain comes in at night and is gone by morning. I'm sure you'll have a beautiful stay." Lightning cracked above like an exclamation point on the receptionist's statement.

Thirty minutes later, Shannon had changed out of her wet clothes and was looking over the courtyard of her hotel toward the ocean. Tulum was filled with small hotels, none of which had more than twenty to twenty-five rooms. Her accommodations were next to where Corrie and her bridal party were staying and one over from where the wedding was scheduled to take place.

The rain had moved away from the flash flooding stage and settled on a proper soak. Much as Shannon would have liked to stay sheltered in place, she needed to find Mrs. Harkin and Corrie and learn the backup plan if the rain ruined the anticipated outdoor wedding.

Donning a pair of sandals, Shannon tucked her room key in her back pocket and left her camera behind.

The rehearsal was supposed to start at six thirty, so she headed toward the venue with an umbrella keeping the majority of the rain away. Dodging puddles and passing cars, Shannon zigzagged up the street and into the venue. She recognized the space from the pictures she'd found on the Internet.

Chairs where the guests were supposed to sit the following day were stacked up against palm trees. The expanse of beach that would house the ceremony appeared much smaller than the images she'd seen. How a hundred plus people were supposed to fit, she didn't know.

Noise from a restaurant behind the beach drifted above the sound of rain. Over her shoulder, she saw the closed sliding doors that obviously opened up to offer the full effect of beach breezes and views on clear nights.

Now it seemed to house anxious faces peering out at the nasty weather. She walked farther into the restaurant, leaving her umbrella at the door.

"Are you here with the wedding party?"

Shannon's gaze found Corrie, sitting in a chair in the far corner, her face buried in her hands. "I am," she said, excusing herself to console the bride.

"This is awful. Nothing is going like we planned." Shannon overheard Corrie's complaints to a young woman sitting beside her.

"It's going to be fine."

Corrie snapped her head up and yelled at her friend, "It's not going to be all right. Look at this place!"

Several people standing around stepped back, and Shannon swooped in. She'd had her share of monster brides and knew when she saw one breaking down under the stress of the day.

She knelt to Corrie's level and grasped the bride's cold hands in hers.

"Hey, sweetie."

Shannon's soft voice seemed to encourage Corrie to cry harder.

"My wedding is ruined, Shannon."

"Your wedding isn't until tomorrow. This can all blow over."

Corrie used the tissue in her hand and wiped her nose.

"That's what I told her," the petite brunette sitting beside Corrie said. "It's an omen. All of it."

All of it? Shannon wanted to ask what she missed but didn't want to open a can of worms with so many people watching.

Mrs. Harkin marched across the room and stopped in front of her daughter. In a tight voice, she said, "Get yourself together, young lady. You're making a scene."

Corrie hiccupped.

"We're going to run through the rehearsal in here. The wedding coordinator assures me the rain will let up by tomorrow."

Shannon made eye contact with Corrie's friend.

A coordinator that could control the weather would be a neat trick.

"It's been raining all day."

Mrs. Harkin lowered her voice. "You're crying like a child. Do you want your husband to think you're too immature to handle a little rain?"

Corrie blinked a few times, opened her mouth.

"Now, go wipe that face and paint on a smile."

Shannon had a strong desire to tell Mrs. Harkin that Corrie had every right to be upset. Instead she took Corrie's elbow and helped her to her feet. "C'mon. Let's freshen you up." She looked at Corrie's friend. "Can you find some face powder, maybe some lip gloss?"

The brunette nodded and took the opportunity to leave Corrie's side.

Shannon followed the hostess to the ladies' room at the back of the restaurant, checked the two stalls to make sure they were alone, and then propped Corrie up on the counter.

Corrie sucked in a couple of deep breaths, her blank stare focused on the back of the room.

Shannon dipped a paper towel into cold water and dabbed the mascara away from under Corrie's eyes.

"There's no guarantee it's going to rain tomorrow. The forecast is saying partly cloudy with scattered showers . . . which is normal for this part of Mexico."

"It's pouring."

"I know. I'm sure it's not what you want. If they have to move the wedding inside, they move it inside. No big deal."

Corrie looked away, her lips in a thin line. "My mother picked this place. Said it would accommodate everyone on the list. The coordinator told me this morning that we had twenty-five more guests than they can seat at the reception."

"I'm sure they can make room. Things like that happen all the time."

Corrie shook her head. "Nothing is going right, Shannon."

She stopped working on the running makeup and captured Corrie's gaze. "What does your fiancé say about the rain?"

Corrie's nose flared, and for a second Shannon thought she'd have a bawling bride on her hands once again. Instead, her chin came up. "I don't know. I haven't seen him yet."

"What do you mean?"

"He flew in a few hours ago. He was supposed to fly here with me yesterday and then told me at the last minute that he had a meeting he couldn't avoid."

Hair on the back of Shannon's neck started to slowly dance.

"He's always working. My mother says that's a good thing, that we won't get tired of each other."

Shannon laid a hand on the countertop. "What do you think?"

Corrie swallowed. "I think it's a crappy way to start a marriage. It feels like I'm just another merger for his company."

Shannon was starting to understand Corrie's point.

"And all this . . . the rain, the screwed up guest list . . . it's an omen."

She took a breath and waited. "Are you having second thoughts?"

Corrie nodded once. Her eyes started to well up again.

"Hey. It's not too late to back out. If you really don't want to do this, you don't have to."

Corrie looked at her like the thought had never crossed her mind that she actually had a choice.

"Trust me. You're better off walking away now than going around faking forever with a man who isn't right."

"I can't do that. My mother would kill me. All the guests are flying in."

Oh, the pressure. Shannon knew it well.

"Listen. I understand that there is a plan here, but you still have a choice. Take it from me, once you say *I do*, it's going to take a lot more to say you *don't*."

"You think I'll end up divorced."

Shannon didn't want to put that on her. "If you both love each other enough, you can work through anything."

Corrie narrowed her eyes. "Did you love your husband enough?"

"I did. But it takes two, Corrie."

She closed her eyes.

"I'm not saying your fiancé doesn't love you." Not that Shannon would know.

The door to the bathroom opened, and Corrie's friend appeared with the makeup. "He's here," she announced.

Corrie released a breath and brushed away the remainder of her tears. "I'm okay."

Shannon stood back and let the conversation drop while Corrie attempted to erase the stress with powder and blush.

"I'll leave you girls."

Corrie painted on the fake smile Shannon had seen the day she'd met her. "I'm fine. It's just rain, right?"

Shannon left the room, anxious now to see who Corrie's future husband was.

Three steps into the dining room, where the waitstaff had already pushed tables aside in an attempt to create a makeshift aisle, Shannon's heart jumped.

Mrs. Harkin stood in animated conversation with Mr. Phone.

Slowly, as if feeling her disapproving gaze, he turned her way. The smile he wore while talking fell.

"You," she whispered under her breath. Maybe he was just a guest here for the wedding and knew the mother of the bride.

Only those hopes faded when Corrie emerged from the bathroom, walked past Shannon, and straight up to Mr. Phone.

He turned his attention to Corrie and kissed the side of her cheek. Their conversation was too far away for Shannon to hear, but it became perfectly clear who the man was, and who his *girlfriend* was.

Not only was Mr. Phone not good enough for Corrie, the man was robbing the cradle.

Chapter Four

Shannon flagged down the bartender and sat at the bar. "I'll have a margarita."

"Make that two."

She turned to the man who moved up beside her.

"It's an open bar, might as well, right?" he said, smiling.

Was it an open bar? She didn't know. "Right."

"Now that the groom finally showed up, we can get this shit show moving so we can do it again tomorrow."

Shannon couldn't stop from laughing. "So that *is* him," she said more to herself than the stranger standing beside her.

He gave her a sly look out of the corner of his eyes. "You must be a friend of Corrie's."

"I'm the photographer, actually."

He sat down. "Then you're not friends with either of them."

"You could say that."

When their drinks arrived, he lifted his glass and said, "Cheers."

She took a healthy drink and tried not to cough. They poured their tequila with a heavy hand in Mexico. Something Shannon was sure Avery would enjoy, once she arrived.

"I'm Justin, by the way."

She shook his hand. "Shannon." His eyes crinkled as he looked at her.

Cute. Had to be in his midforties, with a tiny amount of gray show-ing up in his hair. He'd be someone she might try to get to know better if she wasn't first, working, and second, looking for a baby daddy who could never learn her name.

She instantly removed him from her list of prospects.

He turned his attention toward the bride and groom as they walked around the room. "Since you don't know either party well, what are your thoughts on the *happy* couple?" The sarcasm that laced his ques-tion had her answering honestly.

"To start with, he's too old for her."

Justin nodded and sipped his drink.

"And then there's the fact he's an asshole."

Justin choked on his cocktail, spitting some of it on his shirt.

Shannon handed him her napkin while he recovered.

"Sorry."

He was laughing. "I thought you said you didn't know him."

"I don't." Over the next five minutes, she explained how he'd sat next to her on the airplane and his behavior the entire time they were on the flight. "He never told me his name, so I had no idea he was the groom."

By now she had Justin's full attention.

"That sounds like Victor."

"Is that his name?" He looked like a Victor.

"You really don't know anyone here."

"Only Corrie and her mother."

He twisted in his seat and encouraged her to do the same. "Okay, then. Let me point out the party. Beverly Harkin you know, beside her is her husband, Dale. They like to act like they have money, but from what I can tell, they don't. I'm guessing they want this marriage more than anyone to somehow elevate their world by their daughter getting married to Victor." Justin paused. "Dale seems to like a stiff brandy, or three."

"I take it Victor has money."

Justin shrugged. "Yeah, you could say that." He continued around the room. "Grandparents of Corrie, I don't remember if they're Dad's family or Mom's. I don't know them. The giggling girls continually taking selfies are Corrie's wedding party, Barbie, Bitsy, and Bimbo."

Shannon's mouth dropped open wide.

"Sorry," he immediately said, looking anything but. "They all arrived last night like they'd just been to a frat party. It's just their age, I suppose."

Shannon let the insult slide. "Who are those people in the corner?"

The older man she'd pointed out seemed to know she was talking about him from across the room and looked their way. Justin lifted his glass to the man and smiled. "Parents of the groom. Scott and Renee Brooks."

They didn't fit the groom. "They seem so normal." Unlike Victor.

"About as American grown as they get." He paused, took a breath. "And those two guys over there are old-time friends of Victor's." He went on to point out a grandmother and an aunt on Victor's side, along with a few cousins.

Altogether there were eleven people there for the groom and at least twenty for the bride. A large group for a rehearsal dinner.

Justin turned around and ordered more drinks.

"No, I shouldn't."

"Why? You're not taking pictures tonight, right?"

The bartender hesitated.

"Okay, but just one more."

"There you go. We're laying bets on how long the marriage will last. Did you want to join the pool?"

"That's mean."

"No, it's real. I give it six months."

Shannon licked the salt on the rim of her glass. Considered her bet. "I'll be surprised if they make it through the honeymoon."

"Wow, that's rough."

Not really. Her memory of the earlier airplane ride and the conversation she'd overheard with Victor on the phone surfaced. "Do you know where they're going on their honeymoon?"

"Somewhere here in Tulum. Why?"

"For how long?"

"A week. Then they're off to Cozumel, or maybe it was Grand Cayman . . . I'm not sure."

Then how was Victor going to make his Tuesday meeting back in California? Ditch his wife? "Such an asshole," she whispered.

Justin laughed again.

Annoyed, watching as Victor and Corrie walked the room, Shannon turned around in her seat and sipped her cocktail.

She'd seen enough to know what to anticipate the next day if they moved everything inside. The space would be tight, and she'd likely have to block someone's view of the ceremony in order to capture the right photographs, but there wasn't a way around that. With any luck the rain would stop and give them more space outside. And by this time tomorrow, it would all be over and she could add a shot to her margarita and move on with her own personal plans.

"You never told me who you were to the bridal party," Shannon said once Justin turned around to join her in their drinks.

"I'm the best man."

It was Shannon's turn to spit out her drink. "What?"

He took a napkin from the bartender's stack and handed it to her with a wink.

"Yeah. Sorry. Maybe I should have said that first."

Shannon pushed her drink aside. "You think? I'm dishing out crap on your best friend and you're playing along." She wasn't sure who the bigger jerk was now . . . him or the groom. Or maybe it was her.

"You're only speaking the truth. We all know Victor's an asshole, but we love him anyway. I mean, c'mon, a destination wedding? Who does that? Pretentious and self-centered people who could care less about what the guests have to go through to get there." Justin smiled with a wink. "Not to mention Mexico. Half of his family refused to come because they were worried the cartel would somehow kidnap them and hold them hostage or some such stupid shit."

"Things like that *do* happen."

Justin rolled his eyes.

She stood from her bar stool and straightened her shirt. "Well, if you'll excuse me, I'll just go back to my hotel now and avoid putting my foot any farther down my mouth." She grabbed her drink, needing it now more than ever, and turned to make her exit.

Then slammed straight into Victor, the asshole's, chest.

Her drink went flying, soaking the man's dress shirt. The glass hit the floor but, surprisingly, didn't shatter.

Once again, her lack of grace coupled with humiliation, and Shannon found herself apologizing. "I am so sorry." She reached behind her, past a laughing Justin, to the stack of napkins. She dabbed Victor's chest. "I didn't see you."

"I'm fine." He took napkins from her hands and worked the moisture off his shirt while she continued to wipe with napkins Justin handed to her.

"You shouldn't sneak up on people."

Victor paused. "You pour your drink on me and it's *my* fault?"

She kept dabbing, not really hearing his words. "You snuck up on me."

Justin laughed harder.

Shannon looked over her shoulder. "Stop it."

That didn't work.

Victor brushed her hands away.

She stood back and realized half the room was watching them.

Her cheeks warmed. The need to make a graceful exit crushed down.

"Oh, man, little brother. You sure know how to piss off the women."

Shannon's head swiveled so fast she saw double. "Little brother?"

Justin's playful grin had her seeing red. "Didn't I tell you that?"

No. And if she had a glass with another drink, she might channel her inner frat girl and pour it on him. "It must have *slipped* your mind." Somewhere between betting on his own brother's divorce and spooning out the gossip on the wedding party.

The waitstaff moved in around them and cleaned up the floor.

Mrs. Harkin approached the three of them with a frown. "Oh, dear. What happened?"

Victor smiled at his future mother-in-law. "An accident."

She frowned. "We're going to get started. Do you want to find a clean shirt?"

"I'm okay," he told her, catching Shannon out of the corner of his eye.

"We can wait. You are the groom, after all."

Mrs. Harkin sure knew how to pour on the sugar.

"Not to worry. It matches the soaking from the rain outside."

Mrs. Harkin dismissed the worry as quickly as she had adopted it as a problem and moved on. "I see you've met the photographer."

Victor looked Shannon straight in the eye. "Informally, yes."

"Shannon Wentworth comes highly recommended."

Victor rocked back on his heels, his eyes glued to her. "Is that so."

"Yes. Some of her photographs have even made it into celebrity magazines. Isn't that right, Shannon?"

"Only if the bride and groom want that kind of thing." Very few did. She stared back.

"Of course we do," Mrs. Harkin said on behalf of both parties. "Why wouldn't we want that? Weddings of the rich and famous should be celebrated and shared. Don't you think, Victor?"

Why was he staring at her?

"We'll see."

"Did you know that Shannon was the first lady of California? We're so lucky to have *her* working for *us.* Don't you think?"

He seemed surprised. "You're the governor's wife?"

"Former governor's ex-wife."

"I thought you looked familiar," Justin said beside her.

Victor's gaze narrowed, his lips lifted a tiny bit. "Interesting."

What does that mean?

Corrie approached their little party and tucked her hand into the crook of Victor's arm. She looked like his baby sister, not his future bride. Shannon actually felt a little ill.

"Honey, we need to get started."

Shannon took that as her cue to leave. "Looks like everything is under control here. I'll see you all tomorrow."

"You're not staying for dinner?" Mrs. Harkin asked.

"No. It's been a long day. I want to be fresh tomorrow, make sure I take pictures that last a lifetime." *Unlike this marriage.*

That's all the mother of the bride needed to hear. "We'll see you tomorrow, then."

Corrie pulled Victor away without a second glance.

Justin leaned in and whispered, "Bets are fifty bucks apiece. You in?"

She lifted her hand in a fist. "You're both assholes. But I'm in."

Justin bumped his fist with hers and walked to take his place by his brother.

Chapter Five

Maybe the mezcal the hotel provided in the room was a bad idea after all.

The first shot had tasted like motor oil. Not that Shannon had ever drunk motor oil, but she imagined the smoky, oily taste in her mouth was the closest she'd ever come to such a thing. The second shot wasn't as bad as the first. By the time room service arrived with an order of nachos, the next shots weren't bad at all. Drinking alone wasn't something Shannon did on a normal basis, but watching Victor working the room with his fiancée hanging on his arm prompted the mezcal. By the time she fell asleep, Victor and Corrie had left her head . . .

Until the next morning.

She woke up with the sun, even though her head told her to go back to sleep. The time change always made the first night after flying east the hardest. Not to mention the hangover.

What had she been thinking?

Everything about the past twenty-four hours was completely uncharacteristic for her. She was the quiet one, the one who held her opinion to herself until it was absolutely necessary to express it. She didn't tell strangers off on airplanes or encourage young brides to ditch their fiancés. And for all that's holy, she sure as heck didn't talk to the brother of the groom and tell him what a moron his brother was.

Now, to add insult, she was hungover.

Stomach nauseous, headache, dry mouth hungover.

She needed crackers and ice . . . and a full day to sleep this off.

Sun blazed from outside her window.

Sleep would have to wait.

"This is not okay," she said to her empty room.

Without considering the time, she picked up the phone and dialed.

Avery answered with a groggy voice, "You'd better be dying."

"I am."

"What the hell, Shannon. Do you know what time it is?"

"It's almost seven."

"No, it's five."

Shannon would feel bad about this later, but right now she needed help. "I drank too much last night. I need a hangover cure, fast."

"What?"

"You heard me."

Noise over the phone indicated Avery was talking to her husband and probably getting out of bed.

"You need a hangover cure, so you called me."

"You're my youngest friend. I'm not judging . . . help, Avery. I made an ass of myself and can't be sick today." Her stomach didn't like the adrenaline provided by the memories of the previous night.

"Okay, okay. What were you drinking?"

"Tequila . . . wine earlier, and mezcal."

"Damn, woman. Okay, you need a Bloody Mary or mimosa. Which makes you feel less ill thinking about it?"

"You're kidding. Hair of the dog?"

"Do I sound like I'm kidding? When does the wedding start?" Avery asked.

"Two."

"That's a little time. You could just sleep."

"I have to start taking pictures of the wedding party at noon."

"Then put on your dark sunglasses, go down to the restaurant, order a Bloody Mary and toast, and drink plenty of water. If you start feeling sick, drink another one."

"I can't do my job drunk." Shannon could count on one hand how many Bloody Marys she'd consumed in her lifetime.

"Can you do your job tossing your cookies?"

Shannon rested her head in her hand. "What was I thinking?"

"You weren't, obviously. But it's kinda nice to know you're not perfect."

"Of course I'm not perfect."

Avery chuckled. "Compared to me, you are."

"That's not true."

"Hey, you're the one waking my ass up at five in the morning searching for a hangover cure. Babe, you get points for that, I don't. Bloody Mary. Trust me. Keep a tiny infusion going to ward off all the crap from last night. Then, when it's all over, sleep."

Shannon saw the wisdom, and the stupidity, in Avery's suggestion. "Thanks."

"Oh, and Shannon?"

"Yeah?"

"I can't wait to hear what prompted you to get drunk your first night there."

Shannon shook her head and instantly regretted it. "By the time you get here, most of those reasons should be gone."

Avery laughed as she hung up the phone.

With the aforementioned sunglasses covering her eyes, Shannon left her room wearing a pair of shorts, a cotton shirt, and sandals to make her way to the hotel restaurant.

She asked for a table, because sitting at the bar would make her early morning drinking look obvious. And she really didn't want anyone from the wedding party seeing her.

The good news was the rain had vanished overnight.

The bad news was the rain had vanished overnight and the sun added to the pain in her head.

Note to self: Mezcal bad. Water good!

Her Bloody Mary arrived and she studied it for a good five minutes.

This is a stupid idea.

Best idea ever!

Stupid!!!

"It's meant to be drank, not stared at."

The voice came from behind her. Without looking, she knew the person it belonged to.

And that had her picking up the glass.

"I know that."

"Mind if I sit down?"

The tomato juice, the vodka . . . maybe it was the pepper. *Bad, bad, bad.*

"As a matter of fact . . ."

Victor Brooks sat facing her.

"This is becoming a bad habit," she said, ignoring the roll in her stomach.

"Oh?" He flagged the waiter down, ordered coffee. "What habit is that?" he asked once the waiter left.

"You," she said. "Invading my air space."

He leaned forward. "I'm going to go out on a limb here and suggest you don't like me very much."

The tomato juice wasn't that bad after the second sip.

She lowered her sunglasses long enough for him to see her peering at him with as much disapproval as she could muster with bloodshot eyes. "You'd be right." This man brought out the worst in her.

She shivered.

"Shouldn't you be ass kissing right now? Aren't I the one paying you?"

She could physically feel gray hair sprouting from her roots. "Actually, Mrs. Harkin hired me."

"But I'm covering the wedding."

The sound of reason knocked up beside her temple, but she ignored it.

"Then fire me. I'm sure Corrie's wedding party with their cell phones will be happy to send you their pictures."

He leaned forward. "I can see why your ex-husband divorced you."

Her breath caught in her throat.

There were hits . . . and then there were low hits.

"Does Corrie know you plan on rushing back to LA by Tuesday for your meeting?"

She could tell by the twitch in his eye that his fiancée had no idea.

"Don't pretend to know a thing about me when it's obvious I know a few things about you. I'm here for Corrie, Mr. Brooks. I'll do my best to hide your self-centered, egotistical horns while taking the pictures. But if they pop out, don't blame me." She stood, leaving her drink behind, and walked away.

Let him deal with her bill.

The incidentals of her trip were supposed to be handled by the wedding party, anyway.

By eleven, room service had delivered a replacement drink and toast. Shannon felt seventy percent better, which was sixty-five percent more than she expected.

Unlike the wedding guests, her outfit for the event was about blending in and becoming invisible. In the past, that meant wearing dark clothing, often pants, since kneeling to get the right shot was easier in flexible clothing.

She'd thought ahead and bought tan cotton pants, a simple loose shirt that would breathe while she ran around in the sun, and sneakers. Although she saw herself ditching the shoes if sand getting inside of them became a thing.

Unlike the night before, the way to travel from one location to the next was along the beach.

A vast span of white sand spread for as far as the eye could see. The clear turquoise water faded into deeper shades of blue and disappeared on the horizon. It was spectacular. The gentle waves came on shore like an invitation. Speedboats rushing by or Jet Skis buzzing around didn't interrupt the peaceful scene because that kind of activity was forbidden in the waters of Tulum. It was one of the reasons the location was ideal for beach weddings. In Cancun, where the hotels were bigger and the venues could hold hundreds of people, you had to contend with traffic on the water and more people wandering on the beach during the ceremony. Here, those things simply didn't happen.

Still, it was a destination wedding, and like Justin had said the night before, it was presumptuous to ask guests to travel such a distance to watch someone get married.

This was the kind of place a couple escaped to when they wanted to elope. Or maybe the BFFs came along and everyone hung out for a long weekend while two people just happened to get married.

Shannon pushed the thoughts from her head and angled down the beach to the site of the wedding ceremony.

Already chairs were set up and a florist worked with a team of three people, decorating the space. On each side of the chairs, long benches sat framing the ceremonial space. Shannon frowned as she tried to maneuver the cramped area.

Ida, the event coordinator, was instructing several men when Shannon found her.

Shannon introduced herself and got straight to the point. "The benches are going to get in the way of me moving around to take the photographs the couple want."

"Without the benches, we don't have enough seating for the guests. I explained to the bride that seventy-five to eighty was the perfect number. We could accommodate up to a hundred. Somehow that turned into a hundred and twenty-five."

Shannon looked over the space again.

She'd have to make it work without walking past the guests on the outside lane. Which meant she'd be walking up and down the aisle quite a bit. A distraction to those attending. Hopefully Corrie and Victor wouldn't notice.

The thought of the bet she'd made the night before gave her head some peace. Even Victor's own brother didn't think the marriage would last, which meant the work she was doing would be burned when the divorce papers were signed.

Not that she would let that stop her from doing the best she could.

"I'll make it work."

Shannon walked over to the hotel where Corrie, her wedding party, and immediate family were staying. The party at the beach bar was in full swing. Everyone except the staff was clothed in as little as possible to beat the heat and bronze their skin. It was obvious that not all the guests at the hotel were there for the nuptials.

The paths between the bungalow-style rooms were dotted with palm trees and tropical flowers, all of which would work beautifully for pictures with the bride right before the ceremony. She timed it to arrive an hour and a half early, leaving the last thirty minutes while the guests were arriving to take a few snapshots of Victor and his party. Which Shannon wasn't looking forward to. But she would hike up her big girl panties, paint on a smile, and make nice with the man.

And then photoshop out his horns in the pictures when she returned home.

She found the two-bedroom bungalow that shared a small court-yard. Corrie and her girls took one room, and Mr. and Mrs. Harkin had the other. She heard the girls chattering before she reached the door.

Her knock was answered with a shout. "If you're the groom, go away!"

"I'm not him."

Laughter preceded the door opening.

The room was an explosion of clothes, shoes, half-empty suitcases, and old trays from room service. The girls were in all states of undress. Two wore strapless bras, while Corrie and her maid of honor wore corsets.

Corrie sat in front of a mirror while a stylist worked to add tiny flowers to her hair.

"Good afternoon," Shannon said to everyone as they buzzed around.

Corrie smiled briefly at her through the mirror.

"How are you feeling today?" she asked.

"I'm fine. Nervous. But no rain, so that's good."

Shannon kept a smile in place. "I was just next door. Everything looks fabulous."

The wedding party introduced themselves, but the names that stuck in Shannon's head were Barbie, Bitsy, and Bimbo. Their high-pitched singsong voices didn't help. "How close are you to putting on your dresses?"

Melia was the name of the girl she'd met the night before, Corrie's maid of honor, who answered, "Ten minutes."

"Perfect. And your parents, Corrie?"

"Dad's ready, but you'd think my mom was the one getting married today."

Shannon encouraged the girls to clean up the room enough so that she could get a few pictures of them getting ready without the distraction of panties in the background.

One by one, the bridesmaids slipped into their gowns and helped the stylist with Corrie's.

Shannon focused in on the bride as she watched the others working around her. Her tight smile made the shots fall flat. "Your dress is beautiful," Shannon complimented, focusing closer to capture a true grin.

"It is, isn't it?"

"Perfect. Is it what you always pictured?"

Corrie turned and lifted her arms while Melia helped with the buttons up the back. "Yes."

Still no smile.

"Look over your shoulder," Shannon instructed. "Smile."

She did, but it didn't last. "I think I need to sit down." She lifted a hand to her head to fan herself. The color in her face started to drain.

Shannon grabbed a chair and pushed it close. "It might be the corset."

Corrie slid down, her breathing jumping up a few notches.

"Melia, turn the air on high." Someone handed Corrie a glass of water.

The door to the room opened and Mrs. Harkin stepped in. She frowned when she saw her daughter sitting down and everyone huddled around her. "What's going on?"

"I think she's just overheated," Shannon said.

The door opened wider and Mr. Harkin joined them. "You okay, honey?"

"I'm nervous. Everyone is staring at me."

Her observation had her girlfriends backing up a step.

"Tell you what. I'll take the girls outside, get a few pictures of them. We can wait to get shots with you after the ceremony. I'm sure you'll settle once it's all done."

Corrie nodded a few times.

Shannon exited the room and dragged the girls to the spot she'd scoped out earlier. When she returned, Corrie was feeling better but wanted to wait for the very last second to join the humidity outside.

With her work there done, Shannon left the girls in search of the men.

Unlike the women, the men were propped up on a deck, feet on the railing, wearing shorts and T-shirts.

Shannon saw Justin first and shook her head. "You do know there's a wedding in an hour, right?"

"If it isn't the sassy photographer."

She had to own the title. "That's me. I'm bossy, too."

Victor stuck his head out the sliding glass door. He, at least, was dressed. Gray dress pants and a button up shirt. "Looks like someone knows there's a timeline to this thing," Shannon quipped.

"In an hour," Victor said.

"Yeah, I heard. I need you guys dressed in fifteen. I have what I need from the women, and now it's your turn." She didn't have any trouble asserting herself when it came to doing her job. In her experience, on their own, men waited until the last second to get ready, or for someone like her to bark an order.

Justin pushed off the chair he was sitting in. "You heard the lady. Let's get moving."

Ten minutes later, the men filed out of the room. Hair combed back, dress pants, white shirts. Light jackets. Shannon took the liberty of snapping a few pictures of them standing and joking around with each other. She caught Justin sucking on his finger, a smirk on his face.

Cute.

Using the ocean and a lone palm tree as her backdrop, Shannon posed the men in a series of shots that were both serious and whimsical. Much like Corrie's, Victor's smile for her camera felt forced. She couldn't help but think it was her. It wasn't like she'd tried hard to make a good impression on the man or put him at ease with her instructions.

Then again, she had a fifty-dollar bet with the brother on how long the marriage would last. Maybe he was having second thoughts.

"Okay, Victor. Let's get a few shots with your brother."

She posed them next to a crooked palm tree that stretched horizontally nearly as much as it did vertically. The second she had them in the right frame, Victor turned to her and smiled.

She waved him off. "No, no . . . I want you to talk to each other."

Victor looked confused.

"Natural. I want to capture something real between the two of you."

Justin looked at his brother and laughed softly.

"Act normal?"

Shannon watched them from behind the lens.

"What should we talk about?" Victor asked.

"About how I'm the better-looking brother?" Justin teased.

She captured an eye roll.

"You wish."

She changed her angle, fired off a few more shots.

"What do you think, Shannon? Team Justin or Team Victor?"

Laughing, she knelt. Victor won, hands down . . . but she wasn't about to give him the point. "Oh, I don't know. We have to pull the stick out of Victor's butt before I can judge."

There it was. Shouts of laughter that had both men with genuine smiles filled with good humor.

"Oh, man, Vic . . . she has your number."

Victor turned his smile on her, a smirk reaching his eyes.

"Got it," she said, lowering her camera. "Okay, let's go next door and get a few more with your parents before the ceremony."

Scott and Renee Brooks were polar opposites of the Harkins. Warm and inviting, they didn't seem the least bit interested in taking over anything. They stood beside their son and smiled when asked. Again, Shannon encouraged Justin to stand beside his parents and asked them to talk among themselves. Finding the casual and genuine shot was always more appealing than the staged, plastic moments other photographers reached for.

Guests started meandering toward their seats, saving their places and scurrying out of the direct sun, which would hide behind a white cloud every once in a while. The breeze had picked up a little bit, offering relief, but threatening the flower stands poked into the sand.

With an eye on the time, Shannon let Victor and his wedding party go in search of Corrie and the girls. She found two of the bridesmaids hovering by the door of the air-conditioned room the bride was supposed to stay in right before walking down the aisle.

"Is Corrie here?" Shannon asked the girls.

The taller of the two blondes shook her head. "She's still in our room with Melia."

"Is she on her way?"

The girls smiled. "Her mom and dad just left to go get her."

Satisfied with that, Shannon found Ida and waited for Corrie to arrive.

Minutes trickled by as the guests took their seats. Music played softly in the background.

Shannon kept one eye on the far right of the crowd, where Victor stood in what seemed like deep conversation with his brother, and the other eye on the path Corrie would take to the staging room.

She glanced at her watch.

This wouldn't be the first wedding to start late.

Ten minutes past the hour, Mr. Harkin rounded the corner. Shannon sighed and lifted her camera in anticipation.

And then watched while Mr. Harkin marched straight down the aisle and up to Victor.

The guests paused in their conversations to watch.

"What?" The question came from Victor's lips and was heard from several feet away.

Without a pause, Victor turned toward the adjacent hotel and took the quick path along the beach.

Shannon found herself racing after him.

Some of the guests started to stand.

Justin waved his hands in the air. "Just a delay, everyone. We'll be right back." Then he was gone.

Shannon was a couple of yards behind, holding her camera and chasing the wedding party along the uneven sand.

Victor ran straight into the room where Corrie and her girls had been staying and stopped dead in his tracks. Justin bumped into his brother. Right behind were their parents.

"Where is she?" Victor asked, his voice tight.

Shannon managed to squeeze in between Mr. and Mrs. Brooks and Justin to find Beverly Harkin sitting in the middle of a discarded wedding dress, tears running down her cheeks.

"Oh, no," Shannon whispered.

Chapter Six

"We found this," Mr. Harkin said as he handed Victor a note.

He waved the paper in the air. "'I'm sorry.' That's it?"

"She'll come back," Mrs. Harkin managed between sobs.

"Unbelievable!" Victor's arms collapsed at his sides. "'I'm sorry. I'm sorry'?" He repeated Corrie's written words and paced the room.

"It's okay, son." Mr. Brooks stepped forward.

Victor moved toward the open sliding glass door that led out onto the beach party going on below. He stopped with his back to the group in the room and said, "Does anyone know what is going on? Why?"

He turned then, made eye contact with each person staring.

His scowl landed on Shannon, and the horns he'd managed to hide all day came out. She saw the moment his brain remembered the words she'd said on the plane. *If you were my boyfriend, I'd find the first cabana boy I could and ditch you at the door.*

"You!"

Shannon swallowed her guilt over whatever part she may have played in Corrie leaving the groom at the altar and shook her head. "She didn't say anything to me about leaving."

He took a few steps forward, anger surging through every muscle.

She retreated.

"What did you say to her?"

"This is not on me . . ."

"Okay, little brother, simmer down. You're upset, but this is not the time to start blaming anyone." Justin approached his brother and pulled him outside.

As they went out one door, the bridesmaids and groomsmen walked in another.

"This is bad." Barbie, or maybe it was Bitsy, stated the obvious.

"Did she say anything to you girls?" Mrs. Harkin quizzed them.

They both looked at each other and shrugged. Which told Shannon that Corrie had said something.

"Well?" Mrs. Harkin yelled.

Both girls jumped.

"She was nervous. Said she needed a little time to breathe, so we walked next door."

With all the clothes thrown around the room, Shannon couldn't help but think the girl would be back once the wedding was called off. "Can you look around and tell us if Corrie's stuff is still here? Her purse, passport?"

Her question prompted the girls to take inspection and open the room safe.

The looks on their faces spoke for them.

"Both her and Melia's passports are gone."

"Purses and phones, too."

Scott Brooks patted his wife on the shoulder and followed his sons outside.

When Mrs. Brooks sat beside Mrs. Harkin to console her, Shannon ducked outside. She motioned for the girls to follow her.

Once away from the family, she played big sister.

"She didn't say she was leaving," the tall girl said immediately.

"It's okay. I don't care about that. Check in with Melia, make sure she's with Corrie and that they're safe. You don't have to tell anyone where they are. Just let the family know everyone is okay. That's all that matters."

The girls huddled together and nodded in unison.

⌒๑

Standing beside his brother and telling the wedding guests that his bride had had second thoughts was the single most humiliating experience in Victor's life, though the time in fifth grade when he was mandated to sing in a talent show wearing a green frog costume was a close second. Why that thought surfaced in his head while he was doing his best to make light of the situation, he didn't know.

Justin stepped up and told everyone to stay and eat and drink. It was all paid for, and they wouldn't want it to go to waste.

A couple dozen people left right away, and the others gathered in small groups and quietly ate and drank from the open bar.

Kurt and Arwin, Victor's friends since high school, plied him with alcohol. He allowed them to hand him liquor, but he didn't go out of his way to keep drinking it. Needing some control, Victor approached each and every guest and thanked them for coming. He shook hands with people he'd never met, friends of the Harkin family, and accepted condolences from the people he knew in the crowd.

He heard a chorus of: "Maybe she'll change her mind." "She'll be back when she realizes what she lost." "No worries. There are other women out there."

Yeah, it was all placating crap. The kind of encouragement he'd offer if the shoe were on the other foot.

Only it was his toes stuck in the shit.

And it stank.

What the hell was he going to say to his staff when he returned home? He'd be sitting in the frog suit all over again. Everyone he'd told he was getting married would ask about the missus, and he'd have to relive this moment. He'd worked his whole life to avoid times like this.

A hand on his shoulder snapped him out of his thoughts. He turned, on autopilot, a grin in place.

His mother's soft smile pulled him back to his reality.

"How are you holding up?"

"I'm good."

Her eyes narrowed, concern on her brow. "You know you don't have to stick around here. Your brother offered to take you out with your friends to get *shitfaced*, I think is how he put it."

The closer the evening closed in, the more appealing that became. "I need to make sure everything is okay here."

"No, you don't. Your dad and I will see that everything is taken care of for you."

"I can do it."

She patted his arm. "You were always so independent. Never letting anyone do for you what you could do for yourself. Let us do this for you. This isn't where you want to be tonight. Corrie's parents are already gone, packing up."

"I thought they were waiting for her to come back." To drag her to the altar, not that Victor would accept that now.

His mom looked at her feet, avoiding his eyes.

"Mom?"

"She's not coming back. Noel, is it? Her friend?"

Victor nodded.

"She let us know that she's okay. And that she asked her friends to pack all her stuff and send it with her parents, or ship it home."

Victor turned toward the ocean breeze and caught the last rays of sun on the horizon. What a coward, not even willing to face him. "You were right."

"I was?"

"Yeah. You said she was too young."

His mom stood in front of him and forced him to look at her.

On a deep sigh, she said, "I also told you she wasn't the right woman for you, despite her age. But that doesn't make today any easier." She kissed his cheek. "Now, go with your brother. Let your dad and I handle this crowd."

Victor watched as his mom approached his brother and pointed toward him. Next thing he knew, his brother and friends were pushing him down the beach to a hotel that didn't house anyone who knew him, Corrie, or the whole sordid mess.

∽

"Runaway bride. I kid you not." Shannon sat on an abandoned lounge chair outside her hotel, away from the party atmosphere inside the restaurant and bar, and FaceTimed Avery.

"No way."

"Yeah, I saw her less than an hour before the ceremony, in her dress. She bailed."

"Dude, that's rough."

Shannon sighed. "Yeah, I hope she's okay."

Avery moved the phone closer. "Her? What about him?"

Shannon shook her head. "He's a total tool. Didn't deserve her. Completely full of himself."

"What?"

"Yeah, he reminded me of Paul. Good-looking and knows it. Life is all about work and the next thing that needs to be conquered. Only she refused to be one of them. We could all take a lesson."

"Still, what happens when someone flees on their wedding day?"

"I'm guessing they're both getting drunk right about now."

"Probably," Avery said.

"Anyway . . . I can't wait for you to get here."

Avery grinned. "Meet anyone you might want to have a baby with?"

Shannon stretched out on the beach bed. "I haven't even looked."

"Not at all?"

"No," she admitted. "I've been wrapped up in this wedding . . . or lack thereof. Besides, I told you I wanted to wait until we're at the other hotel to look. People here will recognize me."

"Right, right. When are you going to the new place?"

"The day after tomorrow, when you fly in. I'm planning to spend the whole time on the beach until you get here. Can you believe I've been here a full day and haven't touched the water yet?" She turned the camera around in hopes she could capture the way the moon danced on the sea. "It's remarkable here."

"I'll be there before you know it. I'll call when I land."

"Sounds good. Safe flight."

Avery blew her a kiss and disconnected the call.

What a day. Very few that compared.

"Look who we have here!"

Shannon jumped, the voice behind her familiar.

"Good God. You scared me."

Victor stood behind her, his shirt unbuttoned to midchest, pants rolled up and damp from barefoot walks on the water's edge. The flower that once was upright on his lapel was now smashed against his shirt, with what looked like duct tape holding it on. The perfect picture of the wounded groom.

Turning away, she sat back on the lounge chair and watched the small waves push against the shore.

"Ms. Annoyed is scared," he mocked her.

Yup. He was drunk. Shannon couldn't blame him for that. "You should probably find your room and sleep that off."

"Sassy."

"Bossy," she corrected. "And sober. So you might wanna listen. You wouldn't want to stumble on the wrong beach into some kinda drug cartel situation." She glanced over her shoulder. Saw him swaying as he stood. "Good Lord. Where is your brother? Isn't he watching out for you?"

Victor shook his head. "I told him I was going to bed."

She looked around. "Did you get lost on the way to your room?"

He glanced left, then right. "Misplaced."

Another look around and she knew she wasn't going to find any help. Pushing off her comfortable perch, she made a come-hither motion with her hand in an effort to direct him to his room.

Halfway there, he turned toward the noise of the bar. "I want another drink."

"That's a bad idea."

"I think it's a *great* idea." His words exited his mouth in a slow, steady pace.

She remembered her morning and the need to phone a friend for a hangover cure and paused. The image of Victor spending his morning cussing the world probably wasn't a horrible thing.

She smiled, started toward the bar. "I'm going on record that this is *your* idea."

He grinned. "I'll blame you in the morning."

With that comment, she would see that he did.

They worked their way into the bar. It was late for the resort town, even on a Saturday. Seemed the town wanted to close up before midnight. So things were winding down but not completely empty at eleven thirty. Shannon slid onto a bar stool while Victor did the same with a little less grace. "My friend here would like a shot of mezcal," she said for him.

Victor's eyes opened a little wider. "Two," he said, pointing to the two of them.

Shannon grinned. "I'll take a vodka soda." And when Victor turned his head away, she motioned for the bartender to hold the vodka. With a wink, the man went to fill their order.

"I did *not* get married today," he said, as if that was news to her.

She couldn't help but be amused by his drunkenness. "I know that."

"Flew the coop without saying goodbye. Left a-afloat in the sea all alone."

"Dramatic much?" she asked with an eye roll.

"Hey, you don't know." His elbow slipped on the side of the bar, but he managed to correct himself and look her in the eye. "She could have told me."

"Maybe *she* worried you'd talk her out of it."

"Of course I would have. I'm a very good negotiator."

"Is that right?"

The bartender brought their drinks, setting two shots of mezcal in front of her unexpected drinking partner.

"Then she was right to leave the way she did."

He frowned. "Hey, whose side are you on?"

Shannon lifted her hands in the air. "I'm just the photographer. I'm not on anyone's side." But if she had to pick . . . Team Corrie would win.

He lifted his drink and brought it to his lips.

His expression matched how she'd felt the night before when she'd tasted mezcal for the first time.

"What the hell is that?" He set it down and stared at the oversize shot glass.

She pushed the glass closer to him. "It's a specialty. Trust me, it gets better."

He picked it up but didn't taste it right away. "I'm just saying, she could have done it different."

Shannon sipped her club soda. "According to the song, there are 'Fifty Ways to Leave Your Lover,'" she said, remembering the lyrics.

Victor laughed, concentrated really hard for a few seconds, then said, "She just slid out the back door."

Catching on, Shannon smiled. "Now it's time for you to make a new plan."

Victor hummed the chorus, and they both took turns butchering the lines to the song.

The bartender chuckled at their barroom singing.

They finished the chorus laughing.

Victor tipped the rest of his shot back, squeezed his eyes, and shook his head several times. "You're right," he squeaked out. "Not that bad the second time."

Those wouldn't be his thoughts in the morning. "I guess this means you're going home early."

He took a lazy look around the bar. "No reason to stay," he said. "This might come as a surprise to you, but I don't vacation well anyway."

She mustered up the best look of sarcasm she could. "You don't say?"

His scowl was lost with the half-mast eyes and his elbow sliding off the bar. "You know . . ." He licked his lips. "You're bitchy."

She placed a hand over her chest. "I don't think anyone has ever said that to me. Coming from you, I'll take that as a compliment."

"It wasn't meant as one."

Because he had it coming, she pushed the second shot of mezcal his way. "I don't understand why you're still single, Victor. You talk so sweetly to the ladies."

He slurped up the drink, hardly batted an eye. "I sh-shouldn't be single tonight."

"She was too young for you," Shannon said in all seriousness.

"Did you tell her that?" Every time he blinked, it took longer for him to open his eyes.

"No." Shannon pushed his shoulder up to keep him from falling off the bar stool. If she was less bitchy, she'd be feeding him water and maybe some coffee. Instead, she pointed to Victor's empty glass for the bartender. He came over with the bottle and refilled it.

"Thanks." He looked at the drink, then looked around the bar. "Everyone told me she was too young. Obviously they were right."

He waved a hand in the air. "She just slipped out the back!" He found himself funny and started laughing.

"Yeah, yeah . . . we already sang that song."

"I had a plan."

"Oh? What plan was that?"

"Get a wife. I mean, I'm not bad-looking. You don't think I'm bad-looking, right?"

"Looks don't guarantee anything."

He lifted his glass. "I guess that's true."

Victor silently stared into his drink. The humor drifted away. "I have to make a new plan."

"A backup is always a good idea."

He sucked back his drink and closed his eyes. "I didn't see this coming."

For a minute, Shannon almost felt sorry for him. "I don't think you were looking."

He pushed the empty glass away and folded his arms on the bar, rested his head in them.

"It's okay, Victor. I'm sure there's someone else out there foolish enough to say *I do* to you." She hoped her slur would have him poking barbs back.

Instead, he was quiet.

Really quiet.

She shook his arm.

"Victor?"

Then she heard his snore.

She watched him, passed out on the bar, for several seconds. Would have considered leaving him there but knew the guilt would eat at her if she did.

There was no way she could get him to his room without help.

Patting down his back pockets, she found his cell phone. Using his passed out hand, she pressed his thumb to the reader until it opened.

It didn't take long to locate Justin's phone number. He answered immediately.

"Where the hell are you, jackass?"

"He's passed out *on* the bar," she said with a chuckle.

"What? Who is this?"

"Someone you owe fifty bucks. I can't believe you let this drunk walk on the beach alone."

"Shannon?"

"Yup, it's me. Babysitting your baby brother at your hotel restaurant bar. But my shift is about done and I'm not going to lug this guy to his room."

She heard Justin muffle the phone and shout out to others in the background. "We'll be right there."

She put the phone aside but considered taking a few pictures of Victor facedown on the bar. If Avery were there, Shannon was pretty sure the night wouldn't end without a few embarrassing photos to look at in the future.

Justin showed up with Victor's two friends. They shook their heads as they marched toward her.

"We've been looking for him for the past half hour."

"I would think a bar would be the first place you'd check."

Justin ran a hand through his hair. "He was pretty sloshed. I didn't see him looking for more booze."

She waved at the empty glasses. "You guessed wrong." With a long stretch, she stood and patted Justin's back. "Good luck with that one in the morning. Ending the night with mezcal leaves a nasty taste the next day."

Justin stared down at his brother. "Thanks for keeping an eye on him."

"I'm a team player." She looked to the other guys. "If my friends were here, they'd be taking pictures. Just a suggestion."

That's all she needed to say, and the phones came out.

On her short walk to her room on the opposite side of the hotel, Shannon lifted her chin. It felt good, a little vindictive, even, to know Victor would wake up with a nasty hangover. She might even send over a Bloody Mary as a peace offering.

Nawh . . . let him figure out his own cures.

Because in all the things Victor had said that night, what he failed to proclaim was any love for his former fiancée.

Corrie was right in running off, and even if Victor didn't realize it yet, he was lucky she did.

If anything Shannon had said to the former would-be bride made Corrie flee, then Victor should be thanking her for all the money he didn't have to part with after the divorce.

She doubted that would ever happen, the thanking thing. In fact, she was fairly certain the man's lips would curse her as soon as he realized she'd happily fed more fuel to his already drunk body.

Those were curses she could live with.

Chapter Seven

Something crawled in Victor's mouth and died.

The ceiling fan spun in slow circles over his head, moving air gently around the room.

In careful measures, he scanned the room and his body from head to toe. With each beat of his heart, a solid knock hit his temples . . . hard! The pasty film on the roof of his mouth contributed to the aforementioned death inside. His dress shirt was bunched up around his shoulders, with several buttons missing from the fabric. He was still in his dress pants. The bottoms were damp, and he didn't have any socks or shoes. Rolling over on the bed, he saw his wallet and cell phone on the nightstand, but no evidence of his shoes on the floor. A vague memory of throwing them in the ocean sometime the previous night surfaced. It was one of those "screw the world, I'll be a beach bum" moments.

He forced his body into a sitting position and smacked his lips together in an attempt to find some moisture.

Beside his bed was a bottle of water and a small package of headache medicine, along with a note. *Call me when you're awake. Justin.*

He tore open the packet and washed the sour pills down. He hit the bathroom and then stood over the sink, watching the water run down the drain.

Corrie bailed.

Left him at the last possible minute without one word.

Victor shrugged his shirt off, tossed it in the corner of the bathroom, and walked back to the bed. Sitting on the edge, he looked at his phone.

It was still early. Eight o'clock was entirely too early to wake up after the binge he'd managed the night before.

A text from his mother had come through at six. His parents were on their way to the airport, said Justin was staying an extra day to make sure he was okay, and that if he needed them, to call before they boarded the plane and they'd come back.

He fired off a quick note telling them he was okay and that he'd call them later that week.

Other than his mom, his phone was painfully silent.

No word from Corrie. He'd be damned if he would text or call her first.

No messages from his extended family who had shown up to witness his humiliation. Nothing.

Arwin and Kurt where probably still sleeping, and Justin was probably piling in breakfast.

Victor plugged his phone in to charge and headed to the shower.

Twenty minutes later, he found his brother in the hotel restaurant, sitting in front of an empty plate and a cup of coffee.

When Justin saw him, he put his phone down. "I didn't expect to see you until noon."

Victor pulled out a chair. "I won't be running any marathons this morning, that's for sure."

Justin laughed. "I'm glad to see you up."

"I'm a little surprised I'm vertical. I don't remember going to bed."

"That's too bad. The strippers we hired were top-shelf."

Victor narrowed his eyes. "Yeah, right."

They both laughed.

The waiter brought him a menu and he ordered coffee. His head still had a band playing inside, but his stomach didn't seem any worse for the night. "Thanks for keeping me from following my shoes into the ocean."

"I'm not sure what thought bubble prompted that rebellion. It isn't like Corrie left because of your footwear."

He didn't know where that came from either.

"You made us crazy, taking off like you did last night," Justin said, taking a drink from his coffee.

"I took off?"

"Yeah. One minute you said you were going to take a leak, the next thing we know, you were gone."

The image of the moon hitting the water the night before surfaced in his head. He remembered being pissed the view was perfect. A perfect view on an imperfect night. Then he remembered sitting at the bar with *her*.

Singing.

"Please tell me that photographer wasn't part of last night."

Justin sat in silence.

"Hell, no."

"Sorry, Vic. But you're lucky she stumbled upon you. Or you on her, however that may have been."

"We were drinking at the bar." *And singing.*

"That you were."

Victor shook his head. "She told Corrie to leave. I know it." Her conviction on the plane, the words she told him when she didn't know who he was. The strength and confidence in her couldn't understand how a woman would want a man like him.

Justin sat forward. "You said that constantly last night . . . sober, drunk. What if she did, Vic? No one put a gun to Corrie's head and told her to flake. In the end, she did that all on her own."

"Still . . ."

"Do you remember what you were saying seconds before you realized Corrie wasn't walking down that aisle?"

His back teeth met and didn't let go. "That was nerves."

Justin fixed him with a look. "That was second thoughts. We both know it. So what if Shannon nudged Corrie to walk away? What if her best friends drug her away? It doesn't matter. Her second thoughts stopped her. Why didn't yours?"

"Nerves, not second thoughts."

Justin shook his head. "I call bullshit. If Corrie was the end all, be all, you would have run after her and begged her to come back. But you didn't do that. Did you?"

Victor swallowed. The thought had never occurred to him.

"You're getting a do-over, Vic . . . a new start without going through all the crap that happens when you marry the wrong person for the wrong reasons and end up giving up half your shit for the effort. Trust me on this. Count your blessings." Justin had married in his late twenties and was divorced by thirty-four. No kids, thankfully. His ex did take half.

Victor turned his gaze to the beach outside the open doors of the restaurant. Maybe his brother had a point. "I should just go back to work and forget all this happened."

Justin blew out a frustrated breath. "Or maybe you should take the two weeks you were supposed to be on your honeymoon and figure out why your priorities are all messed up."

He snapped his eyes to his brother. "My priorities are just fine, thank you."

"The hell. You didn't fly in with Corrie like you planned. Why?"

"I had a meeting."

"Did anyone die at this meeting?"

"Don't be ridiculous."

"I'm not being anything. You blew off your fiancée the day before your wedding for a *meeting*. I don't care what was going on . . . a gazillion-dollar deal, a peace offering between the Israelis and the—"

"It was important." Tensions in China were messing with his future.

Justin sat back. "I don't get it. I just don't. You're so damn smart when it comes to finance and futures. You saw Dad working his ass off day and night at the shop, always struggling. When we were old enough to jump in and learn the trade, you were like, 'Hell, no. There's a way to make money on the scraps.' But you're so damn ignorant when it comes to personal relationships."

Their father was a machinist. A master at twisting raw pieces of metal into something that ended up in airplanes flying at thirty thousand feet or rocketing into outer space. With every part he created, there were shavings all over the shop floor.

Shavings of valuable metal that needed to be recycled.

His father had a company come in to pick up the shavings for a price. Only Victor wanted the cut for himself. By the time he graduated from high school, he'd laughingly started Vic Corp. His father and several of his friends gave Vic their shavings . . . for a price, and Victor negotiated contracts with recycling companies to turn a significant profit. Where Justin joined his father at Brooks Incorporated, making parts and working long hours, Victor took a different direction.

He accepted his two-year associate's degree in business from his local community college and went into business for himself full-time. Taking two more years out of his life to accomplish what he was already doing didn't fit his schedule. Vic Corp started with him in his childhood bedroom, he moved to an apartment before he was old enough to drink a beer legally, and by the time he was thirty, he'd stretched his shavings into recycling boats full of garbage to countries that needed the resources.

He was greener than any Prius-driving tree hugger out there.

At least when it came to his business. He knew business. He understood the politics of the game. He negotiated contracts better than anyone on his team. So when there was a last-minute meeting that would mean an annual profit bottom line of five million, he delayed his flight by a few hours.

Victor didn't see the problem.

Only now, his wedding called off and fiancée gone AWOL, he blinked out over the blinding sun just beyond the doors of the restaurant and questioned his own behavior.

"What the hell is wrong with me?" he asked more to himself than his brother.

"Is that a rhetorical question, or do you want me to answer it?"

Victor met his brother's laughing eyes. "I don't have the time to hear your laundry list of answers."

Justin sighed. "Take a break, brother. Enjoy the beach. Maybe find some cute someone to erase Corrie. Or find a cute someone that makes you realize Corrie wasn't the one."

A cute someone.

Yeah . . . he could do that.

Shannon blinked her eyes open and found Justin standing over her.

"Someone is hitting the beach early," he said, smiling.

"Might as well be me." She scooted up on the lounger and pulled her cover-up across her lap. "How is everyone this morning?"

She'd been thinking about Victor, Corrie, and the whole mess from the minute the light penetrated her room.

"If by *everyone* you mean Victor, he's fine. Annoyingly unhungover."

"That's too bad." The man deserved to be cursing liquor all day after the binge the previous night.

Justin shook his head, laughed, and pulled up a seat in a chaise next to hers. "You have an unassuming sadistic side."

"Says the man laying bets on how long his brother's marriage would last."

"Yes, but he's my brother. It's expected. You hardly know him."

"I know his type."

Justin sat back and stared out at the sea. "He's really not that bad. Misguided right now, but not bad."

Shannon wasn't about to debate that with him. She changed the subject. "So when are you pulling out?"

"Tomorrow morning. What about you?"

"A friend of mine is flying in, and we're staying for almost a week."

"Here? Or are you going to Cancun?"

"Here . . . well, not this hotel, but one up the way a bit. I haven't had a beach vacation in a while." She glanced toward the ocean. "You can't beat the view."

"Oh, I don't know. There could be more women walking around topless. That would beat it."

Shannon rolled her eyes and leaned back. "Men."

They were quiet for a few seconds.

"I owe you fifty bucks."

Shannon waved him off. "Keep it."

"No, no . . . I won't welch on a bet. But tell me, did you say anything to Corrie?"

Shannon kept her eyes on two kids playing at the water's edge. "If by *anything* you mean did I tell Corrie to leave, the answer is no."

"So she did say something to you."

Shannon paused, unsure of what she should reveal. "She was beside herself the night of the rehearsal dinner. Between the rain and Victor taking a later flight, Corrie didn't see the silver lining. She was having second thoughts."

Justin kicked his feet up and leaned back. "At least one of them was smart enough to call it off."

She considered him from the corner of her eye. "Was Victor questioning his decision?"

"He called it nerves. I called bullshit."

She settled her sunglasses more comfortably on the bridge of her nose and closed her eyes. "Well, at least he can make his Tuesday meeting without skipping out on his honeymoon."

"His what?"

"Every passenger in first class had the pleasure of hearing Victor tell someone that he'd be at his meeting on Tuesday. And no, before you ask . . . I didn't tell Corrie about the meeting. Although I'd have loved to be a fly on the wall when he explained his need to leave his honeymoon early. Betting the marriage wouldn't last the week was a little like insider trading. Hence why you don't need to pay up."

"In that case . . ."

Shannon smiled.

A few minutes later, after she thought the conversation had dried up, Justin's sigh grabbed her attention. She looked over, found him staring at her.

"I've recently started seeing someone," he told her.

Where had that come from? "That's nice."

"What I meant to say was, I'm seeing someone, but if I wasn't, I would have asked you out. Learned what kind of idiot let you slip away."

The weight of his stare met with a hint of her insecurity. "Well, thank you. I'm flattered. I'm in a strange place right now and probably would have said no." Because starting a relationship while attempting to get pregnant might kill both deals.

"Probably?"

She attempted a smile. "Sorry."

"No, no . . . it's okay."

Shannon returned to the study of the underside of her eyelids.

When Justin remained quiet, she glanced his way. His eyes were closed, his frame stretched out. Team Victor won on the attractive scale, but the man needed a neurorectologist to remove his head from his butt . . . where Team Justin, while still attractive, skipped out on a certain something that she couldn't put a finger to.

Not that it mattered. She'd likely never see either one of them again by morning.

Chapter Eight

Victor noticed Shannon sitting in the open dining area of the hotel the next morning, drinking coffee and reading on her e-reader. He'd spent most of the previous day licking his metaphorical wounds and nursing a headache. Kurt and Arwin flew out the day before, and Justin was an hour away from jumping into a taxi to the airport.

It was Monday, and most, if not all, of the wedding guests had already left the country.

Dressed in cotton pants that went midcalf and a light shirt, she looked like she was dressed for a long plane ride home. As much a pain in the ass as the woman had been, he felt compelled to say goodbye. After all, he was the reason she was there.

He walked up quietly behind her. "If it isn't the woman who fed me mezcal."

The sound of his voice made her jump.

Too bad she wasn't holding her coffee.

"You have got to stop doing that."

Without an invitation, he sat and smiled. She took a deep breath and looked away, came painfully close to rolling her eyes. For some reason, he appreciated the fact she held back and wondered just how much it would take for her to disregard him with such a gesture.

"Please, sit down," she said.

He glanced at his chair. "Thank you."

She set her e-reader aside. "I thought for sure you'd be back at the office by now."

So did he. "I couldn't fly yesterday even if I'd found a flight."

"Oh?"

He didn't miss the tiny shine in the corner of her eye.

"No. I had one too many the other night. Inflicting that on whoever had the misfortune of sitting next to me on the flight home was more than I could take after my flight here."

She smiled, briefly, and lifted her chin. "I'm glad to hear you've evolved since Friday."

Unable to help himself, he laughed.

Her smile returned.

Victor felt a twist in his gut, a pull to something he didn't want to name. "I guess you're leaving today," he said.

She shrugged. "I am."

He nodded. "Justin informed me you made sure I didn't decide to go for a late night swim."

"It was tempting. But then I realized you wouldn't be able to pay me if you swallowed too much water."

"Self-preserving. Very smart of you."

"It's a gift."

When the woman wasn't tossing barbs at him, she was beautiful. Perfect lines in her face, high cheekbones . . . he couldn't tell if her olive skin was from an ancestor or the byproduct of living in Southern California. Not anything like Corrie. Nothing like anyone he'd been attracted to before.

What was he thinking? He wasn't attracted.

Victor shook his head and stood. "Well, I saw you sitting here and thought I'd at least say goodbye."

She stood with him and extended her hand. "For what it's worth, I'm sorry things didn't go as planned this weekend."

Her fingers were long, elegant. Just like the woman. Disappointment saying goodbye was an emotion he had no business feeling. Yet there it was, like a lump in his chest.

"Are you?"

Her smile cracked. "No. But it seemed the right thing to say. I am sorry for the heartache. That's never easy, even if it's for the right reason."

Victor realized he was still shaking her hand and let go.

"Goodbye, Victor. Good luck to you."

"Goodbye, Shannon." And because it was the appropriate thing to do once you said goodbye, Victor walked away. When he turned to take a last look, Shannon sharply moved her gaze to her coffee.

Shannon moved up the beach by half a mile and settled into one of only two second-story suites the boutique hotel offered. With the uninterrupted views of the ocean and a private patio that had its own plunge pool, this hotel was exactly what she'd envisioned while staying in Tulum for a vacation. As planned, there wasn't one familiar face from the Brookses' wedding party. If any of the family or guests had decided to extend their stay, they hadn't changed hotels. Most people wouldn't. Then again, most people didn't plan on the nefarious actions Shannon had in mind for the rest of her stay.

She was on the balcony when she heard Avery enter the room. Shannon stood from the shady spot she'd propped herself up on to greet her friend. Avery held her welcome drink in one hand and her purse in the other.

"Eeeeek. This place is the shit," Avery said, tossing her purse aside and offering Shannon a one-arm hug.

"Beautiful, isn't it?"

The bellhop placed Avery's bag in the room and asked if there was anything else he could assist with. Shannon tipped the man and closed the door behind him.

"Look at this room."

It was pretty nice. A king-size bed and an additional twin was the best they could do without having separate rooms. If Shannon found a baby daddy, it would do well to have a roommate to fall back on if she needed the man to go to his own room when they were done.

"Check out the balcony."

Avery didn't need to be asked twice. She wandered outside and tossed her arms wide. "A private pool?"

More like an oversize hot tub, but yeah. "A great place to wash the salt water off after a day in the ocean."

"This is fabulous."

They talked briefly about her flight and drive from the airport. Then the conversation turned toward the nonwedding.

". . . so I had the bartender pour him several shots of mezcal, and before you knew it, he was passed out on the bar."

"On?"

"I took great pleasure in thinking he was hungover the next day."

They were sitting on their balcony, enjoying the ocean breeze and shade of the palapa.

"I didn't know you had such a merciless side."

"Me either," Shannon said. "I kinda like it."

Avery grinned. "You're either getting to an age where pretending has grown old or I'm rubbing off on you."

"I think it's the former. I don't want a child of mine growing up feeling like they have to hold their emotions back all the time."

"Like we did."

Shannon regarded Avery. "I doubt you did a lot of holding back."

"Yeah, I sucked at it. Still do."

"It's served you well."

Avery swung her legs over the chaise and stood. "Let's find our swimsuits and hit the bar. See if there are any eligible bartenders."

Shannon's stomach twisted.

Avery hesitated. "Unless you've changed your mind."

"No. Of course not."

"You can, you know. Anytime."

Shannon narrowed her eyes. "You came here to help me find a baby daddy, not talk me out of it."

Avery held up both hands. "I know . . . but if you change your mind, at any time—"

"I want a child, and I'm not willing to wait for Mr. Forever to give one to me when he doesn't seem to be out there."

Avery stood. "Okay. Let's do this."

Shannon followed her into the room.

Let's do this.

⌒୨

Victor sat on his perch, watching life go on without him.

Justin had left, the rest of his family . . . people he called friends. And he was on his honeymoon alone.

When he called his office and told his assistant to reschedule all his appointments, the ones he had no right having in the first place, Stephanie asked if he was okay. By now his whole office knew about his lack of a wife. He imagined the place would buzz with gossip while he was gone and turn to silence when he returned.

Hopefully by the time he flew home, he'd have his head wrapped around the entire ordeal and put it behind him.

He attempted to call Corrie once. Needless to say, she didn't pick up.

Probably for the best. He wasn't sure what he would say to her. As the days passed, he started to see the wisdom in his family's words. He looked at pictures she'd taken of the two of them, mainly selfies she'd sent him in texts. Where he was starting to see a little wear around the corners of his eyes, she wouldn't be looking for Botox for a good twenty years.

What had he been thinking?

His grand plan.

Get married, have a couple kids . . .

Coming home to a large, empty house every night had grown old. He'd managed girlfriends over the years, but few tolerated his busy work schedule. His ambition wasn't solely on pleasing a woman. He treated them well, the few he'd seen a few months at a time. He wasn't a cheater. In fact, he never dated two women at the same time, even if they were in a noncommitted relationship. It wasn't his style.

Truth was, he didn't have time to juggle women. Dealing with one was time-consuming enough.

Maybe Justin was right.

Maybe Victor needed to take a hard look at his life and see exactly where his priorities were.

Work.

It fulfilled him. Excited him to make deals and watch his portfolio explode.

It wasn't like he'd grown up poor. His mom and dad gave them a comfortable life. Yearly vacations, sometimes road trips and camping, a few times they'd flown to his uncle's home in Idaho.

When was the last time he sat in front of a campfire and watched the stars?

He'd liked that . . . once upon a time.

What happened?

He leaned over the railing of his balcony toward the party going on at the beach bar below.

People of all ages, families . . .

He heard laughter and found his eyes tracking the sound. Large-brimmed hats hid the features of two women sitting at the bar. They wore cover-ups over bathing suits. Long, tan legs peeped out from under the bar.

He liked long, tan legs.

What kind of asshole was he to think like that just days from when he was supposed to have gotten married?

He'd turned to walk away when he heard that laughter again.

A second look and Miss Tan Legs glanced around, exposing her face.

"What the . . . ?"

No way.

Chapter Nine

The bartender was cute, but not baby daddy cute, nor baby daddy tall. So since the man pouring the drinks was off the list, Shannon relaxed and enjoyed something fruity with coconut while Avery stuck to tequila.

After all, Avery had repeated several times, they were in Mexico.

It felt good to relax and have a friend close by who had no problem talking with complete strangers. Avery was all kinds of social diva. Where Shannon prided herself on the same task in the political, black-tie kind of events, Avery had the bar thing down.

Half-dressed and dripping in suntan lotion lowered all inhibitions. Or maybe that was the coconut thing Shannon was drinking.

The bartender was out, but the two men sitting next to them were both exceptionally good-looking and had all the right parts to give Shannon the baby she wanted. Except for the fact they were married . . . to each other.

Erasmo and Dylan were from Portugal. They were celebrating their two-year anniversary. Like most Europeans, they spoke English fluently.

"Who proposed to whom?" Shannon asked, her head more than a little buzzed from the sugar, rum, and heat.

Erasmo pointed a finger at his chest and Dylan softly smiled at his husband.

"He tries to be a hard-ass," Dylan said, calling Erasmo out. "But inside he's all mushy."

Shannon had so many questions but kept her filter in place. She liked to think she had a diverse group of friends, but she didn't know a happily married homosexual couple. Not personally, anyway.

Avery, on the other hand, had no filter. "How do you know which one of you is the one to ask?"

They turned to each other and laughed. "We get that question a lot," Erasmo said. "I asked Dylan out after we met with a group of mutual friends, and we fell into that pattern."

"Erasmo is more assertive than I am. It isn't any different than any other relationship in this century."

Shannon disagreed. "The hetero world still has the man asking the marriage question in the majority of relationships."

"I would have asked if he hadn't," Dylan said. "Now we're working on an adoption plan."

Avery glanced at Shannon, paused, then smiled. "Adoption, huh?"

Shannon glared back. Adoption wasn't an option . . . yet. She wanted the whole experience . . . and since she was a woman with a few fertile years left, she could get it. Or at least she *thought* she could. Not that she'd tried, and there was always a chance it didn't happen.

"Oh, yeah. We love kids. What about you?" Dylan asked Avery.

"I can wait a little while. I just got married."

"Liam doesn't leave you alone," Shannon reminded her friend.

"There are a lot of factors to getting pregnant. You should know that," Avery teased.

"I'm aware."

"Did you try with your ex?" Erasmo asked Shannon.

Shannon shook her head and sipped her drink. "Not at all. I could tell we weren't going to last long." Mainly because the contract she had with the man lasted two years, or less if he didn't make the office.

But that didn't stop her from dreaming once their relationship became physical and she fell for the man.

"Ohhhh, something unpleasant just ran through your head," Dylan said.

"You're a mind reader?"

"Was he that bad?" he asked.

"Stop prying, Dylan." Erasmo placed a hand on Dylan's arm.

Shannon put her drink down. With a lack of information and facts, people made up their own minds about what the truth was. "He wasn't bad, just not right for me. Coparenting would have made the breakup worse. So I'm glad it didn't happen, even if I wanted kids."

"You still have plenty of time. The right guy is out there," Dylan offered.

Shannon tried not to smile at Avery, feeling as if by doing so she'd give away their ultimate goal for staying in Tulum.

Shannon felt an itch on the back of her head and turned to look behind her.

With purposeful strides, Victor Brooks walked straight toward her. "What is he doing here?"

"Who is that?" Avery asked, following her gaze.

"Victor."

"The asshole groom?" Avery smirked.

"What groom?" Dylan asked.

Victor moved closer.

Shannon waved off the question. "Tell you later." Giving Victor a long look up and down, she determined the man truly hadn't packed for the beach. Black pants, a short-sleeve dress shirt—unbuttoned—and loafers. "What are you doing here?" she asked when he was close enough to hear her.

"I wanted to ask you the same thing. You said you were leaving."

"I did leave . . . the other hotel. What are you doing here?"

"What does it look like I'm doing? I'm on my honeymoon."

Dylan leaned forward. "Congratulations."

Victor glanced up briefly. "I'm not married."

"But you just said—"

"She left him at the altar," Avery informed their new friends.

Victor glared at Avery. "Do I know you?"

She extended her hand. "Avery Holt."

"I don't know you." Victor shook her hand, his eyes hard.

"I'm Shannon's friend. She told me about the marriage mishap. Sorry 'bout that."

"Right." He released her hand, focused on Shannon. "So you go around telling everyone about my personal life?"

It was Shannon's turn to squirm. She always prided herself on being professional, and being caught talking about a client smacked of indecency. There really were no words to excuse herself. But that didn't stop her from trying. "I never thought I'd see you again. Or that Avery would put a face to my explanation of my weekend."

Victor placed his hands behind his back, rocked on the heels of his loafers.

"I'm sorry."

Avery shoved Shannon's shoulder. "Oh my God, Shannon. What are you sorry about?" She turned her attention toward Victor. "I knew she was coming here to shoot a wedding. What would you expect her to say when I arrived and asked how it went? Lie?"

"You were really left at the altar?" Erasmo asked. "That's rough."

Victor continued to stare at Shannon.

Her eyes didn't leave his . . . much as she wanted to crawl into a corner somewhere. The thought of people knowing her personal life, without her telling it, had her feeling sorry for him.

"Ease up." Avery turned in her chair, almost blocking Shannon's view of Victor's quiet anger.

And the man wasn't happy.

"What are you drinking?" Dylan asked in an obvious attempt to break the ice.

"I'm not."

"That might be your problem," Erasmo surmised.

Right before Shannon felt a second apology on her lips, Victor released a sigh. "Anything but mezcal. Seems I don't tolerate that particular liquor very well."

Shannon tried hard not to grin and failed.

⁓

"Don't take this personally . . . but we need to take you shopping tomorrow. This *office on the beach* look thing isn't working for you."

Victor was pretty sure he was being insulted by a gay man he'd just met.

"I'm glad you said it," Avery jumped in.

Shannon shrugged.

"Tell me you packed something appropriate for the sand."

Victor blinked.

Dylan wouldn't have it. "Okay. First thing tomorrow, we shop. Lucky for you, I know what I'm doing. Even for hetero men. So don't worry."

"I, ah . . ."

Shannon finally spoke, after nearly an entire drink and a shot. "If you hate the clothes, you can always burn them when you're back in LA."

Victor glanced at his pants . . . pants that were sticking to him with the heat and humidity smoldering in the air. Unlike any other hotel he'd stayed at in the past, this one didn't have a dry cleaning service.

"Fine."

"Good call." Avery lifted her glass and ordered another round.

Seemed the five of them were taking up residency at the bar while most of the crowd found lounge chairs on the beach. Victor couldn't remember the last time he'd met complete strangers and drunk with them at a bar just for fun. Anytime he was in a social situation with people he didn't know, he had an ulterior motive. Finding new contacts, learning more about his competitors, finding clients on both the buying and selling ends of the recyclable goods . . . these were his top reasons for drinking in bars. He would meet with his brother every once in a while, or his buddies, but never complete strangers with no connection to his working life.

Yet here he was.

He'd learned that Avery was in estate sales for the wealthy. And that she'd recently married.

Erasmo was an investment banker in Portugal and Dylan was a physical therapist.

Then there was Shannon . . . the wedding photographer who sat across from him but avoided eye contact. She seemed genuinely embarrassed when caught talking about him. He couldn't blame her, he supposed. He might as well get used to it. He wouldn't avoid the talk when he returned home.

"Why wedding photography?" Dylan asked Shannon.

"I've always wanted to be a photographer. Weddings just kinda happened in the past couple years. I had a studio before my marriage but couldn't keep up with it."

"Why not?" Erasmo asked.

"Shannon was married to a governor," Avery explained.

Victor had somehow forgotten that since he'd first learned of her political husband. He had a strange desire to look up her ex and see if he could find any pictures of the two of them together.

"That had to be exciting," Dylan said.

"Sometimes," Shannon told them. "Most of the time it was full of fake smiles, fake friends, insincere accolades from strangers, and a whole lot of gossip."

Dylan reached over and patted Shannon's hand. "Good thing you didn't have kids with him."

Victor watched a smile come and go from her face.

"A very good thing," she said.

"Do you have a boyfriend back home?"

Shannon looked at Victor briefly, then played with the straw in her drink. "No."

"The men in California must be blind and stupid," Dylan said with a wink.

"Hey," Victor said, reacting to the direct insult on his location and gender.

Dylan waved him off. "You don't count. You were engaged."

That made him feel marginally better. He considered Shannon with a tilt of his head. "I bet you intimidate a lot of men."

"Why do you say that?" she asked.

"You speak your mind. Have no trouble telling strangers they're rude . . . and we know you're sassy."

She seemed to like his definition of her, if the smile on her face was any indication.

"Are we talking about the same woman?" Avery asked.

Victor's eyes locked with Shannon's.

"I did tell him he was rude."

"And Justin said you called me an asshole before you knew who he was," Victor told her.

Her cheeks started to flush.

"Who is Justin?"

"Victor's brother," Shannon told Avery.

"Ouch."

"You're the only one who has accused me of being full of sass," she told him.

"I can vouch for that," Avery added.

"I find that hard to believe."

"Nope. Shannon's the reserved one. Always watching but almost never speaking up unless asked."

Victor moved his gaze to Avery. "Now I know we're not talking about the same woman."

"I've known her longer than you, buddy."

He smirked. "She sat in my lap on the airplane."

"I fell," Shannon corrected him.

He met her stare, lifted an eyebrow. "You didn't get up right away."

"There was turbulence."

"Then you blamed me."

"I needed to get back to my seat, and you stretched out and fell asleep when I was using the restroom."

Victor grinned. "See the sass?"

Shannon rolled her eyes.

Avery's mouth hung open. "You did *not* just roll your eyes. Shannon never rolls her eyes."

Dylan started to laugh. "Looks like you bring out the best in our new friend, Victor."

Shannon seemed to bite her lips together to keep from speaking. But man, did he want to know what she was thinking.

"Looks like I do."

Chapter Ten

"I just need a couple more hours." Avery rolled back over when Shannon nudged her awake after eight the next morning. "I think I drank too much last night."

"Can I get you anything?"

"No. I'll meet you on the beach in a few. Jet lag and drinking. Bad combo."

They hadn't been out that late, closing the beach bar and grabbing a bite in the hotel restaurant.

"I'm within shouting distance if you need something."

Avery lifted a hand and then tucked it under her cheek.

Five minutes later, Shannon left their room with a beach bag slung over her shoulder.

Instead of going straight for the sand, she detoured to the hotel restaurant, sat, and ordered coffee. She picked up her e-reader and clicked into a book written by and about a single mother by choice. There were a lot of things she'd considered before making her decision to have a baby . . . and many she had not. Hearing from women who had done it helped boost her confidence in her plan.

She sipped coffee and ordered a plate of granola, fruit, and yogurt and enjoyed the quiet before the restaurant and beach outside filled with people.

Deep in a chapter about the support system needed to be successful at raising a child as a single woman, Shannon nibbled on her breakfast, ignoring everything around her. Her thoughts wandered to her parents . . . people she had tried to please most of her life but ultimately felt she disappointed. They'd been ecstatic with her marriage to Paul. What affluent parents wouldn't be? Little did they know it was all a calculated plan to obtain financial security for her future. It wasn't that Shannon was afraid of work. She wasn't. Her liberal arts degree was for her parents, her minor in digital photography was for her. Except photography didn't pay well, and as a new graduate, she couldn't afford her rent. And her parents refused to help her financially so long as she pursued a career in taking pictures. Shannon ended up opening a small studio and had been working with wannabe actors who needed headshots and budget weddings. But she wasn't getting ahead, and her parents were already one daughter short since Angie had run off. Since Shannon was a people pleaser more than she cared to admit, she started to look for alternatives that would make her parents happy and give her the financial freedom she needed.

She'd met Samantha Harrison, owner of Alliance, the company that arranged her temporary marriage to Paul, at a holiday party at her father's firm. Sam, as she liked to be called, clued in right away that Shannon was looking for stability while building her business. With her pedigree and poise, coming from a wealthy family, it was an easy match between her and Paul. Sam introduced her to Meg, one of her colleagues, and the facts of a temporary marriage were spelled out to her.

When Shannon realized she only had to pretend to be the man's happy wife for two years and then leave with six million and a house worthy of the governor's wife, Shannon signed the contract.

Falling in love with the man wasn't part of the plan.

Spending three years after her divorce mourning the loss of her temporary marriage wasn't expected either.

With her fertility clock ticking away and the desire to not put her heart out there only to be stomped on again, Shannon felt she was making the best logical step to making her future better.

Her parents no longer nagged her to get married, and while they didn't openly support her work as a photographer, they didn't continually put it down either. Her mother referred to it as a hobby. And since it didn't truly support her, Shannon couldn't disagree. Then again, she wasn't attempting to fill every extra hour with work. There wasn't a need. Which led to her desire to have a child. She had love to give, and who better than her own baby?

Like the woman who'd written the book she was reading, Shannon had enough money to support a baby on her own, and with her friendship pool filled with strong women with equally solid men, she knew she and her child would be fine.

Shannon flipped through the virtual pages of the book discussing the lesbian choice of conception and moved on to the single straight woman.

"It's either a boring book or you're a speed reader."

The voice behind her made her jump.

She set the reader down, heart in chest. "Stop scaring me, Victor."

He slid into a chair, signaled the waiter, and sat back with a smile. "Good morning."

He still wore ridiculous pants, loafers, and what looked like a T-shirt from the hotel staff. "You're up early," he said.

"I can't help it."

He looked around. "Where's Avery?"

"Sleeping."

"Ahh. She seemed very protective of you yesterday."

"She is. Good friends are like that." She looked at his shirt. "Did you bum the shirt off the waiter?"

"Concierge offered a lost luggage pack."

She smiled. "Did you tell them the airline lost your suitcase?"

He leaned forward, lowered his voice. "That was my first thought, then I realized they'd be on the lookout for when the airline found it and sent it here. So I told them my runaway bride ran off with my luggage by mistake."

"Sneaky, but resourceful."

The waiter brought his coffee. "I'm meeting Dylan here before we shop. Although I'm sure I can manage on my own."

"When was the last time you bought casual clothes?"

"I order stuff online."

Shannon shook her head. "You need his help. Don't worry, I know it's a stereotype, but most gay men know how to dress. I'm sure he won't lead you wrong."

"Everything I've seen since I've been here has a hippie, bohemian theme."

"I can think of worse looks."

Victor shrugged. "I guess."

"Isn't today the day of your important meeting?" It was Tuesday.

"I rescheduled."

She smiled, waited a beat. "Any word from Corrie?"

"No."

Because she needed to know. "How are you doing with all that?"

"I didn't get wasted last night . . . so better, I guess."

"Progress."

"What about you guys . . . what are your plans today?"

"Beach, swimming, dinner plans tonight. Tomorrow we're doing the tourist thing." *And searching for a baby daddy away from the hotel.*

"What are the tourist things to do here?"

"You can visit the ruins, the cenotes, do some snorkeling. Do you dive?"

"Scuba?" he asked.

"Yeah."

"No. If I were meant to breathe underwater, I'd have gills."

"There's kayaking, windsurfing. You can rent ATVs, ride through the jungle, find the monkeys, maybe a jaguar or two. I'm sure you can find plenty to do." Shannon had a strong suspicion that Victor didn't plan on doing any of it.

"I'll figure it out."

They both noticed Dylan approaching at the same time. He greeted Shannon with a kiss to the cheek. "Good morning, lovely."

"Good morning."

He turned to look at Victor, frowned at the shirt. "You're a fashion emergency if I ever saw one."

"We're going to fix that, right?"

Dylan stood back when Victor got up from his chair.

"Good luck," Shannon said.

"I'm going to need it," Dylan said.

"I know when I'm being insulted," Victor added. "Let's get this over with. I'm not a shopper. The sooner we start, the sooner I can walk around without looking like I just got off the plane."

Shannon waved as they walked away. "Have fun." She couldn't wait to see what Dylan would dress Victor in. Anything would be better than dress slacks on a beach.

What had he been thinking?

Curiosity, she told herself. To see him in something casual. Maybe a change in clothes would help him loosen up. He'd seemed a little more relaxed than the day before. When she'd asked about Corrie, he didn't show much in the way of emotions.

She remembered when she and Paul had split. The day their agreement was up, he handed her divorce papers. She was devastated, made worse by the fact she couldn't show him how much. They were adults. They agreed to get married platonically, and somewhere into the first year of their agreement, they fell into bed.

They both agreed it was just physical. Two adults having an affair within their temporary marriage.

For Paul, that was exactly what it was.

For Shannon . . . not so much. For months she couldn't talk about her divorce without a world of pain. The fact that Victor didn't even flinch with Corrie's name just days after she'd jilted him told Shannon everything she needed to know about where his heart was.

His heart wasn't in the game.

Maybe he was coming to that conclusion on his own. Or maybe he'd always known it wasn't.

Shannon stared toward the door the two men had left through and asked herself why she was concerned in the first place.

Curiosity?

She shook her head, lifted her e-reader, and continued where she'd left off.

The chapter was titled "Consciously Conceiving a Child without a Partner." She sat back to read, and pushed Victor from her mind.

∽

Hours later, Shannon and Avery walked up the beach along the water's edge to scope out prospective hotel bars.

They walked past several spaces of land that were boarded up and others that looked closed to the public. "I'm guessing private residences," Avery suggested.

When they came across an active beach scene, they'd meander toward the bar. Several employed female bartenders, and the men didn't fit the daddy checklist. But staff circulated, and there was always a chance the right guy would be there the next day. Or so Shannon told herself as they walked away.

They were a good mile from their hotel when Avery suggested they turn around.

Shannon heard a party up a little farther on the beach. "Let's find out where the music is coming from."

They walked around a grouping of palm trees and hesitated.

Avery leaned in. "Well, at least you know what you're going to get if you find the guy here."

Shannon scanned the crowd but didn't see one face.

Everyone was buck naked.

Unlike a few topless sunbathers they'd seen on the beach, this was full-on, nothing-covered-up adulting like Shannon had never witnessed before.

"We're overdressed." Shannon found herself staring at a woman putting oil on a man lying next to her. It would be one thing if she was covering his back, or even his legs . . . but Shannon couldn't imagine the man wasn't able to reach his own penis.

Shannon turned away, grabbing Avery's arm when she realized there was more than one couple doing more than nude sunbathing. "Let's go."

"But this is—"

"Not where I want to find a father for my child."

Avery twisted around and looked over her shoulder. "She's full-on stroking him right there."

"Yeah, I saw. And I don't want to see him finish. C'mon."

Thirty feet back in the direction of their hotel, Avery started laughing. "I can't believe that."

Shannon squeezed her eyes closed, still saw the oiled couple. "That falls into the category of things I can't unsee."

"I say we go back," Avery said.

"I say you're crazy."

"I bet no one asks your name there. People will be too busy staring at your body to see your face. Could be perfect."

Shannon walked faster. "I like to think I'm progressive, but that is way outside my comfort zone."

"Fine, fine." Only Avery kept looking behind her as if she were missing out.

Back at their hotel, Shannon ditched her cover-up and walked into the water. It was bathtub warm without the crashing surf that spotted the shores of Southern California. In one word, it was *relaxing*.

They ate lunch on the beach, decided to skip the alcohol and stick to bottled water until dinner, and gave up on the hot sand altogether after a few hours.

Shannon found herself scanning the beachfront for Victor. Curious as to what he'd be wearing when she saw him again. Only he never manifested. Neither did Dylan or Erasmo. Maybe they were still shopping. Though she doubted a man who normally shopped online would make a full day of picking out resort wear.

When Avery suggested they go up to their room and spend time in their private plunge pool, Shannon agreed.

The second they were on their balcony, Avery removed her swimsuit and jumped in. The guests from the beach couldn't see them unless they stood on the edge of the balcony, and the only other room that had a view was the second penthouse on the other end of the beach. From what Shannon could tell, no one was in the room. Not surprising, considering the price.

"This is perfect." Avery leaned her head back and floated toward the surface of the water.

"I've never skinny-dipped."

Avery peeked at her with one eye open. "Doesn't really count if there isn't a guy around. This is more like girl time at the spa."

Shannon shrugged and slipped out of her bikini. Like Avery, she let gravity float her body toward the sun once she was in the water.

The water soothed her warm skin and calmed her nerves. Strange how being naked in a public place had that effect.

"I think I need to swim naked more often."

"We need to go back to the nude beach."

"That place looked more like an orgy than a hippie colony." Then again, those things sounded like the same thing.

"Those are the stories you tell your children about when they're teenagers so they know you were *cool* once."

"I don't know if I wanna be that cool," she said, laughing.

"I do. I'll probably go without you."

"You can't do that."

Avery looked at her. "I can't?"

"No. I mean . . . of course you can, but what if someone comes on to you? What would Liam say?"

"My husband trusts me, and if anyone can fend for themselves, it's me."

Avery had been studying krav maga for over a year, and while Shannon hadn't seen her in action, Liam had told her that Avery could put a man twice her size on the mat and make him cry.

"Of course it would be better if you came with me. Just in case I need someone to call my lesbian lover."

"Parading around as a lesbian might not be the best way for me to find someone to father my baby."

"A lot of men get turned on by that kind of thing."

"Why do I get the feeling you're going to win this conversation?"

"Because you secretly want to display that goddess body and cut loose the ties society has bound you in. Personally, I think you're more apt to find a stranger to sleep with if you shed all the proper bullshit you've been fed all your life."

"Am I that pretentious?" Shannon truly thought she'd evolved in the last five years.

"Not pretentious, just not the kind of woman who sleeps with strangers. I've never seen you flirt. Do you even see the men who smile at you?"

"I don't turn as many heads as you'd think."

Avery ran her hand along the top of the water. "You turn twice as many. You just don't see them. And you don't see them because you don't want to. The second you let that guard down, men will line up.

If they're eligible and single . . . and even if they're not, you're going to need me there to knock them away."

Shannon couldn't comment on the effect of dropping her walls, but she knew they were there. "I don't know how to break out of this rut, Avery. I've been trying."

"Here's my advice, like it or not. Treat all the men like they're not a threat. Look at Dylan and Erasmo. Two guys, nonthreatening on any level . . . you relaxed around them, laughed. I even saw some of that sass Victor said you had."

Just hearing the man's name made the hair on her neck stand up. "Victor riles me."

"I noticed. He is a prime example of a man watching you and you don't see it."

"Oh, please. The man's fiancée ran out on him three days ago, and he placed some of the blame on me. If he's looking, it's only to make sure I'm not sabotaging something else in his life."

Avery smirked. "That man is a bee to your flower. Even more . . . you like him."

"I do not—"

Avery held a hand in the air. "You don't *want* to like him, you could even say it's not *right* to be attracted, considering the circumstances. But you do."

Shannon opened her mouth to dispute, only to have Avery cut her off.

"You argue with him. When he looks at you, you turn away if he catches you staring. The tension between you is there. Don't mistake it as anger."

"Ridiculous."

"He's an attractive man."

"Looks aren't everything. His social manners are that of a preschooler."

"Why does that bother you?"

"Because he's an adult. Established. He should know better. Victor has no idea how to treat a woman."

"And he lost his fiancée because of it."

Shannon grew warm just thinking about it. "Corrie was too young, and what the heck was he thinking, wanting to marry her to begin with?"

Avery was silent.

Shannon looked over at her friend.

"Like I said. You're attracted to the man. If you weren't, you would have blown all that stuff off and not given him another thought. Inside, you want to know the answer to those questions, and I bet you've been thinking about what the preschool executive will be wearing the next time you see him."

"*If* I see him."

Avery just laughed.

Chapter Eleven

Victor was pretty sure if he looked up the word *voyeur* in the dictionary, he'd find a picture of himself staring back.

Shannon was naked.

Full-on, head-to-toe, in-the-buff naked. No peeking into windows to see it either. Quite by accident, he'd caught a glimpse of her lean backside as she'd slid into the water. But sitting in the shade of his balcony, hidden by a windblown palm tree, he waited patiently for the woman to emerge again. Nothing accidental about that.

He doubted the women knew they were being watched, or they'd have kept their suits on. Well, Shannon would have. He wasn't sure about her friend.

A decent man would have looked away.

He kicked his feet up and watched.

The view was worth it.

Long and lean, with legs that went on forever. He wasn't close enough to see the color of her nipples, but the shape of her breasts stirred heat deep in his belly.

He shouldn't be attracted to her.

But damn it . . . he was.

It's physical, he told himself. A rebound attraction.

Taboo, even.

He wanted to refresh his drink, which he'd finished in one gulp once he realized who he was staring at, but he wasn't about to miss it when she emerged from the pool. So not only was he a voyeur, he was masochistic.

The woman got under his skin. Called him out at every turn. In short, she irked him. If he'd had a sister, he imagined she would be just as annoying. But then he wouldn't be looking at his sister naked.

Bad analogy.

Maybe his best friend's girl.

But then he'd be violating the man code . . .

Never mind. She was just Shannon, the sophisticated female who called him on his shit without invitation.

Damn, she was something to look at. Strange how seeing her naked from across the span of the hotel's beach made him take a better look at her other features. Or maybe a second look. He'd noticed her beauty on the airplane but dismissed the woman after she gave him crap about his phone call.

It had been important.

Although for the life of him he couldn't remember what the call was about now.

He needed to pee.

Victor shifted in his chair and ignored his bladder.

Shannon moved to the other side of the pool but didn't get up.

"I've been reduced to a thirteen-year-old," he said to himself. It wasn't like he hadn't seen a naked woman before.

But this was Shannon. A woman he would never have an opportunity to see nude.

She was the one parading around a public place in the buff.

Maybe parading was a *slight* exaggeration . . .

He really needed to pee.

Ten minutes later, with his knee shaking up and down like a kid holding his goods and hopping on one foot, Victor gave in and left his vantage point for the bathroom.

He'd never peed so fast in his entire adult life.

When he returned, both women were standing outside the pool, wrapped in towels.

He cursed the universe but did so quietly. He wasn't about to give up his location and make the women think they didn't have complete privacy.

Oh, no. He would be out there watching every chance he could.

He wore linen . . . or something like linen. White pants fit for the beach and a soft gray shirt that floated on his shoulders. He leaned against the edge of the reception desk at the front of the hotel, arms crossed and searching the people walking by.

"Is that Victor?" Avery asked at her side.

Shannon nodded.

"Mmm, mmm."

Shannon bumped Avery's side in an effort to stop her obvious appraisal.

"Dylan did well," Avery said.

"I never had a doubt."

A few steps closer, and Victor twisted his gaze their way.

They both wore dresses that showed off the sun they'd managed to get after a day on the beach.

Acutely aware of his evaluation, Shannon found her heart skipping.

"Do you hear that?" Avery asked.

"What?"

"The buzz."

That man is a bee to your flower. Once again Shannon nudged her friend.

Victor stepped in front of them and smiled. "Don't you both look refreshing?"

Avery turned a full circle as if on a runway. "Why thank you." She reached out and touched the edge of Victor's shirt. "Much better for Tulum."

He lifted both palms to the air and cocked his head to the side. "I have to admit, shopping with Dylan wasn't nearly as painful as I thought it would be." His eyes found Shannon's and held.

"I'm impressed," Shannon said after searching for the right words to offer approval without too much personal praise.

His grins were starting to appear more often. "I'll take that as a compliment."

"I'm sure they won't come often," she teased.

He laughed.

"We were just headed to dinner. Would you like to join us?"

Avery's invitation caught Shannon off guard. Inviting Victor had not been on the agenda.

Shannon opened her mouth to quickly offer Victor an out and subtly brush him off but found him talking over her.

"I would love that, Avery. Thank you."

She snapped her lips shut, held her hands in front of her, and smiled.

His eyes lit up and he paused. "Unless you'd rather not, Shannon."

He knew he was pushing his way in and was testing her resolve. "I'm sure the restaurant can accommodate three instead of two on the reservation."

Victor turned toward the busy road and looked both ways. "Taxi? Or can we walk?"

"It's less than a New York avenue block," Avery said before leading the way.

They walked on the side of the road in single file to avoiding being run over. Not that the cars were going very fast, but the pedestrian shoulder was barely two feet on either side. Avery led, Shannon walked behind her, and Victor caught the tail.

Shannon felt the heat of his gaze. Every time she glanced behind her, Victor wasn't looking at her, but she felt his eyes when she turned back around.

"I didn't realize how many places there were to eat here until I went shopping today," Victor said.

Small talk? He's making small talk?

"Where did Dylan take you?" Avery asked.

"The better question would be where he *didn't* take me. We grabbed a taxi that took us up the road a good two miles and then walked back. I'm sure the last time I shopped like that my mother had been involved and I was returning to school after summer."

"Sounds like a good day," Shannon said.

His voice moved closer behind her.

"I had my fill for the year. I bought enough clothes to last the rest of the vacation and a few things I'm sure I won't get around to wearing."

They crossed the street to the jungle side of Tulum's beach road and approached the hostess at Arca. The five-star restaurant specialized in the unexpected, cooked on a wood burning stove, and had a swanky atmosphere you would expect in the heart of a major city and not the wooded section of Tulum. The entire restaurant was outside, including the kitchen.

Avery spoke to the hostess while Victor and Shannon stood back to avoid crowding the small podium the greeters used.

Victor pointed to a smoldering pot at the entrance to the space framed only by an outdoor bar and the outdoor kitchen in the back. "What is that for?" he asked Shannon.

"I'm guessing the mosquitos."

He nodded once. "They must have a lot of them."

Shannon and Avery had practically bathed in repellant before leaving the hotel. On the beach side, with the breeze off the ocean, the nasty little bloodsuckers didn't stick around. But out here, where the air was still and the forest was thick, they might be in need of a blood transfusion if the insects had their way.

"You put on bug spray, didn't you?" she asked.

The expression on his face said he hadn't. "I haven't had a problem so far."

Avery waved them over, and they followed the hostess to their table.

Victor took a seat opposite the two of them and studied the wine list. "Would you mind if I picked?" he asked.

Shannon glanced at Avery.

"You know your wines?" Avery asked.

"I've tasted a few."

Not only did Victor know his wine, he knew his food pairing as well. Then he surprised her by carrying much of the conversation with stories about his and his brother's teenage years.

Unlike Shannon and Avery, Victor had grown up in a middle-income family with financial restrictions that depended on frugality to afford vacations. "A place like this would never have been on the radar," he told them. "I've tried to send my parents on trips, but my dad won't accept my help."

"Who suggested Tulum for the wedding?" Shannon asked.

Just the mention of the wedding shifted a little of Victor's smile. "Corrie." He paused. "I think. Maybe it was me." He lifted his wineglass. "I should know the answer to that. Anyway, I encouraged it and knew my parents would come."

Shannon didn't want to think that the man had picked his wedding location in an effort to give something to his parents. By shifting Victor out of the selfish category in her brain to the thoughtful side, her equilibrium was thrown off. In fact, she'd felt a little unsteady most of the night. Their dinner came in multiple small courses that had them holding their stomachs by the time they finished off the second bottle of wine.

Shannon swatted at what had to be the fifth mosquito that broke the repellant barrier under the table. "I'm starting to become part of the food chain," she told them.

"Are you ready to go back?" Victor asked. "Or did you ladies have something else planned for tonight?"

Shannon and Avery exchanged glances. Their plans had been to flirt with the waiter at the restaurant if he was cute enough . . . and he was, now that Shannon thought about it. But that idea hadn't been put into action. "We're on vacation, playing everything by ear," she said.

"I told Dylan and Erasmo I would try and find them at our hotel bar later. I heard there was a band playing . . ."

"I love live music," Avery said.

Shannon smiled at Avery. Looked like they were going to listen to a band.

Victor stood and smiled. He excused himself to the bathroom while they waited for the bill.

Shannon ducked her head close to Avery's once he walked away. "Inviting Victor to dinner probably wasn't the best way to attract another man's attention," she told her.

Avery pretended to look around the busy restaurant. "The guys here are barely out of diapers." An exaggeration, but they were all young. "Maybe there will be someone back at the hotel."

Shannon moaned.

"He was pretty charming tonight, don't you think?"

"Victor?"

Avery rolled her eyes. "No, the cook."

Shannon looked past where Victor had disappeared in search of a bathroom. "He picked a decent wine."

"Decent . . . it was perfect. I wouldn't have guessed he had a palate for anything but whiskey."

Shannon couldn't argue that.

"You know, for a man without social manners, he didn't wipe his mouth with the back of his shirt or thank the chef with a burp."

Now Avery was teasing her.

"Okay, okay . . . maybe he isn't that bad."

They both looked up to see him talking with the waiter and pulling out his wallet. "He doesn't need to do that," Shannon said.

"Let him. Part of attracting a man is letting them do things for you that you can do for yourself. It empowers them."

"I don't know if I want to empower him."

"Then consider it payment for crashing our dinner. Don't over-think it."

Shannon slapped at a mosquito buzzing in her ear and stood when Victor walked over. "I'll try."

～∽

For the first time in Avery's life, she was the observer and not the active player in the mating game. Victor buzzed Shannon so loudly an exterminator would be needed to detach the man. Knowing he was humming around made Avery's life so much easier.

She'd been against Shannon hooking up with a stranger since she'd first mentioned it months before. Even though she hadn't set out to sabotage Shannon's efforts, she had every intention to play devil's advocate for the men who may have suited the baby daddy bill.

Victor was making it so much easier.

He wasn't the one-night-stand, baby making man Shannon wanted. But with him close by, the other men at the resort, the restaurant, the bars, they didn't approach. And Avery didn't point said men out to Shannon when she realized they were watching her friend.

Like now, Avery sat at a small table with Dylan, Erasmo, Shannon, and Victor, talking over loud music. Erasmo had his arm comfortably

103

around Dylan's back, resting on the chair, Avery sat next to Dylan, and Victor had taken a seat between her and Shannon. A dance floor had been set up in front of the band, and several couples were swinging around on their toes.

Avery zeroed in on the posse of men that had joined the crowd and were searching the guests for single women. Their eyes would settle on Shannon, then slide to Victor, who seemed to always lean forward and say something to Shannon right when someone approached.

The third time a man walked by, eyes trained on Shannon, Victor placed a hand on her shoulder and had her turning around to hear what he had to say. That was when Dylan did the same to Avery.

"Are you watching what I'm watching?" he asked, eyes on Victor and Shannon.

Avery nodded with a smile.

"I didn't think she liked him."

"She doesn't."

Dylan sat back with a wink.

"Why aren't you two dancing?" Avery asked Dylan.

"Erasmo doesn't like to dance."

"Not my thing," Erasmo said with a shrug. "I do it for him, once in a while."

"In the privacy of our own home," Dylan added.

"I dance for you. Take Avery," Erasmo suggested.

Dylan sat forward.

Avery leaned in, aware that Shannon and Victor hadn't noticed their conversation. "Ask Shannon. I'll ask Victor."

Dylan rubbed his hands together. "You're one sneaky friend." It seemed Dylan was just as sneaky, since he rose to his feet and moved around Victor and extended a hand to Shannon. "C'mon, beautiful . . . let's dance."

Shannon turned toward Avery, narrowed her eyes. "I don't know how to salsa."

"It's easy, I'll show you."

Victor shifted in his seat. Avery tapped his shoulder. "Can you salsa?" she asked him.

He shook his head.

She stood and extended her hand. "Then I'll lead."

The people on the dance floor obviously knew what they were doing, and in order to dance without being stepped on, the four of them stayed on the outside perimeter and started to move. Avery had danced salsa a couple of times in her life and knew the basics, so she grabbed Victor's hand and spoke loud enough for him to hear. She called out steps and counted each one. Victor seemed to catch on pretty quickly, and it was obvious that Dylan knew what he was doing.

Shannon laughed when she messed up her footing, but Dylan corrected her step and kept her moving.

By the time the first song was done, Avery had Victor twisting her around a few times, all with a few stubbed toes, but she didn't bring attention to his lack of grace.

Dylan took the opportunity in the change of songs to hand Shannon off to Victor as he grabbed Avery's hand.

She followed his lead, zigzagged in and out of Dylan's arms as he got into the music. When they came close together, Dylan spoke in her ear. "They're both stepping on each other."

Avery glanced toward her friend.

It was great to see Shannon laughing, and not with the superficial laughter that often came out of her, but with this deep abandon that only came with real joy.

Dylan moved the two of them to the opposite side of the dance floor and eventually pulled them away from the crowd.

"I have to ask you something," he started.

Avery fanned herself and attempted to slow her breathing down. "Go for it."

"Why Victor? He's obviously on the rebound. Those never end well."

Avery tried to find Shannon and Victor through the couples on the dance floor and couldn't see them. "She's on a rebound, too."

"I thought her divorce was a few years ago."

"It was. And she hasn't dated since. Like at all."

Dylan looked at her as if she were lying.

"I know Shannon. She won't let anything happen with Victor, but he is bringing out the blush in her. And that's a step in the right direction. I'd rather see her flirting with him than hooking up with a stranger."

"She doesn't seem the hooking up type."

"She's not. Victor seems safe enough."

Dylan nodded. "Harmless, if you ask me."

"Clueless, if you ask me."

They both laughed.

Avery leaned in close, lowered her voice. "I want my friend to discover she has a vagina again, but not give it up to someone who will hurt her. She knows the score with Victor." Though again, Avery was pretty sure the man couldn't charm Shannon's panties off her.

Not with the risk of her getting pregnant with a man she knew, who would find out if she had a child.

They both turned to see Shannon and Victor walking back to their table, his hand on her arm and both of them smiling and out of breath.

"I hope you know what you're doing," Dylan said.

Avery felt a slight doubt in the back of her head. "I do."

Chapter Twelve

"I know what you're doing," Shannon said once the two of them were down to their birthday suits and floating in the pool under the light of the moon. The sidewalks rolled up early in Tulum, and the party below was down to a few die-hards at the bar after the band had finished for the night.

Dylan and Erasmo said their good nights, and Victor bowed out shortly after.

"What do you mean?"

"Don't even try and pretend. Dancing with Victor, invites to dinner . . . I'm surprised you didn't suggest he join us in the pool."

Avery looked down at her reflection. "Good idea."

Shannon splashed water at her friend. "He isn't the right guy to sleep with."

"I never suggested he is. But he is the right guy to flirt with."

Which was exactly what she'd done all night. Avery's words swam in Shannon's head continually about the man's attraction to her. Her hyperfocus on his actions made it hard to see anything but the soft brown of his eyes or the way they smiled when he laughed at how clumsy the two of them were while attempting to salsa dance. If she were honest with herself, and right now she was doing her best to lie, the man was slowly tugging on her inactive libido. Men had led her on and off the dance floors in social situations many times in the past few years . . . since Paul . . . but she hadn't paid attention to how their palms molded into the small of her back, or how they lingered on her shoulder. Probably because those dances were obligations during her friends' weddings or the occasional fundraising event where saying no would have proved awkward. Again, the people pleaser in Shannon would come out, and she'd dance with strangers she felt nothing toward.

Just thinking about Victor's long fingers and laughing smile warmed her. He was different.

"Look at it this way," Avery started. "Victor is safe, right? I mean, he just broke it off with his fiancée, and the chances of you really falling for the guy are pretty slim, right?"

Shannon instantly agreed. "He's not the keeping kind."

"Exactly. But he is a decent transitional guy. You haven't put yourself out there in forever. And yet you somehow expected you'd be able to come here, pick up a stranger, have sex, and move on. C'mon, Shannon. You had to know you'd stutter a few times before your sexual engine starts to hum."

Shannon lifted her chin, wanting to deny Avery's claim. "I've been running low on fuel for a while."

"Men like Victor are the gas station. Let him flirt. Flirt back. Enjoy his attention and learn to cut it off. Something I don't think you're all that practiced on. He's on the rebound and can't be looking for more than the same thing you are. Positive opposite sex attention."

"I'm not sleeping with him."

Avery was quiet.

"I'm not."

"Fine. Don't."

"Avery. I'm as fertile as they come." She'd taken her ovulation tests over the past few months and mapped out her best days to conceive.

"Condoms still work."

"I know, but no. I'm not going there. If something happened and I did end up pregnant with Victor's . . ." She shook her head, unable to let the image continue in her head. "That would be wrong for everyone."

"Relax. No one is getting pregnant tonight. Enjoy the attention, Shannon. That's all I'm suggesting. When was the last time someone looked at you the way he did tonight?"

His eyes did hold hers a lot.

"It's been a long time."

"The man was undressing you with his eyes every time he thought no one was looking."

"That sounds sleazy."

"If he was open about it and added a 'hey baby, your place or mine,' then yes. But he only looked when he didn't realize anyone watched. Know the difference between him and the 'your place or mine' guy. That is the guy you were looking for this week. Mr. Temporary. Mr. Hot Attraction Baby Daddy Material. Not Mr. Jilted Groom Bleeding Heart Guy."

"I don't see a bleeding heart."

Avery sighed. "Me either. Whatever. It doesn't matter. Consider Victor a practice run."

Practice run . . .

She could do that.

‍᠎᠎᠎᠎᠎᠎᠎᠎᠎᠎᠎᠎᠎᠎᠎᠎᠎᠎᠎᠎᠎᠎᠎᠎᠎᠎᠎᠎

If it made a difference, Victor looked away when Avery stepped out of the pool.

The heat of the day had disappeared with the sun, but the warmth of the Caribbean kept the evening temperatures well into the low eighties.

The only thing that would make the habit-forming ritual of watching Shannon skinny-dip better would be if he could eavesdrop on her conversation. She felt their attraction, even though she seemed to squirm away from it whenever he leaned in close. Avery was making it easy, pushing it, even.

He had to respect a friend who approved enough to create opportunities for him to seduce. Which was why he looked away when Avery stepped out of the pool.

The moon didn't offer much in the way of light, but that didn't stop him from finding his perch moments before the women slid into the water.

Avery wrapped herself in a hotel issue bathrobe and disappeared into the room. Shannon lingered outside. She toweled off outside and turned around. Victor was sure that would be the end of it.

She surprised him.

Shannon dropped the towel on one of the many chairs on the deck and walked straight to the edge of her balcony. Anyone walking on the beach would have seen her . . . all of her. He glanced down at the sand and felt some relief to see it deserted.

She, too, scanned the space before leaning her elbows on the balcony to display her curves against the silhouette of the sky.

Victor squirmed in his chair, the soft erection of knowing she was naked in the pool now pressed firmly against his cotton pants.

Light went on inside their room, and Victor saw Avery pacing with a phone to her ear. Shannon seemed to notice, too, and instead of going inside, she pulled a chair closer to the railing, sat, and perched her legs so she could lounge in the moonlight.

No wonder sailors wrote stories and songs of mermaids and sirens on the shore, calling their name.

Shannon was a goddess stretched out, nude, with her head tilted back. He imagined the smile on her face and strands of her hair falling above the curve of her breasts.

Much as he wanted to free his dick, he refrained and just enjoyed her image. He had no doubt he'd recall this moment in the not too distant future when his body needed release, but doing so now, with her right there, didn't feel right.

Yeah, and making a sport out of watching her walk around naked when she didn't know it was anything but right.

This was his little secret. One he planned to keep to his grave.

Victor stretched out, ignored his teenage dick, and committed Shannon's moonlit curves to memory.

⁀๑

If Shannon hadn't heard Avery in the bathroom first thing in the morning, regretting the drinking from the night before, she would have thought the woman was faking illness to push Victor into her day.

"I didn't think I drank that much," Avery said, crawling back into bed.

"We did have wine with dinner and martinis at the bar, after."

"Mixing is always a bad idea."

Shannon did the mom thing and placed the back of her hand on Avery's forehead. "You don't feel warm."

"I'd rather be hungover than sick."

She pushed off the side of the bed. "I'll go get some toast from the restaurant."

"Yeah, that might help. If you see Victor, give him my seat for the tour today."

They had planned a private tour that included kayaking, snorkeling, and a dip in the cenotes.

"We can skip the sightseeing."

"No, go. I'll feel bad with you sitting around here all morning. I'm sure this will blow off by the afternoon."

She wasn't sure about inviting Victor out for the day.

"I'll be able to rest if I don't think I'm ruining your vacation."

Shannon imagined she'd feel the same if it were her. "I'll see what I can do."

The waiter at the hotel restaurant smiled when he saw her and asked if she wanted the same table as the previous day. Seemed her routine of dining alone first thing in the morning was being noticed. She accepted the table and ordered coffee, fruit, and yogurt and watched for a familiar face.

If Victor didn't show up, she'd take it as a sign to skip the tour.

On her second cup of coffee, after her breakfast was finished and she was waiting on the toast for Avery, Victor snuck up behind her as she was checking her e-mail.

"Working on vacation?" he said close to her ear.

She jumped.

"I swear, Victor. You're going to get hit doing that."

He grinned, unfazed. "Violence . . . that will be new for us."

"Us? There is no us."

He sat opposite her. "Was that breakfast?" he asked, looking at the remainder of the fruit platter.

"After last night, I'm surprised I could eat at all."

He glanced around. "Where's Avery?"

"Not feeling well. I think she's coming down with something."

"I'm sorry to hear that." He looked sincere.

"Me too. We scheduled a tour today at nine thirty." Shannon looked at her phone, checked the time.

"Where are you going?"

She told him where they'd planned on spending their day.

"You can always go without her."

If she was going to ask him, now was the time. "I wouldn't want to go alone. There are still single-female travel advisories for the area."

He didn't buy it. "You traveled here alone to begin with."

"But that was work. I didn't plan on leaving the hotel where people knew me until Avery arrived. I can try and reschedule for tomorrow . . . unless Avery is still under the weather."

Victor sat back, a smirk on his lips. "If you want me to go with you, just ask."

She opened her mouth, pretending surprise. "The thought never crossed my mind."

"Really?"

She didn't meet his eyes. "No. You probably have plans."

"My plans slipped out the back door on Saturday, freeing up my life's schedule." He leaned forward, grabbed her bill, signed his name and room number, and stood. "Go get your bathing suit on. I'll meet you out front in thirty minutes."

He left without waiting for her reply.

"This is a bad idea," she whispered to herself, right before she left to do exactly what he suggested.

Chapter Thirteen

Shannon wore large rimmed sunglasses, her hair pulled back into a ponytail, and a cover-up that hid her swimwear underneath.

Victor didn't have much of a chance to say hello before he jumped in the back of the van in board shorts and a T-shirt. Something he hadn't worn in years.

Shannon tensed at his side.

Leo, their private tour guide, drove them away from Tulum's beach road and out onto the main highway. He explained the history of the area and the booming tourist trade that had popped up over the past dozen years. The more the twentysomething-year-old kid talked, the more relaxed Shannon became.

Thirty minutes into their drive, Shannon unfolded her crossed legs and tight arms. She asked Leo several questions as they moved toward their first destination.

"The government doesn't help to provide electricity and water to the hotels where you're staying," Leo told them. "Each hotel has their own generator and drives in their drinking water."

"That must be quite an expense," Shannon said.

"Part of the bill you pay to visit, yes?" he asked.

"It isn't cheap."

Victor knew firsthand how much Shannon and Avery were spending for their deluxe accommodations. Lesser hotels and smaller rooms without views probably did cost less, but it still wasn't a budget vacation, even though some might think anything in Mexico would be.

"Worth it, I hope," Leo said. "We need all the tourists."

"Is the cartel as bad as what our media tells us it is?" Shannon asked.

Leo glanced in the rearview mirror. "Every country has their problems."

Translation: yes!

Victor glanced at Shannon. Maybe her line about female traveler alerts was a thing. Sometimes he forgot how great it was to own a Y chromosome.

Leo pulled off the main road and down a rutted dirt path surrounded by the rain forest. He stopped at a checkpoint and said something in Spanish to the man standing there.

"I have an arrangement to visit this part of the beach. All these homes are private. No hotels."

They drove for about two miles. Shannon pointed out the homes to him, suggesting the ones she liked and those she didn't.

Shannon could see that even though the road leading to the place wasn't anywhere close to what you'd find in the States, the houses were for the wealthy. Various stages of construction were taking place, building materials piled up along the short driveways or monitored gates.

"I keep looking for the monkeys in the trees," Shannon said, staring out the window.

"We have tours for that, too."

"Trying to sell us on another day, Leo?" she teased.

"A man needs to make money." He laughed.

"Let's do today first."

Leo pulled into a small clearing that looked like it could be a parking lot and cut the engine. "You have sunscreen on, right?"

Shannon nodded, looked at Victor.

"I'm sure I'll be fine."

Leo looked over his shoulder. "Americans always fry."

Shannon dipped into her bag and removed suntan lotion. "Here."

Becoming a lobster was probably not the best way to spend the rest of his time in Tulum.

They stepped out of the car, and Victor poured a generous portion of lotion into his palm. He yanked off his T-shirt and oiled up his chest, arms, legs, and what he could reach on his back.

Shannon watched him while Leo stepped toward the man with the kayaks and snorkel gear.

After making a few slapping motions on his flanks, Victor turned to her and smiled. "Would you mind getting my . . ." He turned his back to her and handed her the sunscreen.

"If I didn't know better, I'd think you planned this," she said before he felt her small palm slide over his shoulder blades.

He hadn't planned any of it, but that didn't make her touch any less inviting. There was nothing suggestive or sexual about it, but his mind didn't seem to know that.

"I'd have planned it better," he told her.

Her fingers ran to his lower back, right above the waistline of his swim shorts.

"How so?" she asked.

"I'd be lying down instead of standing on the side of a road."

"If we were back at the hotel, I'd suggest you lie in the shade."

He glanced over his shoulder, caught her staring at his back. "Not sure I buy that."

She snapped her hand away, closed up the sunscreen, and handed it to him. "You might want to get your face. Skin cancer leaves holes after the doctor cuts it out."

"See, you care."

Shannon rolled her eyes and walked toward Leo.

Victor followed, laughing.

❦

Shannon waited for the last second to shed her cover-up. Even though all the important parts were covered, she couldn't help but feel naked when Victor looked at her.

In his defense, he did try to look away, but failed.

She didn't spend any serious time at the gym, never really had to. The yoga studio she had a membership with saw her a couple of times a week, but she wouldn't say she had one of *those* bodies. Still, Shannon knew she looked better than a lot of women wearing bikinis on the beach. She'd always thought of her body as long and willowy. Partly because she never grew out of a B cup bra. In her college years, she'd wanted more curves. But as she grew older, she embraced the body she'd been given and dressed to enhance what she had.

Like now . . . with her sun-kissed tan, her white bikini crisscrossed over her back, holding her breasts in place, while the adequate bottoms hid enough but showed off a lot.

Avery had whistled when she helped secure the top before Shannon left that morning. "Way to pull out the big guns," she'd commented right before returning to the bathroom and revisiting the liquor from the night before.

If it wasn't for Avery yelling at her to leave her to die in peace, Shannon would have bailed on the day.

But she'd been in Avery's position before and preferred to suffer alone.

Shannon looked up to find Victor staring.

Channeling her inner Avery, Shannon turned to the side and cheated her butt to the man. "Do I have something out of place?"

He narrowed his eyes, cleared his throat. "That suit should be illegal."

His honest groan empowered her. "It probably is in Dubai."

Leo heard them, laughed, and handed them their snorkeling gear.

On the shore, Leo helped her into the front of the kayak and encouraged Victor to climb in the back. Once they were all set, Leo rowed in front of them into the bay.

"I haven't done this in years," Shannon told Victor over her shoulder.

"I can beat that. I haven't done this at all."

"Really? Not even at summer camp?"

She matched Victor's pace with the paddle, digging left and then right, until they found a rhythm that would take them away from shore.

"I never went to summer camp."

"That's a shame. The best things in life happened at summer camp."

"What kinds of things?" Victor asked.

"Things like this. Kayaking, getting dumped in the water from a canoe. Campfires and ghost stories. First kisses."

"Ohh, tell me about those."

She grinned. "The ghost stories?"

He splashed her with his paddle. "The kisses. What was his name?"

She looked back at the memory. "Russell Lipski."

"Lipski? You're making that up."

"Why would I lie about a name like that?"

Victor laughed. "How was Mr. Lipski?"

"Cold, wet hands. Dry lips. It was over before it started. I ran back to my cabin to tell the other girls that he'd kissed me. What about you? What was her name?"

"Wendy Simmons," he said in a dreamy voice.

Shannon looked over her shoulder, caught him smiling. "That good?"

"She was older than me."

The image of a teenage cougar came to mind. "How much older?"

"Fifth grade when I was in fourth."

Her jaw dropped. "Your first kiss was in fourth grade?"

"It was the last week in school before summer."

"I'm not sure that's any better."

Victor laughed. "I think Wendy did it on a dare, but that didn't stop me from bragging about it all summer long."

"So it was never repeated?" Shannon turned around, kept rowing.

"Nope. Wendy's parents moved them away that summer. I was devastated until Halloween."

Shannon was afraid to ask. "Why Halloween?"

"Because Mia Fletcher dressed up like a cat and made me forget all about Wendy."

Laughter caught in her gut. "Men are so easy."

"That we are. Isn't that right, Leo?"

Shannon glanced at their guide, rowing alongside them.

"It's a curse, I'm afraid."

They all laughed.

Since they were talking so candidly, Shannon risked a couple more questions. "Can I ask you something?"

"Go ahead."

"Why do you work so hard?"

He was silent as they rowed a few times.

Shannon glanced over her shoulder to see if he had heard her.

Victor was concentrating on the oar in his hands, his lips in a straight line.

"Never mind, you don't have to answer that."

"No, no . . . I'm trying to think of a quick answer."

She turned back to the sea in front of her. "We're going to be out here for a while. A long answer is fine."

It was still a few breaths before he started to talk. "It's my company. When I started it, I was only twenty. Granted, it was only me back then, but now I have employees and plants, and teams. I'm responsible for keeping this company going and the jobs it provides. People depend on Vic Corp to put food on their tables."

His answer was unexpected. Not to mention completely selfless. The image of the self-centered *all about me* man she'd met on the plane dissipated with his explanation.

"That sounds like a lot of stress on one man's shoulders," she told him.

"Most days it is."

Once again, she looked over her shoulder. Their eyes caught and he smiled.

"But not today," she said.

"No. Today would be the opposite of stressful."

"The word is *relaxing*," she teased.

He pushed his oar deeper into the sea, let his muscles ripple as he put his back into the job of pushing them forward. "I have a feeling this *relaxing* might need a good massage once we're done."

Leo ended their conversation by stopping them by a buoy to tie up their kayaks. They left their life vests aside and donned their snorkeling gear. In the water, Shannon watched Victor working his way into his mask. "You've done this before, right?"

"In Hawaii."

Good. She didn't need Victor strutting to gain her attention only to drown in the Yucatán.

᧠

When he was twelve . . .

He'd snorkeled in Hawaii when he was twelve. How hard was that to say?

Apparently impossible, since the words never left Victor's lips, and he followed Shannon's example and put on his mask.

How hard could it be? Keep the water out of your eyes by tightening the mask, keep the pipe clear of the water, and breathe out of your mouth.

He sputtered the first time he stuck his face in the water. Lucky for him, Shannon had already kicked her fins up and was skimming the surface with her white bikini ass leading him into the deep.

The memory of mermaids and his thoughts of the night before surfaced as he attempted to rid his mask of water and put it on tight.

He kicked his feet and caught up with Leo and Shannon, who were several yards ahead of him, looking at the reef below. Once he was close, he placed the mouthpiece again and attempted to view the ocean floor.

Shannon's long legs kicked out beside him, her arms helping her tread water.

Leo waved his hand and pointed to something moving below.

A stingray hid in the sand, their presence obviously disturbing its peace as it swam away. Victor didn't mind seeing it go. He tried to remember the name of the wildlife expert that had recently died from a stingray, and he didn't want to become part of that club.

Victor worked to keep his breathing normal and found it hard to concentrate on the beauty around him. All he really wanted to do was make it through their snorkeling part of the day without drowning.

He sputtered again and came to the surface to clear his mouth.

"You okay?" Shannon asked from a few yards away.

"I'm fine," he lied. He put the mouthpiece in again.

You can do this, Vic. Thousands of people do this every day.

Once facedown, he didn't even try to see the fish, the color of the reef, or the sea turtles below. All he did was follow Shannon and concentrate on breathing.

She either caught on to his plight and took pity or wanted to be by his side. Either way, she was there, catching his attention by tapping his shoulder and pointing at something below. Purple coral . . . fluorescent blue fish. Some of the rocks looked like someone had carved the image of brains into them.

Yeah, the ocean was a perfect disguise for the world below. So much life surrounded them, welcomed them as guests.

Shannon reached out and held on to his arm right as a school of fish, thousands of them, swam around them.

Victor held on to her arm, felt several fish brush past his legs.

He followed her lead and popped his head out of the water once they were gone.

"Holy cow, that was awesome," Shannon said. "Have you ever seen something like that?"

"Only in the movies."

She played with her mask, chasing the fog away, smiled, and ducked back into the water.

Yeah, Victor would take on more water just to have her smile at him like that again.

The first of the two cenotes Leo took them to was what the locals called *the garden*. He explained the underground rivers of fresh water and how important they were to the ecosystem. Shannon knew instantly that Victor was much more comfortable swimming without a facemask than he had been in the ocean. She'd recognized his discomfort early on in their snorkeling and made a point to stay by his side. If he knew she caught on to his lack of snorkeling skills, he didn't say.

The tiny fish in the fresh water were much more his speed. Even when those fish started to volunteer a pedicure for them as they sat on the steps leading into the water. "People pay good money for this back home," Shannon told him as the fish tickled their toes.

"We're paying good money for this here, too," he replied.

They ended their tour in a cave. This time they wore life vests as Leo swam them deep inside, where flashlights were needed in order to see where they were going. It was filled with stalagmites and stalactites, everything Mother Nature created where most people would never see.

The deeper they went, the cooler the water became. Still, the view was worth every second of the trip.

"What feels like sand below your feet is actually calcium from the sides of the cave," Leo told them.

Shannon reached down and brought it to the surface, rubbed her hands in the gritty substance.

"Exfoliating?" Victor teased.

"Hey, for all we know the cure for cancer is down here somewhere."

They ended their tour with a lunch cooked by the locals. Fresh fish tacos on homemade tortillas, rice, and fresh fruit. They each drank a beer with lime, which seemed appropriate for where they were.

Back in the car, she sat on a towel and covered her shoulders with her cover-up.

Victor poked her arm with one finger. "Looks like you got too much sun."

She was a little pink.

She poked him back. "You did, too."

The ride back to the hotel was a lot more relaxed than it had been driving away.

With soggy hair, fried skin, and a few more mosquito bites to add to the equation, Shannon felt her shoulders relax.

They somehow fell into a conversation about their siblings. She told him about her sister.

"Your sister is in the Peace Corps?"

"That's what I said. You wouldn't think joining would make her the black sheep of the family, but for my parents, it did."

"How's that possible?"

"They didn't approve. They wanted us to marry up and add our family name to more guest lists."

Victor considered her from the seat across from hers. "Is that why you married a governor?"

Should she deny it? "He wasn't a governor when we married."

"I'll pretend you didn't avoid answering that question."

There was no way she would directly. Let him guess all he wanted. "For what it's worth, I didn't want my marriage to end. But things happen and we split."

There was a brief pause in the conversation. "Can I say something and risk it sounding like a pickup line?" Victor asked.

"Go for it."

Victor looked her in the eye. "He's an idiot."

She should have expected his words.

She didn't.

Unexpected moisture gathered in her eyes. "No accounting for taste." She blinked away her emotions.

"I mean it." Victor looked away, giving her the ability to hide her instant response to words so many had said before. "I know you and I didn't start out on the best footing . . ."

"To say the least. I fell in your lap."

". . . and blamed me."

She rolled her eyes, feeling laughter instead of pain. "Whatever."

"But today was good," Victor said.

"Don't forget the salsa dancing. If we can call it that."

"I'm ignoring the bruise on my instep."

"You do *not* have a bruise."

Victor lifted his foot to prove her wrong.

Shannon saw sand, but nothing else. "I don't see anything."

"It's on the inside."

They laughed together.

∞

Thirty minutes into the ride back to the hotel, Victor put his head back and closed his eyes. "For the first time in a long time, I feel like I escaped the rat wheel of my life. I owe that to you," he told Shannon.

"Even rats need to recharge once in a while."

"Yeah." He turned and watched the landscape outside the window. "I've been thinking about your question earlier. About working too hard."

"Your explanation told me a lot about you."

He shook his head. "It made me sound like a saint. I'm not. I like the perks, the money . . . the path to decent tables at restaurants and first-class seats on airplanes. My ego gets a charge quite a bit with this company."

"There is nothing wrong with enjoying the benefits of your labor," Shannon told him.

He shrugged. "Until it's not enough. I need more of this. Days where I don't have a phone to my ear and my biggest worry is if the big fish looks at me as if I'm lunch." Just saying the words made him envision their snorkeling adventure taking a turn for the worst. "I need balance."

"Was that what Corrie was?"

Her question couldn't have been more spot-on.

"My attempt, I guess."

Shannon must have sensed he was sorting out his own feelings on the topic and gracefully changed the subject.

Leo pulled up to their hotel a short time later, and Victor gave him a generous tip.

It was just after three, and the beach party was in full swing. "I had a good time today. Thanks for stepping in for Avery," Shannon told him.

"I hope she's feeling better."

"I'm sure she's fine."

"Thanks for inviting me out," Victor said. "And for listening to my . . . well, my current drama."

"I'm a therapist on the side. I'll send you my bill," she teased.

"I'll look for it."

CATHERINE BYBEE

The awkward goodbye lingered above them. "I need to get out of this suit."

Victor lifted an eyebrow. "That's a damn shame." He hadn't meant to say that out loud.

Backing up, she lifted her hands to the air, a mischievous smile on her lips. "Okay, I'm gone."

"We'll touch base for dinner," Victor called after her.

"If Avery's up to it," Shannon said as she continued to walk away.

He didn't say goodbye, and neither did she.

But his eyes followed her as she left his sight.

Chapter Fourteen

Avery had recovered but spent the day on their deck nursing a headache. Shannon joined her outside and received the inquisition.

"Did he hit on you?"

"If you're asking if he made a pass, the answer is no."

"No inappropriate touching?"

"Nope."

Avery frowned. "What about comments? I'm sure he had something to say about that swimsuit."

"He had plenty to say about the suit."

Avery smiled. "Give it up."

Shannon looked down at the suit she had yet to take off. "He said it should be illegal."

"That's something."

"He was a surprisingly good sport with all of it. It was obvious that he hadn't snorkeled in a while, or at all. But he kept a smile and made a good show without complaint. The cave was incredible. We have to come back here and bring Trina and Lori."

Avery rubbed her temple. "But no pass."

"No. But it isn't like I gave him the opportunity. I'm enjoying the flirt, like you suggested. No one said anything about physical contact." Although the more she thought about it, the better it sounded.

"We still have three nights left. I'll be sure and leave you alone with the man to give him an opportunity."

Shannon glared. "Don't you dare, Captain Obvious."

"You're right, you're right," Avery backtracked. "If he wants it, he will create his own opportunity."

She thought about his confessions about work, about his life. There was a lot more to the man than she first thought. Not that she was going to reveal any of that to Avery right at that moment. Doing so would get the woman going more than she already was.

Shannon pushed up off her chair to walk inside. "I'm taking a shower and a nap before dinner."

"Good idea. Rest up before the night comes, in case you need your energy."

Shannon walked away shaking her head.

Avery was like a dog with a bone.

A bone named Victor.

❧

Victor kicked back on his bed, wrapped in a towel. The air conditioner and the fan spinning above him were the only sounds in the room.

He'd purposely left his phone behind for the day, and in fact was making a concerted effort to avoid logging into the real world or risk being sucked into his normal life. Except a text from Corrie waited for him when he returned to his room.

> In the off chance you care, I thought you should know I'm not
> dead in a ditch somewhere.

Her words evoked a desire to immediately text her back to let her know he was quite aware she was alive and well, that her parents had informed his parents, who had told Justin, who revealed the information to him.

What was the point?

His conversation with Shannon about balance had him rethinking why he'd asked Corrie to marry him in the first place. She was a beautiful girl . . . woman, he corrected his thoughts. Except now when he thought about her, he realized she was immature in many ways. Just like her text suggested. She and her friends liked to hang out in clubs and wake up late. Things he learned when he called her early in the morning and found her sleeping in after stumbling in past two.

He didn't see Shannon doing those kinds of things. Even in Tulum, the lady didn't overindulge. And her friend Avery obviously didn't drink all that much if she was getting sick after their wine at dinner and maybe one cocktail. Comparing Shannon to Corrie was like the apple and the orange.

Corrie accepted his need to overwork.

Shannon challenged it.

Corrie had openly flirted with him when they first met.

Shannon blew him off.

Corrie ran off.

Shannon stayed.

He supposed the last part wasn't truly for or because of him. But Victor owned it anyway.

The opportunity to miss Corrie, even when they were dating . . . yeah, that never really happened. She was right there, ready to jump when he called. She fell into place, and asking her to marry him was as much about closing a chapter in his life and moving forward as any business deal he'd been a part of.

He was an asshole.

Marriage wasn't a business.

At least it isn't supposed to be.

Marriage and love are about the welled up emotion that surfaces at the most unexpected times. Like with Shannon today. He hadn't missed the tears in her eyes when she spoke of her ex.

Victor kicked his feet off the bed and retrieved his laptop.

He ignored the three hundred new e-mails in his inbox and logged into the hotel's Wi-Fi. He googled Paul and Shannon Wentworth and scanned through their public pictures.

"Jesus." He blew out a whistle.

He knew she was attractive, obviously. Between his voyeur tendencies, the killer white bikini, and the relaxed sundresses she wore, it was hard to miss her beauty. The pictures he looked at now were of her and her ex-husband in black-tie attire, floor-length rhinestone studded dresses, full makeup, and jewelry fit for a princess.

Victor stuck to his earlier conviction.

Paul Wentworth was a fool.

Victor removed Paul's name from the search and found a new thread of society page photographs. Pictures ranging from gossip magazines after her divorce to her attending celebrity weddings. In fact, on closer inspection, it looked as if Shannon and Avery had both been in the wedding party of a well-known country singer and an oil heiress.

Yeah, Shannon Wentworth was a lady, where Corrie stuck out like a college student.

He had an itchy desire to read the articles about her divorce, then decided against it. He considered it a violation of her privacy, even in light of it being public knowledge.

"Yet you secretly watch her swimming naked," he said to himself. "Twisted, Vic . . . really twisted."

He glanced again at the number inside the red circle above his e-mail inbox, clenched his fists, and closed his computer.

It could wait.

Whatever it was . . . it could wait.

Stephanie was told to call him only if the sky was falling.

Victor peeked out the window. Nope . . . the sky was still there.

⌒

Clouds rolled in as the sun started to go down, and the rain that made the region tropical started to fall.

Shannon and Avery ended up having dinner at the hotel restaurant, where Victor joined them. They took their time with their meal but ended the night early.

Avery still wasn't a hundred percent, and Victor didn't suggest they extend the night longer.

The next morning, Shannon sat on the side of Avery's bed, placing a cold washcloth on her head. "I think you need to see a doctor."

"I must have eaten something bad."

"Food poisoning doesn't last this long. Unless you ate something that has a parasite, it wouldn't linger."

Avery's eyes widened. "I've heard horror stories of stuff in the food here."

"That has to be it. We didn't drink last night, and I didn't buy a hangover from the night before. No offense, my friend, but your liver is seasoned better than that."

Avery attempted to smile through her misery.

"I could just be sick."

Shannon thought that, too. "What do you want to do? We can find a clinic."

Avery shook her head. "A Mexican hospital isn't something I want to experience, not when I don't speak the language. If I'm not feeling better by tonight, we'll go."

"You sure?"

"Yeah. I'm sorry, Shannon. I know this isn't how you pictured the week to be."

She stood. "It's okay. I wasn't ready for meaningless sex yet, anyway. I'll go out to the beach and check on you by lunch. If you're not feeling any better, I'm going to drag you to the nearest doctor."

Avery rolled over, tucked her hands under her cheek. "I might let you."

Shannon grabbed a coffee from the hotel coffee bar and parked herself in her usual beach spot.

She opened the book she'd been nibbling away at and lay back to take in the morning. It didn't take long for Dylan and Erasmo to find her and settle in, and soon after, Victor worked his way down.

"Good morning."

It was a simple greeting. One she'd just received from Dylan and Erasmo . . . yet his had her smiling on the inside.

"Morning."

He spread out under the palapa to her left and glanced briefly at her body. "No white swimsuit today?"

She blushed. "I need to switch up the tan lines."

Today she wore a more conservative navy blue number without all the crisscross strings.

"Still nice," he said. "But yesterday's wins."

"I didn't know there was a contest."

He leaned back, put sunglasses over his eyes. "Now that you do, I'll look forward to tomorrow."

"Look forward to disappointment, then. I only brought two. One to wear, one to dry."

Dylan overheard their conversation and spoke up. "I can help you with that."

Shannon picked up her e-reader, woke up the screen. "Victor can have his own little fashion show in his head. I have plenty of suits at home. No need to shop here."

"Where's Avery?" Erasmo asked a few minutes later.

"She's still not feeling right. I want to take her to the doctor, but she's not cooperating."

"She's not drinking the water out of the tap, is she?" Victor asked.

"No."

"She didn't drink alcohol last night," he added.

"Even if she did, of all my friends, she's the one with the iron stomach."

"She seemed fine last night."

"I know. It's like she's allergic to the morning." Sick in the morning . . . fine by the evening. It reminded her of when she wanted to skip school as a kid.

Only Avery was skipping her vacation.

"Is that the new e-reader?" Dylan asked.

Unless . . .

"Yeah," Shannon answered on autopilot.

She flipped forward several chapters in the book she was reading and came across the one titled "Pregnant and Single." She skimmed several pages and read a passage on morning sickness.

"Oh my God."

"What?" Victor asked.

Shannon dropped her e-reader and jumped up. "I'll be back."

She all but ran through the sand, around the beach chairs, and up the stairs to their suite. She swung the door open, startling Avery.

"Geez, Shannon . . . you scared me."

"You don't have a parasite," she said, smiling. "You're pregnant."

Chapter Fifteen

Victor watched as Shannon ran off. "What is that all about?" he asked the other guys.

"Who knows. I don't try and figure out the actions of women," Erasmo said.

Victor laughed.

Dylan moved over to Shannon's spot and picked up the e-reader he had been asking her about. "I've been thinking about getting one of these." He waved it around. "It's waterproof. Perfect for the beach."

Things like that didn't interest Victor.

He looked around the shade of his palapa to see if he could get a glimpse of Shannon up in her room, but his vantage point wasn't nearly as good as it was across the beach.

"Oh, wow . . ."

Victor glanced over to Dylan, who looked at him, and then the device in his hand.

He dismissed Dylan's excitement over the new technology and folded his arms behind his head and started to close his eyes.

"Oh, oh . . . no."

"What's so exciting?" Erasmo asked.

"Nothing." Once again, Dylan looked at Victor, then the e-reader.

Dylan dropped the device and scooted back to his spot next to Erasmo.

Victor started to close his eyes again.

"Do you read for pleasure?" Dylan asked him.

"No time," he replied.

"That's too bad. You can learn a lot about a person by what they read."

Erasmo laughed. "Which would make you a serial killer with all the thrillers you go through."

Victor felt the weight of someone watching him.

He opened his eyes and saw Dylan. When his gaze moved to where Shannon had been sitting, or more importantly, the e-reader he'd been so fascinated with, Victor caught on.

He sat up. "Waterproof, huh?"

Dylan nodded. "Lightweight, too."

Victor looked up, didn't see Shannon, and saw his hand reaching toward her stuff.

He touched the screen and it came to life. It took him a few sentences to comprehend what he was reading.

A book on pregnancy? No . . . not exactly.

He flipped through and found a chapter heading and the title of the book.

No, no. Why would Shannon . . . ?

"Pretty cool, right?" Dylan asked.

He had to be mistaken. Was the woman pregnant? He thought of the bikini hugging her body. A bathing suit like that was what a woman wore to attract a man. Not to mention the alcohol. Shannon seemed like a responsible woman. Pregnant women didn't drink.

Victor knew it was wrong, but he clicked on what looked like a menu and the images of book covers popped on the screen. *Single Mothers. Single Motherhood by Choice. Skip the Syringe, Just Have Sex. What the . . .*

He clicked back into the book she'd been reading, flipped back a few pages, uncertain where he'd picked the device up, and left it next to her bag and hat.

"I might have to take up reading again," Victor said, staring at Dylan.

Dylan offered a sad smile.

So many questions came at once. Shannon was considering a baby, which was obvious. Skipping the syringe meant sleeping around, trapping a man? No, no . . . single mothers. No dad needed for that. Except in the baby making part of the deal. Kinda hard to have a baby without a man or the implied syringe.

Victor tried to find some kind of incriminating behavior to point the finger toward Shannon working some kind of scheme to get pregnant without the man realizing what was going on.

Except all he came up with was the time she'd spent with him and the gay couple from Portugal.

Which left him.

Only his fiancée had walked out, and here Shannon was at his honeymoon hotel, *by accident.*

Was she playing him?

Was she playing anyone?

Son of a . . .

There was really only one way to find out.

Shannon skipped back onto the beach ten minutes later, much happier than when she'd left.

"Is everything okay?" Victor asked.

"Everything's great." She sat on her perch, waved a hand at the server on the beach. "I'm up for a Bloody Mary, anyone want one?"

"I'll take one," Erasmo said.

She looked at Victor.

"I'm good."

"Dylan?"

"Too early for me."

"How's Avery?" Victor asked.

Shannon grinned and bit her lip. "Much better."

"What's so funny?"

She shook her head. "Nothing."

The waiter approached, cutting off the conversation.

As Victor watched Shannon sipping what he would call a *vacation cocktail* or something given a name that made it okay to drink before noon, he completely ruled a pregnant Shannon out.

Her playing him, however, was still on the table. He had two days to figure out her game.

If there was one thing Victor had come to realize, it was that she was up to something.

❦

Nothing could dim her mood. Even Avery grumbling around their room and checking her stomach's profile in the full-length mirror while in complete denial.

Like clockwork, Avery's transient stomach issues disappeared as the morning ran on, leaving her tired but hungry around two.

"We've been using protection."

"Apparently not all the time."

"I knew going off the pill was a bad idea." At thirty-three, her doctor had suggested she take a break to test her hormone and thyroid levels. Add to that the fact that she and Liam had talked about having a baby . . . someday. "All your talk about getting pregnant scared me into thinking I wouldn't."

"Obviously not your concern."

Avery paced the room, as she had most of the day. "We just got married."

"Liam is going to be thrilled."

"I know that. But he isn't the one puking. I'm going to get fat." She sat on the edge of a bed. "Maybe it's just some kind of parasite."

Shannon giggled. "Yeah, the nine month kind."

"This isn't funny."

She took Avery's hands in hers. "You're going to be a great mom."

Avery's eyes opened wide. "Oh my God. I'll be like my mother."

"Not a chance."

"What if I screw up?"

"You're not going to screw up."

Avery shook her head. "I'm not ready for this."

Shannon knew her friend. It had taken her a long time to allow a relationship between her and Liam, even longer to admit it. Then one step after the other, Liam had put them on the fast track to getting married. Now this. "You're ready. Liam is going to be the perfect father. You have me, Trina, and Lori. Everything is going to work out."

Avery reverted back to her earlier argument. "I just got married."

It was going to be a long night.

Victor found Dylan and Erasmo at the space reserved for their party before Shannon and Avery joined them.

He'd barely taken a seat before Dylan brought up their discovery earlier in the day. "What are your thoughts on Shannon's choice in reading material?"

Victor glanced beyond Dylan to his husband.

Erasmo smiled. "We share everything. He already told me about it."

Victor looked over his shoulder, didn't see Shannon or Avery in sight. "Honestly, I'm confused."

"She doesn't act like she's pregnant."

"I don't think she is," Victor added. "She seems a lot more responsible than to be drinking during a pregnancy."

"That's what I pointed out," Erasmo said. "But if she's reading books on being a single mother, then maybe she's considering her options."

Dylan lowered his voice. "We know a lot of same-sex couples, and the women have talked openly about hooking up with a guy long enough to get the job done."

"One even asked one of us to step in," Erasmo told him.

Victor's jaw dropped. "Seriously?"

They both nodded.

"Some of us have explored the other side before coming out, so it's not terribly uncommon. And with fertility clinics being slow on the diversity train, same-sex couples haven't always had the same options as hetero couples." Dylan sighed. "We said no, in case you were wondering."

Victor lifted his hands in the air. "Not my business."

"Do you think maybe Shannon is here to find a guy to do the job?" Dylan asked.

The thought had crossed Victor's mind more than once. "That's where I'm confused. If she is, she isn't going about it very aggressively."

"She doesn't seem to be the aggressive type." Erasmo looked over Victor's shoulder, lifted his chin. "We could just ask her."

"Sure, and confess to invading her privacy by reading her book. Women don't like that," Victor said.

Dylan smiled. "He has a point, hon. I say we keep this to ourselves."

Somehow Victor thought invading Shannon's privacy by watching her skinny-dipping every night might be the bigger sin, but he wasn't about to go to confession on that one.

c⑨

"Don't say anything to anyone," Avery said as they made their way to the beach barbeque and bonfire that night. As the afternoon moved on and Avery's morning sickness eased, her denial ramped up. Although

Shannon had slipped out of the hotel in a cab and returned from a pharmacy with an at-home pregnancy test, it said to use it in the early morning, so it sat in their bathroom waiting for the next day. "Probably a false alarm."

Shannon rolled her eyes. Let the woman live her fantasy for another night. By morning, she'd confirm what they both already knew.

The sun had yet to set, but the small fire was heating the warm air on the beach. The guys were already there, reserving seats for the two of them.

"It's not cold enough for a fire," Avery said as she sat down.

Shannon scratched at a bite on her arm. "Maybe it will help with the mosquitos."

"Vicious little shits, aren't they?" Erasmo said.

Victor moved over, giving her room to sit at the low-lying table surrounded by cushions. "They don't seem to like me," Victor bragged.

"Lucky you."

His eyes traveled the length of her, and he smiled. "You both look lovely tonight."

Avery flopped beside Dylan. "I should . . . I've been sleeping all damn day."

"I'm glad you're feeling better. Nothing worse than getting ill on vacation."

Avery wasn't amused. "I'm over it."

The waiter arrived to take a drink order. Shannon hesitated until Avery spoke. "Iced tea . . . wait, no—caffeine. Juice."

"Orange? Cranberry? Apple?"

"Apple . . . wait, no. Orange."

The waiter paused. "Any tequila in that?"

Avery looked around at the group and sighed. "No."

"And you?" He turned to Shannon.

She glanced at Avery, wanting to support her.

"She'll have a margarita," Avery ordered for her, removing her choice.

"I will?"

"Yes. Just because I shouldn't, doesn't mean you shouldn't."

Shannon smiled. "Fine, I'll take a margarita."

The waiter walked away.

"We're glad you could join us," Dylan told Avery. "Our flight leaves in the morning."

"This was your last day?" Shannon asked. How did she miss that?

"Work calls."

"If you're ever in LA . . . ," Victor offered.

"I'm sure we'll make it there sooner or later." Erasmo put his arm around Dylan's shoulders. "Our place is small, but you're welcome anytime—"

"No long goodbyes. The night just started," Avery snapped, cutting them off. "It's a small world. Made smaller by airplanes and shit like that."

Everyone stopped talking and stared at her.

Avery looked around, oblivious to the effect her words had on the group. "God, I'm hungry."

Shannon hid her smile behind her hand, counting the hours until the morning when Avery wouldn't be able to deny her fate any longer.

If there was one thing she was well read on, it was pregnant women and single mothers. She was happy that her friend was only half of that equation—not that Avery couldn't handle taking on a child by herself. She could. Liam, however, would balance out all of Avery's insecurities.

Once her drink arrived, Shannon lifted it in a toast. "To new friends."

Victor touched his glass to hers. "To surprising friends."

Their eyes caught and gooseflesh prickled on her arms.

Gooseflesh and *Victor* were words that had no right belonging together. Her gaze moved to his lips. It had been a long time since she'd noticed a man's lips.

"When do you girls leave?" Dylan asked, pulling Shannon out of her thoughts of first kisses and butterflies.

"Day after tomorrow." Their time had flown by.

"What about you, Victor?"

Victor watched Shannon as he answered, "I'm booked through Monday, but ah . . . I don't know."

"I thought Corrie said you had two weeks," Shannon said.

"Another week in Cozumel . . . I'm not feeling it. I took a whole week, that's big for me," he said, directed at Shannon.

"I'm pleasantly surprised. I didn't think you had it in you."

He chuckled. "Me either."

"At least now you have the right clothes if you ever come back." Dylan nudged Victor.

"Why would he come back?" Erasmo asked Dylan. "This is where the ex dumped him."

"Hello, Mr. Sensitivity!" Dylan scolded.

"Sorry."

Victor brushed them off. "I have less memories of her here than I do of all of you."

Shannon doubted he would ever be able to return and not think of Corrie.

"Have you thought about what you're going to say to her when you see her again?" Avery asked.

Victor looked away. "No. I've actually done very little thinking about the whole thing."

That explains his flirting, Shannon thought. Ignore the woman at home so you could concentrate on the woman in front of you. In this case, her.

"Lots of fish in the sea. I'm sure you'll find someone new to swim with." Avery smiled at Victor when she spoke.

"Lots of sharks out there, too," Dylan added.

Avery narrowed her eyes. "Shannon's not a shark."

"I didn't say anything about Shannon."

Shannon jumped in. "I'm not swimming in anyone's ocean."

"What are you guys talking about?" Erasmo asked.

"Duh, Victor and Shannon," Avery said.

Shannon wanted to duck under the tiny table. "There *is* no Victor and Shannon." Shannon attempted to bury Avery with a look.

It didn't work. "We'd all have to be blind to not see this thing that's going on here." Avery waved her hand in the air between the two of them.

Erasmo caught on and smirked. "She has a point."

"See?" Avery sat taller, as if she'd made her case known. "So no talking about sharks in the Victor and Shannon Ocean."

"Now you lost me again." Erasmo frowned.

Dylan leaned over. "Avery said there were lots of fish in the sea, I said beware of sharks—"

"Shannon's not a shark," was Erasmo's reply.

"Exactly!" Avery lifted a hand in the air for him to fist bump.

It was like watching a skit of "Who's on First," only Shannon was standing on second.

"This is a ridiculous conversation. There is nothing going on between Victor and me." She looked at Victor for his agreement.

He stared at her.

"You were engaged six days ago."

"That's true."

"I thought you were a complete asshole."

Okay, what had she said to pull that cocky smirk from his lips?

"What?" she asked him.

"Thought? Past tense."

She backed out. "I'd go back to thinking that if you were hitting on me six days out from a near-marriage breakup. I mean, c'mon. Corrie's perfume still lingers in your hair."

It seemed the whole table leaned forward to sniff Victor.

"I've showered," he told them.

Erasmo laughed.

"Figuratively speaking!" These people were exhausting her.

Victor leaned back on his hands, amused with himself, the conversation.

She wanted to hit him.

"So what is the appropriate time frame for hitting on someone after a near-marriage breakup?" Victor asked.

"I have no idea. But it's a hell of a lot longer than six days." She glared at him.

"Three months," Erasmo said.

"That's about right. Otherwise it's just a rebound thing, and those never have a chance." Dylan and Erasmo were on the same page.

"A lot can change in three months," Avery said, staring away from the table. "Three months ago I was getting married, and now I'm knocked up."

Victor snapped his gaze toward Avery.

Dylan and Erasmo opened their mouths in awe.

Shannon smiled and shook her head.

"What?" Avery asked as if completely clueless to the bombshell she'd just revealed.

"You told everyone you're pregnant," Shannon told her.

"No, I didn't."

"Knocked up . . . pregnant. Same thing," Dylan said, his gaze flickering to Victor.

"Might be. Maybe . . . oh, God." Avery dropped her head in her arms.

Shannon looked over at Victor. "This is what denial looks like," she told him.

"I take it you just found out," Erasmo said.

With Avery at a loss for words, Shannon answered for her. "She pees on the stick in the morning."

Avery gently hit her head against her folded arms.

"Can I say congratulations?" Victor asked Shannon.

Avery moaned.

Shannon laughed.

And the men lifted their glasses in a silent toast to the woman in denial.

Avery lifted her head long enough to glare. "I'm not the one with the biological clock ticking here—that's you."

Shannon offered a nervous glance toward Victor.

"If hormones are any indication, I'd say you can skip the pee stick in the morning," Dylan said.

Avery must have caught on to what she was saying and backed up. "I'm a horrible friend. I'm sorry, Shannon. This week was supposed to be about you."

∽

Avery's bombshell pulled the focus away from him and Shannon. Good thing, since he felt Shannon was pretty close to making an excuse to leave the table.

Their dinner was Mexico's idea of barbeque, which meant open fire cooking of fresh fish and a big slab of beef. They had family-style service, with the table filled with sides and spices.

For the first time since Victor had met Shannon, she was silent and observant throughout the whole meal. Maybe she was pissed at her friend for pointing out his attraction, but he wanted to believe that it was her attraction to him that had Shannon miffed. He suspected that the biological clock comment was more to blame. Whatever it was, it kept her deep in her thoughts with only minimal comments about Avery's pregnancy.

It was only when Avery started doubting her ability to be a parent that Shannon snapped out of her trance.

"I'm still a kid," Avery started. "I can show my child how to skip school and spend their tuition on trips to places like this. How to sneak out of the house."

"First of all, you're not a kid, you're thirty-three . . . didn't we just talk about this?"

"Still a kid."

Everyone denied Avery's attachment to that argument.

"Second of all, you have so much more to teach your child than sneaking out of the house. If you have a girl, she'll learn how to break a man's arm before he can get to second base."

Avery seemed to like that.

Shannon looked around the table. "Avery studies krav maga."

"That explains the tattoo on your arm," Erasmo said. The word *warrior* was illustrated with a small spider.

"You're overprotective of those you love. You insisted on coming here this week for me."

Avery nodded a few times. "That's true."

"You needed a bodyguard?" Victor asked.

"Not that, just . . ."

"Part of the girl code," Avery continued for her. "We don't go to clubs alone if we have a friend to come along. Keeps the creeps away or helps vet the guys you want to know."

"So you were on the prowl this week?" Erasmo asked. "You should have told us, we could have helped."

Victor didn't think Shannon's face could turn redder.

She started to shake her head.

Avery stopped her. "Girl, your face isn't gonna lie for you."

"Okay. Fine. I'm single. I'm allowed."

They all laughed.

Victor and Dylan exchanged a look. The woman was on the prowl all right. But did she want a seven-pound reminder of her trip to Tulum?

"You still have time," Avery told her. "There's a couple cute guys at the bar."

They all turned their heads.

Victor frowned.

"Are you talking about the blond guy that looks like he lives on a surfboard?" Shannon asked.

"He *is* cute," Dylan said.

"He's twelve," Shannon pointed out.

"He's drinking at a bar, I doubt that," Victor said.

"Okay, eighteen . . . we *are* in Mexico."

He looked more like midtwenties to Victor.

"If he's single and straight, you could tap that in ten minutes," Avery challenged.

"You know you sound like a dude, right?" Erasmo asked Avery.

"Hey, women talk as much smack as men."

Victor saw the game as it was rolling out. He also noticed how Shannon started rubbing her hands on her thighs. He'd bet money that she wouldn't even try hitting on Mr. College Kid on Spring Break.

"I'd have given my left nut for a lady like you when I was his age," Victor said.

Shannon snapped her eyes to his. "Are *you* suggesting I hit on him?"

He couldn't believe the next words out of his mouth. "I can't ask you out for three months, apparently. A lot can change in three months." Like she could find someone to take care of that biological ticking clock. Suddenly his challenge sat like acid in his stomach.

The table went silent.

Shannon pushed back from the table and came to her feet.

Victor's mouth went dry.

There was no way . . .

"Challenge accepted."

She'll turn around.

She'll turn around . . .

Oh, damn, she isn't turning around.

Chapter Sixteen

Damp palms and a racing heart . . . you'd think she was at a junior high school formal, asking the popular boy to dance.

The eyes from everyone at Shannon's table bored into her back as she approached Surfer Boy.

Hearing Avery's words in her head, Shannon moved in beside her target and leaned against the counter as if she were attempting to gain the bartender's attention. "I hope you don't mind me squeezing in," she said over the noise of the bar.

Surfer Boy turned her way midsentence with his buddy, did a double take, and blew off his friend.

She pushed her hair over her shoulder and smiled.

"Well, hello." As hellos went, his was suggestive.

"Hello." She smiled and ignored the nerves jumping in her gut. Okay, so he wasn't eighteen . . . but it was highly possible he was in his early twenties. Very cute, but *cute* being the key word. His gaze did a quick up and down. Not gay, she concluded.

"I'm Steve." He put his hand out to hers.

"Shannon." She reached out to shake his hand, and he turned it around and kissed the back of it. She wanted to find the gesture endearing, but all it did was make her want to laugh. Like where had he learned that? TV? Netflix?

"You're stunning," he said with a wink.

She took her hand back, placed it against her chest. "You're sweet." Okay, okay . . . she'd proved her point. The last thing she wanted to do was lead this kid on only to cut him off.

"What are you drinking?" he asked.

"Margaritas, but I can buy my own drink."

He reached out and placed a hand on her arm.

She looked over her shoulder to see if her party was watching. Three sets of eyes were pinned.

Victor was gone.

"Let me buy you one. It's our first night here," he said.

Without being terribly obvious, she wiggled out from under Steve's hand.

"Is that right? How long will you be here?" Shannon smiled at her admirer and glanced away.

Where is Victor?

"A week. Then it's back to the grind."

"Work?"

Steve shook his head. "School. One more year and I'll be out."

The bartender stopped in front of them.

"The lady will have a margarita."

She tried to wave the bartender off. "It's okay, I can—"

Steve reached for her hand and placed it on the bar. "I insist."

Okay, no more touching.

She pulled away.

"There you are!" Victor appeared behind her, a hand on her shoulder. "I've been looking all over for you."

She sighed in relief.

"Is she bugging you, young man?" Victor asked Steve.

Steve dropped his hand, his smile gone. "Excuse me?"

Victor turned Shannon toward him, both hands on her shoulders. "Do you really want to blow sixty-two days of sobriety now? You've come so far." His eyes twinkled with amusement.

Lost for words, Shannon stared and blinked.

Victor placed an arm over Shannon's shoulders and glanced at Steve. "It took me six months to get her into AA."

Steve stiffened when the bartender delivered the margarita.

All three of them looked at it.

Victor reached into his pocket, tossed a few bills on the counter, grabbed Shannon's hand, and dragged her away.

"AA? Really?" she asked when they could no longer be overheard.

Victor didn't answer, he just kept moving. She had to jog to keep up with him. Instead of heading back to their table, he pulled her toward the beach, away from the people, the music . . . the lights.

"Slow down."

Victor stopped without warning, and she ran into him.

The amusement in his eyes was replaced by something much more heated. "How far would you have gone?"

"What?"

"With the twelve-year-old? How far?"

Oh my God, what was he accusing her of? "He wasn't twelve, and hello . . . you challenged me."

"Is that all it takes? A dare?"

His angry questions made her blood boil. She snapped her hand out of his. "You started it."

"He was pawing you."

"He was trying to pick me up."

"And getting somewhere, apparently."

She couldn't believe what she was hearing. "What is this? Jealousy?"

Victor opened his mouth, closed it.

"You have no right to be jealous. I've known you for what, six days? All you've done was toss a couple compliments and flirtatious barbs. If I want to hook up with College Boy, I will!"

Victor's nose flared, tension snapped in the air.

"Fine," he gritted out between his teeth.

"Fine!" Shannon turned on her heel and made it three steps.

Victor caught up with her, grabbed her hand, and spun her around. "Not fine."

His lips crashed down to hers, heated with the same emotion she felt bursting from her skin.

She sucked in a breath, stunned still, and let him fold her into his arms.

Victor kissed her with such fierce abandon the only thing she could do was hold on and try to breathe. Her mouth was open, gasping, and he was laying claim everywhere he could.

He's kissing me.

Oh, God, it had been so long.

The scent of him, the need in him . . . in her.

Shannon's body caught up with his. She tilted her head and kissed him back, full, open-mouth kisses that skipped anything timid and went right into overdrive. Raw and needy, she wrapped her arms around his back, dug her fingernails into his shirt.

His hands were in her hair, the back of her neck, her spine. He didn't let her up for air, just kept kissing her for what felt like hours.

Only when his pace slowed down and his kiss became softer did her brain engage. *Bad idea* . . . it didn't matter that she wanted this man or that her body was damn near begging for him.

Perfect timing for a baby.

The second the thought popped in her head, Shannon slammed on the brakes. She dragged her swollen mouth away from his. "I can't." Her breath came in pants.

"You want this," he whispered.

No denying her desire, her reactions proved he was right. "But I can't do this to you."

He smiled down at her in the moonlight.

Slowly, their breathing returned to normal.

"I want to see you again."

"We aren't leaving until—"

"Back home," he clarified.

She wanted to deny him. "Victor—"

"In three months. Give me three months and then give me a chance."

What the hell was she supposed to say to that?

He lifted a palm to the side of her face, traced her lower lip with his thumb. "Wait for me. Let me be the next man to kiss these lips."

"Victor . . ."

"Please, Shannon."

Three months? Her emotions clashed with common sense. Confusion muddled her brain. "Where did the asshole I met on the plane go?" she asked.

He reached around to the back of her head, moved in close. "A woman in a white bikini chased him away."

He kissed her one last time, slowly. Thoroughly.

∾

"He was pissed! Holy shit, I didn't think he could come out of his seat fast enough when that guy started touching you."

Shannon listened to Avery's take on what went down at the table after she'd left. They lounged in the plunge pool, as they had nearly every night they'd been in Tulum. The price of the room was worth every penny to shed the suit and swim naked. Maybe the people on the nude beach had found the answer to life.

"He doesn't have a right to be jealous."

"Maybe not. But he was seething."

Shannon had told Avery that he'd kissed her the second they walked away from the bar. Avery's response was a hard look at her lips and a comment about bruises.

"He asked me to wait for him, Avery."

"What do you mean?"

"Three months. He asked me to wait three months and allow him to see me."

Avery pushed to the other side of the small pool and looked her in the eye. "What did you say?"

"I didn't say anything. I mean, I didn't agree, didn't disagree. He isn't what I expected. He was a total piece of work when I met the man, and now . . ."

"Not so much," Avery finished for her.

"Not so much."

"What do you have to lose?"

"What if it doesn't work? What if he turns back into the selfish guy he was on the plane?"

"Then you cut him off and go back to your other plan. Consider this: What if you'd met him a month from now, two months from now, and Steve-o at the bar ended up being Mr. Baby Daddy? Call me naive, but a pregnant girlfriend who is carrying a child that isn't yours is a little harder to juggle."

Avery's logic rang true.

"I haven't been touched by a man since Paul, and I'm considering letting this guy put me on the hook, pushing off my plan for three months based on one kiss." *One spectacular kiss.*

Avery shrugged. "I guess when you put it like that . . ."

"See?"

They were both silent for a few breaths.

"How good was the kiss?" Avery asked.

Shannon closed her eyes and shivered. "I've never been kissed like that. With such abandon and need. It was like he had this one shot of making his point, this one moment, rolled up in a single kiss." She opened her eyes, found Avery smiling. "I think it was the best first kiss I've ever had."

"Doesn't your best first kiss deserve a chance?" Avery asked.

"Why are you so congenial about Victor? The man was engaged to another woman less than a week ago." A big red flag in anyone's book.

Avery kicked her feet up in the water. "Oh, that's easy."

"Why?"

"You. Because of you! The First Wives Club is going on, what, three years? I have never seen the kind of smiles on your face that I have since we've been here. Even when Victor ticks you off, there is a glow in you. So if he ends up being the selfish douche guy you spoke of, right now the man is pulling you out of the muck that Paul drug you through. And I'll take it. You're quite the catch, Shannon. I don't think you've ever allowed yourself to acknowledge that li'l fact. Hell yeah, I'm gonna promote Victor. For worse or for better, the man is empowering you."

"I don't want to get hurt."

"Then don't let him."

"How do you do that?"

"By keeping it honest with yourself. You fell for Paul, but he didn't fall for you. You couldn't just walk away because of the marriage contract. I get it. But that isn't the case with Victor. If you start diving off the heart-filled cliff for the guy and he's waving as you're going over, get out. If he wants to date you and other women at the same time, then be sure and do the same. Enjoy what he has to offer, and don't take any crap that you're not okay with."

"Should I wait for him?"

"In a normal situation, I'd say hell no. You just met the guy, you've had one kiss . . ."

"A fabulous kiss."

Avery grinned. ". . . he just got out of a serious relationship, and the chances of him jumping around right now are pretty high."

Shannon heard a *however* coming.

"But," Avery continued, "I've never been on this 'get pregnant with a stranger' bandwagon, and the last thing you want is an accident with the wrong guy. Therefore, waiting a little longer, three months . . . I think that's the way to go."

"I had a plan," Shannon said.

"Change the plan," Avery suggested.

Three months . . .

Shannon stood in the reception area of the hotel, her suitcase by her side. Avery stepped away so they could talk without an audience.

"You're a surprise I wasn't expecting this week," Victor told her.

"I would hope so, considering."

He wanted to pull her in his arms and kiss her but decided that a public display might not be what she wanted quite yet. He reached out his hand. "Can I see your phone?"

She removed it from her purse and handed it to him.

He typed in his number and pushed a call through. His phone rang and he hung up. "I'm going to call you."

Her ride to the airport pulled into the drive.

"If you change your mind . . ."

He narrowed his eyes. "Don't count on that."

She sucked in a breath. "One thing."

"Name it."

Vulnerability crossed her face. "Don't play me."

He wasn't sure he'd know how to play a woman like her. "I won't."

She leaned in, kissed the side of his cheek, and moved to the waiting car.

He held the door open for Avery and accepted her hug. "Congratulations," he said in her ear.

"I'll thank you when I stop throwing up."

He laughed.

She lowered her voice. "Absence makes the heart forgetful," she told him. "You might want to remember that."

"I will."

Victor watched the car drive away and felt the sunshine all around him dim.

Chapter Seventeen

A mausoleum would have been noisier than Victor's office the day he returned. He purposely walked in late in the morning, yet a week earlier than he'd told Stephanie that he'd be back.

He walked past the receptionist in the main lobby, smiled, and said good morning. As he walked through the maze of halls and cubicles of desks and various employees, his presence seemed to stop all chatter midsentence.

By the time he walked into the foyer of his office, Stephanie was standing by his door, folders in hand, with very little expression on her face.

"Good morning, Mr. Brooks."

"Morning, Stephanie." He walked past her and into his vast space.

"Did you tell me you were returning today?" she asked, following him.

She knew he hadn't.

"No. I did not." He sat behind his desk and glanced at the open stack of mail. But all of that could wait. "Call a meeting with the executive team in one hour. Is anyone out today?"

She shook her head. "No. You asked that no one take time off when you were gone on your honeymo—" Stephanie stopped midword and dropped her eyes to the floor.

"Right. Good . . . one hour. You and I will meet directly after to go over anything I've missed." He picked up the first paper on his desk, dismissing his assistant without asking her to leave.

Stephanie hustled out of his office, closing the door behind her.

Victor dropped the mail in his hand, leaned back in his chair, and sighed. The images of surprised faces surfaced in his head. Of all the people in the office, their silence.

None of them had been at his botched wedding. Why was that? Oh, that's right, he needed things to run while he was gone, and asking staff to attend could stop the machine he'd put into motion.

His plan seemed to have worked.

Everything appeared to be running as normal in his absence. The closest Victor came to checking in was when he left a voice mail for Stephanie to reschedule his Tuesday appointment. A meeting he had no business making during his honeymoon. A fact Shannon had pointed out before he'd gotten off the airplane.

The thought of her brought a smile.

He wondered how she would handle a staff that refused to look her in the eye after a personal disaster. With grace, he determined.

His fascination with the former first lady of the state had prompted him to look up as much information as he could about her once he'd returned from Tulum and had been sitting in his quiet, empty home alone. The staff at the governor's house had reported that they never knew of any problems with the couple, and that they were all very sorry to see her leave. No one had anything negative to say about the woman. Gossip magazines tried to find dirt, and all they came up with was a pretty hefty payment that a prenuptial agreement spelled out in detail before the couple married.

Her ex-husband had been seen with other women socially during his term, but none were pegged as the reason for the split.

Shannon was only seen with friends, or husbands of friends. Twice he found images of Shannon and Paul speaking cordially at an event after their breakup. Both times the magazines talked of a reunion, which obviously didn't manifest.

Victor was pretty happy about that. Not only would he have never met Shannon, since he highly doubted she'd be running around taking pictures of other couples' weddings . . . she wouldn't have been available to flirt with him and hold him in her arms.

The look on her face when he'd kissed her would live with him forever. Surprise, excitement . . . yielding. She'd been as wound up as he. He was shocked that she didn't push him away the second he touched her, and even more stunned when she told him she couldn't go any further because of him.

"I can't do this to you." Her words had repeated in his head from the moment she uttered them. What had they meant?

In addition to searching the magazines and articles on the lady, he'd also downloaded the book she'd been reading on the beach.

The book was solely geared toward a woman contemplating having a child without the benefit of a husband or partner. Coupling that information with what Avery had suggested—they were there to find someone for Shannon—it stood to reason that maybe Shannon had moved past the contemplating stage of having a child on her own and on to the execution stage of her plan.

So he'd asked her to wait.

Not that he'd be silent for three months.

In fact . . .

He removed his cell phone from his pocket and found her number. He clicked on her number and opened a text message.

He asked one question.

Are you still waiting?

It took a few seconds for the knowing little dots to tell him she was responding.

Victor?

He had no right being this happy.
Good answer, he replied.

I thought for sure you'd be back to work by now.

He smiled. I am. No one is looking me in the eye.

That's rough.

He stepped out of character and asked, How would you handle it?

You want my advice?

Yes.

Ignoring the elephant in the room never makes it go away.

Victor rubbed his chin and grinned. Wise and beautiful.
The telling dots went on for quite a while, as if she were typing something, changing her mind, and then restarting.

You said three months, Victor. Now go away.

He laughed out loud.
The phone on his desk buzzed.
"Yes?" he answered.
"Everyone is gathered in the boardroom, Mr. Brooks."
Had it been an hour? He looked at the time.
Daydreaming about Shannon was very time-consuming.

"I'll be there in five minutes."

He opened his phone to a different app and slowly made his way to the meeting.

No one looked at him as he walked the hall, and many people scattered out of his path to avoid contact.

He was the elephant.

Inside the boardroom, the talking came to an abrupt halt with his presence.

"Good morning," he said.

A chorus of replies similar in nature returned.

Then silence.

He placed his phone on the table and pressed play.

His staff exchanged nervous glances as the drum riff of Simon and Garfunkel's hit about all the ways to leave your lover started to fill the room. When the words started to sink in and the chorus played, the nervous looks of his employees turned to smiles and laughter.

Victor was pretty sure he burped up mezcal at the memory of singing the song with a near stranger in a Tulum bar.

The song ended and the air in the room eased.

"Seems Corrie realized I was a workaholic asshole, wised up, and ran in the opposite direction as fast as she could."

No one in the room disagreed with him.

Not one.

He laughed. "Okay . . . tell me what I missed."

Shannon's studio was a tight, comfortable space with a room in the back fit for photo shoots. Her small office sported a TV-size monitor where she could scroll through the images she'd taken and narrow down the best shots without clicking on each one.

Even though Victor and Corrie's wedding was one that would never have the bride and the groom skimming the images, Shannon found herself sifting through the pictures anyway.

The tightness in the faces of the bride and groom had been passed off as nerves at the time, but now when she was looking at them, Shannon saw something completely different.

Doubt.

Easily deduced in light of Corrie taking off, but even with Victor. He'd been so uptight when she first started taking his photograph with his groomsmen.

She came across the pictures she'd managed of Victor and Justin. Their resemblance really popped on camera, especially when they smiled.

Shannon filed a couple of the better, more natural shots in a folder and continued through the pictures. She'd taken several shots while the guests were being seated . . . of Victor standing on the sidelines, waiting for word that Corrie was on her way. She zoomed in on an image where Justin was saying something to Victor that drew out a heated response. Then she found one of Victor looking at his watch.

From then on, the images she caught were pictures no one realized she was taking. Her lens had focused on Victor when he'd told his guests that his bride had cold feet. His gaze looked over the people, avoiding eye contact. Embarrassed? Upset? Shannon couldn't decipher his mood.

The somber mood of the people that lingered after Victor left could be felt in the photographs. They huddled in small groups, drank the free liquor, ate the food. At some point someone made an executive decision to set the food up on a long table, and the local families that walked up and down the beach tempting tourists with their handmade trinkets were offered a free meal.

That was when Shannon took picture after picture.

The local children laughed with their siblings with bright eyes and animated faces. They stuffed their bodies with food and their souls with their family. These kids had next to nothing in terms of things. It was apparent in their lack of shoes that fit and the clothes that looked as if they'd been passed down six times before reaching their backs. But they had what so many people didn't.

Each other.

For the first time in a long while, Shannon thought of her own sister. Where was she now? Angie had dropped out of school to join the Peace Corps years ago, eventually finished school in Spain, and had continued her volunteer efforts tutoring English in remote locations in Brazil. When she didn't come home for the holidays again last year, her mother had hinted that Angie was considering traveling to Africa next.

"That girl won't be happy until she contracts some incurable disease."

Their parents didn't approve.

On impulse, Shannon fished her cell phone from her purse and dialed the only number she had for her sister.

The phone rang four times and went to voice mail, a common occurrence with a woman who frequented places that didn't have running water.

"Hey, Angie . . . it's Shannon. I was thinking about you and wanted to catch up. Where the heck are you now? It's been too long. I love you, sis. Call me sometime."

She disconnected the call with a shrug. She'd left messages like that in the past, only to hear back six months later in the form of a card or word passed on through their parents.

Somewhere around the time Shannon married Paul, her sister had faded out of her life without explanation. Shannon asked herself why. They never crossed words, agreed on most political positions, and got along when she did show her face.

Shannon had never come right out and asked her sister what she had done to be ignored. Probably because she wasn't prepared to hear the answer.

Who was she kidding? Alone with her own thoughts, she couldn't be honest with herself.

Angie had never approved of Paul. When they'd announced their engagement and rapid trip to the chapel, her sister sent a brief letter. The words had been etched in Shannon's brain for years.

What happened to my sister with her big dreams of fixing the screwed up world one revealing photograph at a time and ideals that weren't spoon-fed by our parents? You're selling out. You're more than some man's political wife.

Her sister had been right, which hurt to hear. But at the time it solved so many problems. Shannon was *outsmarting* her parents by signing a temporary contract to be Paul's wife.

The arrangement was a two-year job she was utterly skilled at performing. She hadn't dated anyone seriously since college, so when presented with a marriage that would end with six million in her account and a home—and her parents off her back—she took it. The only downfall Shannon foresaw at the time was if she'd met someone during her marriage and couldn't act on it.

She didn't expect that *someone* to be the man she was married to . . . and she didn't expect to leave her marriage rich yet in shambles.

Shannon's sellout had backfired.

At least that's how she viewed her brief time as a political wife. That was, until she met the women in the First Wives Club. Lori, Trina, and Avery became the supportive sisters she needed. They didn't judge her with condescending eyes, they understood her with loving hearts.

They lifted her up and gave her the courage to take an active step forward in her life.

She came out of hiding the year Lori pushed the four of them to take a Mediterranean cruise together. Her small wedding photography business had picked up, giving her purpose.

Shannon looked at the images of the fragmented Brooks wedding.

Flowers and finery . . . dressed up guests and grooms. She was good at wedding photography, but she'd be lying to herself if she said she had true passion for it.

Earning money for posed pictures was not what Shannon had studied in college.

In a way, she was still selling out.

Wedding photography was safe.

Marrying Paul had been safe.

Kissing a jilted groom, not safe at all.

She was tired of the safety net. Wasn't that why she was considering a one-night stand in an effort to have a baby? Was it rebellion, or was she playing it safe to have a child alone in an effort to save her heart from breaking again?

Shannon powered down her computer, grabbed her camera bag, and locked the door behind her as she left.

Chapter Eighteen

Two weeks after his return from Tulum, the remaining bills from the wedding came due.

Victor ignored the mail for several days. When the weekend arrived and he sat in his home office taking care of his personal finances, he tore through them.

The caterers had been given their payment the night of the reception, but they failed to bill him for the overage, since the guest list had increased nearly twenty percent. It didn't matter that many of the guests had immediately left. The food had been ordered, cooked, and served. To whom, Victor couldn't say.

The florist sent a receipt . . . he'd forgotten how much he wrote the check for.

He glanced at the envelope from a jeweler. It wasn't the person he'd purchased Corrie's ring from. He opened the mail and read the receipt. It was for a male wedding band.

Victor looked at his left hand.

Two thousand dollars?

The receipt stated paid in full, but it was in Victor's name.

He logged into his personal bank site and opened the separate account he'd opened for Corrie to use for wedding expenses. In light of the fact that they weren't yet married when he opened the temporary account, both their names were tied to it.

Not that she'd put any money in.

Weddings are expensive, she'd told him. If he wanted to be bugged constantly for questions like, "Do we want to add bacon to the salads and pay a dollar more a plate?" then he could stop working every time or just allow Corrie to take care of it.

Having more money than time, Victor cut a check and stepped back.

He looked at the balance on the account.

To her credit, it wasn't at zero.

No, there was a $23.67 balance.

He compared the jeweler's name to a check written against the account. Not that he cared to have a two-thousand-dollar wedding band instead of a bride to go with it. The names matched and he pushed the receipt aside.

He'd put twice as much money in the account than was the estimated need, which had him digging.

Early checks were written in deposit, some were posted the day of the botched wedding . . . and it appeared some were still due.

He skimmed the list, trying to muster up a little anger that he was paying for something he didn't get. Although when you thought about it, he did get what he'd paid for. He paid for flowers, he saw them. He paid for food, his guests ate it. The bar bill . . . yeah, he'd gotten his money on that. He also paid for Corrie's friends to fly to Mexico and their stay in the hotels. Even his friends refused him when he offered to pay their way.

What did he expect? Corrie was fifteen years younger than he.

He found Shannon Wentworth Photography and a check written for one thousand dollars.

Now, call him naive, but he didn't think for one minute that was her total fee for flying to Mexico to be their photographer. And yet there wasn't a second bill in the pack that he was sifting through.

He smiled at his resourcefulness as he picked up the phone.

Shannon answered on the second ring. "You're seventy-five days early," she said instead of hello.

Victor sat back in his office chair and propped his feet up on his desk. "Do you have a countdown clock like people use when they're excited about a major life event?"

"Are you suggesting a phone call from you is a major life event?"

He heard laughter in her voice.

"Hello, Shannon."

She sighed. "Hello, Victor."

"Aren't you going to ask me why I called?"

"No. I'm sure you'll get around to it."

She made him smile. "You sound good. Did I catch you at a decent time?"

"It's two o'clock in the afternoon on a Saturday."

"I'll take that as a yes."

"Oh my God, Victor . . . yes. It's a good time. Why are you calling?"

He could see her eyes narrowing, her lips pulling into thin lines. "Miss Annoyed is back. I kinda liked her."

"Victor!" His name was a warning.

"Okay, okay, I actually did have a reason other than wanting to hear your voice."

She paused. When she spoke again, her voice had lost some of its edge. "What's your reason?"

"I think I owe you money."

"Excuse me?"

He glanced at the pile on his desk. "I'm going through the wedding bills, and all I see is a deposit for the photographer."

"Oh, that. Uhmm . . ."

"Shannon?"

"I don't expect to get paid for something I didn't do."

"You flew all the way to Mexico for a job. You deserve to get paid for your time."

"Thank you, I appreciate that."

He kicked his feet off the desk, reached for a pen. "How much?"

"We're even, Victor."

"Shannon!"

"Oh, Mr. Annoyed has arrived."

"I'm serious."

"So am I. We're good."

"Do you want me to guess what your fee is and send you a check?" Because he would.

"I won't cash it."

"Then tell me a number."

"Fine. Two hundred dollars."

He started to write down the amount and paused. "That isn't possible."

"That's my number, take it or leave it."

"Why are you being difficult about this?"

"Because I don't want your money," she told him.

He dropped his pen. "That might be the first time I've ever heard that."

She laughed. "That's too bad."

"You're refreshing," he told her.

"I have no business being anything to you for at least another seventy-five days."

The fact she had the days down like a calendar made him grin as if he were a kid skipping school on a sunny day. "I'm looking forward to it."

"Goodbye, Victor."

"Goodbye."

He stared at his phone for five minutes and replayed their conversation in his head. Then he opened his calendar, counted seventy-five days ahead, and started a countdown clock. He titled it: Major Life Event.

∽⊙

Shannon hung up the phone as she sat surrounded by the portfolios she'd done when she was in college.

Victor calling didn't surprise her, but his reason did.

There was no way she was taking any of his money. Not after she'd kissed the man. Not with a pending romantic date in seventy-five days. On some level, she knew her job as his photographer and going on a date were entirely different things, but it didn't stop her from cutting him off.

Shannon Wentworth was finished taking money from men.

Especially men she kissed.

"Miss Annoyed," she said to herself.

Shaking her head, she ducked back into the project in front of her. Each collection of photographs had a different purpose for the class she'd taken. In the beginning, she took her professor's direction literally. When he assigned an urban setting, she went out and photographed all the angles and textures of Los Angeles. She remembered vividly the moment she saw her grade as a D. The doubt she'd harbored inside her heart about picking the class as her minor soared. Her second assignment had been "Through the eyes of a child." The grade went to a C minus. Again, she pulled her hair out. The images she'd captured were exactly what the professor asked for. When she turned in her third assignment, her professor called her into his office.

He told her that if she was going to continue delivering photographs that anyone with a cell phone could take, that she should drop his class right then and there.

She was so upset to see her dream explode before she could even exercise it.

As she was leaving his office, tears down her face, he stopped her.

"How do you feel?" he asked. "One word. Tell me how you feel in one word."

She had turned around, looked him in the eye. "Despair."

"Good. Now go out there, capture despair . . . in the city, and the eyes of a child . . . anything. Prove to me you should be in my class."

And she did.

Shannon picked up the portfolio of those pictures she'd taken all those years ago and flipped through them. With one word, one emotion, she found exactly what her instructor wanted. Her first stop was an animal shelter, where she found the solemn face of an emotionally wounded mixed breed dog. It took everything not to spring the animal and take it home. Then she took the same emotional wound on the face of a child sleeping in a makeshift tent with her parents under one of the many overpasses of the 405 freeway in Los Angeles. That was when Shannon found her voice behind the camera.

She'd proved she belonged in the class and went on to capture the attention of the head of the photojournalism department. Some of her work ended up in the school newspaper.

When her professor encouraged her to reach out to the more mainstream media, Shannon retreated back into her shell. The turmoil of her sister's independence had started to shake their parents' patience and made life for Shannon more difficult. They expected her to fall in line even faster since her sister couldn't find the damn thing. By the time Shannon was graduating college, Angie had long since dropped out.

Shannon sold out to the commercial end of photography. Because she came from an affluent family, she managed to book the occasional wedding. But her meals came from the stream of kids wanting their starts in Hollywood who were in need of reasonably priced headshots.

Somewhere in all of that she'd met Sam and was told about Alliance. She met with Lori for the first time when they discussed a marriage contract with Paul.

Stupid plan.

Well, except for the money. That part worked out rather well. Although she wasn't sure it was entirely worth it.

She put aside her infant work and picked up her senior project.

Gritty stuff, nothing smooth and perfect about it. Even if she was taking pictures of beautiful people, she'd seized the moments their facades fell and real life crashed in. Then she framed the same subjects and added the filters they wanted . . . like her life as Paul's wife, and then her real life when alone with her thoughts.

The striking contrast earned her honor awards.

And what did she do with it?

Shannon flew to Tulum to take pictures of a spoiled girl's wedding. That was how she spent her independence.

In her defense, there wasn't a way to take the images she'd managed in her college years after she became Paul's wife.

She was the subject of speculation and gossip for years following their divorce.

Was that the case any longer?

There really was only one way to find out.

Shannon lifted herself off the floor and went to her closet.

The walk-in room housed all the finery one would expect of a woman who spent much of her time on the other side of the camera. She sifted through her jeans, designer, but nothing that had a logo that would scream money.

From her workout clothing, she chose a T-shirt with a cat and pulled it over her head. Next came a ball cap, and she tugged her hair through the back in a ponytail.

In her bathroom, she removed her jewelry and lipstick and looked at herself in the mirror.

Not exactly what anyone would expect her to be wearing.

With her camera bag in hand, she set the alarm in her house and walked out the door. Seeing her car, she stopped short.

Ten minutes later, Shannon rode in the back of an Uber to test her popularity. If she went unnoticed as she wandered the streets snapping photographs, then maybe her identity as the governor's wife was truly behind her.

And she could see if she still had something else to give this world other than pretty pictures of people faking the perfect life.

Chapter Nineteen

Victor sat in a Starbucks on Ventura Boulevard with one eye on the door.

She'd agreed to meet him. Public place, no possibility of physical contact outside of conversation . . . not that Victor had any intention to touch anyone.

He caught sight of Corrie before she waltzed through the door. She walked up with a friend and was talking to her outside. With what looked like a breath of courage, Corrie pushed through the entry, scanned the room, and paused when she saw him.

Dressed in a flowing-sleeved shirt in pale yellow and white jeans that stopped just below her knees, she crossed the room, turning a few heads.

Victor stood as she approached.

Should he kiss her cheek? Pull out her chair?

She didn't give him the option.

"Hello, Victor."

"Good morning."

She tugged her chair back and sat, removing the sunglasses hiding her eyes.

"Did you want a coffee?"

"No. I don't," she said.

Okay . . . He sat across from her and tried to find the name of the emotion floating to the surface of his feelings in that moment. Nothing came.

"Thank you for meeting me," he told her.

Her chin was tight, her eyes scanning the room instead of looking at him. "I'm surprised you found time in your *busy* schedule."

She was angry.

"I—"

"And you're here on time? Do you know how many times you were on time when we were together?" she interrupted him.

He opened his mouth, didn't utter a sound.

"Zero. Even on our first date you showed up ten minutes late."

"There was traffic." He regretted the words the minute they sputtered from his lips.

She dropped a hand on the table. His coffee jumped.

"You're right, Corrie. Okay. I know I wasn't the most attentive boyfriend."

"Fiancé."

"Right. Fiancé. There isn't anyone who will argue against that."

She lifted her chin, an indignant smile on her face.

"I'm not sure I deserved how you ended things, however. When did you know you didn't want to be my wife?"

He asked the question because he'd asked himself the same one several times in the past three weeks. When did he start questioning his future plans with her? Looking at Corrie now, no longer feeling like he could place his hand on her arm, kiss the side of her cheek, take credit for the fact the men in the Starbucks turned to look her way, he saw her differently. She was beautiful, no denying that. Her stubborn jaw and curt attitude, however, when she was the one who had walked out on him, felt displaced. Adolescent, even. And yes, she was young.

"Once the newness of wearing your engagement ring wore off," she told him.

"When was that?"

"Two months after you put it on."

He glanced at her hand, wasn't surprised to see she wasn't wearing the two-carat ring he'd spent a small fortune on. Other men would have asked for it back.

She must have noticed his attention on her hand. She lifted it up, wiggled her fingers. "I sold it."

That, he didn't expect.

"If you knew you didn't want to go through with the wedding, why did you plan it? Why wait until the last moment to run away? Was I so impossible to talk to? Didn't I deserve a face-to-face conversation saying you were leaving?" Because while he admitted he didn't give the woman as much attention as he should have, or maybe even the love she deserved, he had never fought with her or denied her whatever she wanted when it came to their wedding plans. He gave her gifts . . . what woman didn't like gifts? They went to nice places . . . yeah, he was sometimes late, and there were times his phone interrupted.

"I got caught up in the process and waited until no one was looking." For a nanosecond, her hardness ebbed and her eyes moved to her lap.

He reached across the table, and she snapped her arm away. He opened his mouth to say he understood her position, but she didn't give him a chance to speak.

"Then I realized that you'd kept me waiting over and over again, and it was my time to return the favor." Her anger was back.

Around them, people hushed their personal conversations to watch them.

Victor lowered his voice. "I'm sorry you didn't feel you could talk to me."

She leaned forward, her voice tight. "You don't know me. I was told you addressed our families with a *nice* speech about me getting cold feet and then you mingled. How could you mingle?"

"I thanked our guests for coming and encouraged them to enjoy their stay regardless of what happened."

"Then what did you do? Catch the next flight home to go back to work?"

He was not going to have this pissing match with her. Not in public. What was the point, anyway?

Closure, he told himself, he was searching for closure. For him, for her . . .

Victor's silence had her sitting up as if he'd answered her question with a yes.

"While you were mingling, I was out getting laid."

She was trying to hurt him.

He couldn't muster a jealous ounce of adrenaline.

Her nose flared. "He was fabulous."

And there it was . . . the age gap in Technicolor.

Scooting his chair back, he picked up the keys to his car and paused. "I have a box of your things at my place. Should I send it to your parents?"

"Burn it." Her foot tapped against the air.

He wouldn't, but he stood and finished their conversation. "Goodbye, Corrie. I hope you find someone who deserves you."

Outside of the coffee shop, he took a deep breath.

That didn't go well.

∽

"I need advice." Shannon looked out over her secluded backyard under the shade of her patio, her phone to her ear.

She could count on one hand how many times she'd been in her pool, and twice had been after her return from Tulum. Both of those times she'd ditched her swimsuit and hoped none of the neighbors was flying drones in the area.

"Is this about getting pregnant?" Lori was on the other end of the line. It was just after three in the afternoon. Shannon wanted to catch her friend before the end of the business day in hopes of luring her over for an hour after work.

"No. Nothing to do with that at all, actually. Is there any chance you can swing by after work today?"

"Oh? It's something important?"

Shannon rubbed the back of her head with her free hand. She'd been up late, huddled over her computer, and woke with a crick in her neck.

"To me, but nothing you have to drop everything for. If you're busy—"

"You never ask for me to drop by after work. I'll be there. Should I bring wine?"

"I have plenty, just bring yourself."

"Since there seems to be a lift in your voice, I'm going to assume I can leave my lawyer hat at work."

Shannon laughed. "I haven't done anything illegal in at least a week, you're good."

"If Avery said that, I'd worry."

"Liam is taming our willful friend."

They shared a laugh and hung up with the promise of seeing each other later in the day.

She set her cell phone in her lap, leaned her head back, and closed her eyes.

Slowly her body melted into the chaise lounge. Normally she'd feel a little guilty about having nothing to do during the middle of the day and move to try to change that. But since Tulum, she didn't feel the drive.

Not for the first time that day, her thoughts shifted to Victor. What was he doing? At work, of course . . . but what did that look like?

She brought up the thread of texting he'd managed to sneak in since they parted in Mexico. Basically it was a series of numbers followed by something snarky from her.

The day after he'd called her, he sent a text. 74 Days

She replied with a rolling-eye emoji.

73

Are you going to ping me every day? she'd texted back.

Maybe.

And he did, until day sixty-seven. Much as Shannon hated herself for looking forward to his attention, she couldn't deny the fact that she looked at her phone several times . . . waiting.

He caught up on day sixty-five by texting 65.5 and then a few hours later, 65.

Now they were on day sixty-two. It had been nearly a month since she'd seen him, a month since she and Avery were in Tulum. It dawned on her at that moment that she was once again entering her fertile time of the month. Maybe that was why she was finding herself looking for more attention from the only man on her radar.

She hadn't initiated contact once with him. She only responded.

Shannon tapped her finger on the side of her phone . . . what would it hurt?

∽

Victor sat across from Ray, his personal finance manager, and Manny, his accountant. Victor's quarterly estimates were fanned out in front of them.

"I think it's time you start diversifying, Victor," Ray said.

"Projections for expansion aren't looking favorable this year." Besides, he already had three operating plants on the West Coast, two on the East Coast, and a hub in Texas and another in Michigan.

"He isn't suggesting expansion. More like new ventures. Men with your wealth do things like buy newspapers or become partners in football teams."

Victor laughed. "I wouldn't know the first thing about owning anything like that."

"You understand business. You don't have to run a newspaper to own one. Racehorses on the track are never ridden by their owners."

"You want me to buy racehorses?"

Ray sat forward. "I want you to consider something, anything, that makes money. Yes, I can continue to roll your money in the market like I've been doing for years. You own several pieces of property, all tied into the business. Let me play the devil's advocate here. What happens if the scrap metal business starts to tank?"

"That isn't going to happen. There will always be recycling of scrap."

"You said yourself that exports are down. Projections are steady, but they aren't rising like they have in the recent past, right?" Manny asked.

"I'm not closing any doors," Victor told them.

"What if China stopped needing our resources, or war broke out and halted trade? Those are things that aren't in your control and would affect Victor Brooks's bottom line. I wouldn't be doing my job if I didn't suggest diversifying now, when you have the money and energy to take on new things. Would it hurt to consider other avenues without giving up this one?" Ray asked.

Victor leaned back in his chair and picked up the summary statement of his market investments. "Where would I start?"

Manny started packing away the papers he came into the office with. "Start with something that interests you. You have a team here for acquisitions and mergers, right?"

"Yes, of course."

"Hand them a new task."

Victor had stood to let the men out when his cell phone buzzed on his desk, catching his attention. He looked briefly at the text that flashed on the home screen.

62

He stared at his phone. *What is* . . .
Shannon.

His heart did a rapid thud in his chest, his lips spread into a grin. The woman had finally texted him.

"We'll see you in three months." Manny's words snapped Victor out of his thoughts and back into his office.

He reached out, shook their hands, and walked them to the door. "Thank you, gentlemen."

Victor snatched his phone and dialed Shannon's number the second he was alone.

She picked up on the second ring.

"Hello, Victor."

He liked hearing his name from her lips.

"Good afternoon."

"You didn't have to call me."

"Yes, I did." He crossed to the window of his office and looked out over the skyline. "We don't really have to wait sixty-two days."

"Three months. That was the agreement."

Victor scratched his head. The image of her with her head tilted back and the moonlight on her freshly kissed face reappeared from his memory. "I think of you. All the time."

"That sounds distracting," she said, a lift in her voice as if pleased to hear his confession.

"Terribly. My assistant keeps shooting me strange looks."

"They probably think you're reflecting on your relationship with Corrie."

Hearing Shannon say Corrie's name so effortlessly made him pause. "Even Mr. Clueless knows that talking about an ex with someone new in your life is frowned upon."

There was silence for a breath. "When did I slip and call you Mr. Clueless to your face?"

He smiled. "I don't know, but I didn't pull that title out of the air."

She sighed. "Well, in this case, Mr. Clueless, I think talking about your ex is important. It's only been a month since everything blew up. Waiting three months is all about your reflection on Corrie and working through whatever emotions you're dealing with."

He knew she was right. Even if he didn't feel any pressing emotions. "Do you really want to hear my thoughts and dealings with her?"

Silence again.

"I'll take that as a no."

"No, wait. I was there when it happened, the breakup, anyway. I'd rather we have conversations about her now, when it's expected that she'd be on your mind, than two months from now."

"That means we would have to have conversations that were more than a number texted on the phone," he told her. He liked the idea of hearing her voice instead of having to pull it from memory.

"I don't know—"

"I want to be transparent. You asked that I don't play you, which means you've been played before. I've thought about that statement a lot in the past month."

When she spoke again, her voice had changed. "No one likes to feel used."

"Was it your ex-husband?" he asked.

His question was met with silence.

"Okay, you don't have to tell me."

"No, wait . . . if you can talk about Corrie this early, I will discuss Paul."

He waited.

"He didn't care for me the way I did him."

"But you were married."

He heard her sigh.

"When was the last time a single man was elected to the governor's seat?"

He scratched his head. "I don't know, but I'm sure it's happened at some point."

"Three times in the state of California. That's it."

"Are you saying—"

"I knew Paul wasn't emotionally connected when our marriage started, Victor. But once we were there, and we spent more time together, he made me feel as if nothing would break us apart."

"What did?" As soon as he asked the question he wanted to pull it back.

"Nothing catastrophic. He was busy being the governor; I was busy pretending to be the perfect wife in our cookie-cutter life. He asked for a divorce and I gave it to him."

Victor couldn't see anyone letting Shannon go that easily.

"This happened after he was elected."

"Obviously."

Paul used her to get elected. Dumped her once he was.

"I won't use you, Shannon. I want to shed the title of *clueless*, but I might need some help learning how. I took your advice with my staff, and everyone is more relaxed around here. Before you, I would have ignored what everyone was thinking until it went away."

"I'm glad it all worked out. But don't give me credit. Your experience with Corrie had to help you realize what happens when you push problems aside."

He started to argue her point and stopped. Victor hadn't considered what he took from Corrie running away the way she did, but maybe Shannon was right. He'd been shocked that she'd taken off and oblivious as to why . . . until Shannon pointed out his faults.

"What makes you so wise?" he asked.

"I'm observant. Part of my profession as a photographer. I watch while others do."

The phone on his desk rang. "My phone is—"

"I hear it. Go."

It rang again.

He wanted to say something to make her understand what he felt just talking to her. "I'm going to call you again."

She giggled. "Goodbye, Victor."

"Until next time."

Chapter Twenty

Shannon hugged Lori when she walked into her house later that day. "Thank you for coming."

Lori handed her a bottle of wine. "I can't do it empty-handed."

Shannon graciously took the bottle and closed the door behind her. "I'm not sure if that's good upbringing or a guilty curse," she said.

"Both."

She led Lori through the foyer and out the back door to the patio. "It's such a beautiful day. I hope you don't mind if we sit out here."

Lori dropped her purse on the kitchen counter before following her. "I've been in this house five times since you moved in, and each time you entertain outside."

"I like it out here. It's the place I feel most comfortable."

"Is there a reason for that? You mentioned something about selling last year."

Shannon looked around at her midcentury modern home, made a little warmer by the darker wood tones than were normally seen in the style. "I picked this home two months after Paul executed the contract for divorce. Somewhere I thought maybe he'd realize he didn't want to split, and he and I would spend time here together. This home is more his style than mine."

"I should have guessed."

Shannon crossed to her outdoor kitchen and found a corkscrew. She'd already set up glasses and a cheese plate for them to soak up the wine.

"When I think of all the pining I have done over that man. What a waste."

"Some breakups are harder than others."

The cork lost its hold on the bottle with a pop.

Shannon filled their glasses and lifted hers for a toast. "To positive change."

Lori eyed her with speculation. "Since we're drinking wine, I have to assume that means you're not talking about pregnancy changes."

Shannon sipped the cabernet and took a seat. Lori followed. "No. Nothing like that. I'm closing my business."

Lori stopped midsip. "What? Where did this come from?"

"I don't know. A combination of things, I think."

"I thought you loved photography."

"I do. Just not what I'm doing. It's like this house . . . wedding photography is a compromise. I didn't realize how much of my life has been a sellout until I watched Corrie run away on her wedding day."

"Avery told me all about that."

"It was quite the show. You hear about those things happening, but to see it go down . . . crazy. I noticed how upset everyone became when they realized she'd ditched the dress and ran off, and I thought . . . that is exactly why I never confronted anyone in my personal life. I was too concerned for everyone else's feelings and needs. But you know what I witnessed after Corrie left?"

"Other than the groom getting hammered?"

Shannon smiled at the memory. "Other than Victor singing in the bar, yeah. I realized that everyone who had come to the wedding had a moment of shock, and then they went on with their lives. I'm sure

Corrie's parents are giving the girl hell, but they have to go back to living their lives eventually. Like with my sister completely shedding the things she was told she needed and gallivanting around other countries, living on pennies . . . my parents were upset about it, still complain on occasion, but it doesn't rule them."

"You've given this some thought."

"I have. I've reflected more in the past month than I have in years. My only rebellion was marrying Paul. And when that ended, I faded away. Literally. I fell into commercial photography because it was a respectable job. It didn't hurt that my name and status as Paul's ex-wife landed me contracts that paid top dollar. I guess I knew on some level I was using his name, but I didn't care."

"But you care now?"

"Not about using the name. Not really. But I don't want to just be Paul Wentworth's ex-wife. I can hide in my studio and book a wedding a month to keep myself from being bored, but where is that leading me?"

"What about having a child?"

Shannon closed her eyes, still saw what she thought her baby would look like. "I still want that. But if I have a baby to fill a void, what happens when that child grows up and has a life of its own? I'll be right back here, or worse, I'll put my needs on my kid and make them hate me for it."

"I think you're too observant to allow that to happen."

Shannon sipped her wine. "Maybe. Maybe not. I need to find something external, something other than a relationship or a child to help find meaning in this life." She placed her free hand on Lori's. "I know I have you and the others, but what I really need is to rely on me."

Lori sat back, crossed her legs. "You called to ask my advice, but it sounds like you've already made up your mind."

Shannon set her wine down and unfolded from her chair. "About closing the business, yeah. I didn't call you about that." She stepped through the open door leading inside and brought out a stack of photographs she'd taken over the past week. "I wanted your opinion on these."

She handed them to Lori.

Slowly, Lori looked over each individual picture without saying a word. At one point she put her glass of wine down and peered closer.

Her silence had Shannon wondering if maybe she was premature in closing her business. Maybe her dream was born from a childish desire and not talent.

After what felt like an hour, Lori finally flipped through the last image and lifted her gaze to Shannon. "Let me start by saying I don't know a thing about photography."

She felt her heart sink.

"Stop that!" Lori scolded her. "I don't have a *professional* foot in this platform, but I know what I like. Holy shit, Shannon. Why are you sitting on this talent?" She thumbed through the pictures and isolated one. It was of a homeless woman, but not as you would expect to see her, full of despair and pain . . . no, Shannon had captured this woman as she sat beside her dog. The love in her eyes and happiness she had for the animal were palpable.

Shannon had offered to buy the woman a meal as she pet her dog. She seemed surprised that Shannon was even talking to her. They shared a few minutes. Shannon asked if she could take the woman's picture and promised to return with a copy. Only the woman wasn't in the same spot when Shannon returned a few days later.

"I forgot I had it," Shannon told Lori. "I've been so busy feigning a happy life I misplaced the things that made me smile."

Lori set the photographs aside, picked up her wine, and lifted the glass in the air. "To closing one door and opening another."

Shannon could drink to that.

Lori cleared her throat. "Does any of this have to do with Victor?"

"Avery told you." Shannon wasn't shocked.

"Guilty."

She waved Lori's concern away. "I suppose me flirting with any man is newsworthy."

"Ah, yeah!"

"I'm not sure what Avery said. Most of it's probably true." Her friends didn't embellish like so many others did.

"He was the groom?"

"Yeah, that part is true. But to be clear, I thought he was an absolute jerk until after Corrie ran off. I'm still not completely sure he's able to be anything but self-centered."

"Avery implied that he was dialed into you like a bear to honey."

Shannon took a bigger sip of wine. "Which could be because he had just been dumped. That's why I'm waiting another two months to meet with the man. If there is still a spark, I'll go out with him. If not, no harm, no foul."

"How very calculated of you."

"Isn't that how I am? I think everything through. I usually mess up the outcome, but I do try and consider all the possibilities before making any decisions."

Lori smirked. "Two months is a long time."

"Sixty-two days, actually."

She laughed. "Not that anyone is counting." Lori paused. "So does this mean you've put the baby daddy thing on hold completely?"

Shannon cut off a piece of cheese and nibbled as she spoke. "It might be a little awkward to go on a first date pregnant with another man's child."

"To say the least."

"It's only a couple of months. Besides, I don't feel as settled as I did before going to Mexico. I have two more weddings booked, and

I'm closing my doors. I've already contacted a couple of colleagues to send referrals. I should sell this house, truly cut my ties to anything that reminds me of my other life."

"Not your new friends, I hope."

"Goodness, no. You guys can't get rid of me that easy. You're the ones who have kept me fueled. I need experience walking in these new shoes."

Lori regarded her feet. "What shoes are those?"

"The ones that close the doors on what everyone else thinks I should be and start living for myself again. My aunt Joan, on my mother's side . . . she pulled me aside the Christmas after Paul and I split. She said to me, 'Shannon, wait until you're fifty. You won't give a crap about what anyone else thinks about you. Wear the red hat and dare people to look.' She'd been referring to the magazines that jumped on the divorce, but I heard her message. I don't want to wait until I'm fifty."

"I can't wait to see who this new Shannon is."

She rolled her eyes. "Don't expect sweeping change. I'm not going to dye my hair pink or anything. Although I might change my name back to Redding."

"I think that's a great start."

"It's been long enough to where the public doesn't really know my name, or my face. Or if they do, they can't place it. Which works for me. I like the anonymity."

Lori smiled over the rim of her glass. "Or you can wait and see if someone comes along and changes your name for you."

"Or I can just keep my maiden name and skip being identified as belonging to someone else." It was easy to say that to Lori, since she hadn't changed her name legally. Although many people referred to her as Mrs. Barnum.

"Belonging to someone else isn't a bad thing when it's the right man."

"Now you're starting to sound like Trina." Their friend absolutely loved being called Mrs. Wade Thomas.

"Speaking of . . . she called me yesterday. She and Wade are coming to town for a spot on *Good Morning Los Angeles*. She wanted to host an intimate party for Avery and Liam."

"A baby shower? Isn't it a bit early?"

"She didn't call it a shower. She actually suggested getting a little dressed up, giving Avery a reason to wear something pretty before she starts showing and complaining about her figure."

"That's very thoughtful of her."

"I think she just wants an excuse to visit."

"She doesn't need an excuse."

"Okay, maybe she has something to share."

Shannon's eyes lit up. "Is she pregnant, too?"

Lori shook her head. "If she is, she didn't tell me. I'm just guessing that maybe there is something cooking in two of our friends' ovens."

Shannon was giddy just thinking about it. "I'm in. Just tell me the date."

❧

"Mr. Brooks?"

"Yes?" Victor answered the phone in his office two days later.

"There is a Mr. Holt on the line."

Victor searched his memory bank and came up on empty.

"I don't know a—"

"He says you know his wife, *Avery*."

And like a switch, Victor's entire body tensed. Why would Avery's husband be calling him unless something bad had happened? "Yes. Put the call through."

The line clicked and Victor answered. "Mr. Holt?"

"Call me Liam. Victor Brooks?"

Victor smiled. "Looks like we have the names right. Is Shannon okay?"

The man on the line laughed. "She's perfectly fine. I hope it's okay that I'm calling."

Victor blew out a breath. Adrenaline dumped into his system. "Of course. How's Avery? The last time I saw her, the mornings weren't treating her well."

"This last week seemed to be the end of that. I'm hoping for smooth sailing from here on out."

Liam sounded like a man Victor would like to know.

"Congratulations, by the way."

"Thank you. I'm beside myself."

Victor couldn't imagine. He'd have to wait a little longer to get there. "What can I do for you, Liam?"

"I'm calling to invite you to a small dinner party. It's last-minute. But that's the way the women seem to work."

The women?

"Trina wanted to throw a party and asked that I made sure you could come."

"Do I know Trina?" Victor asked.

"No. But she knows Shannon and Avery . . . and in turn, knows about you. Therefore, since—and I'm quoting here—'I'm the one responsible for Avery's condition,' I needed to find a way to get you to the party—and again I'm quoting—'if I knew what was good for me.'" Liam blew out a breath.

"Your wife is a handful," Victor said.

"And I love her for it. The party is this Saturday. I know it's last—"

"I'll be there."

Again, Liam sighed on the phone. "Perfect. Hurdle one . . . now. You can't tell Shannon."

"Excuse me?"

"Victor, I'm just telling you what my wife requested. It's up to you to decide what's best. Her directions were this: 'You knocked me up. Get Victor here and don't let Shannon know he's coming or she might bail.' Word for word."

Not only could Victor see Avery saying all that, he could hear her voice utter each syllable.

And since he would do just about anything to see Shannon at day . . . he calculated in his head . . . fifty-six, he would keep his invitation silent.

"What should I wear?"

Chapter Twenty-One

Beverly Harkin called and asked to meet Shannon at her studio later that week. Why Corrie's mother wanted to talk with her was a mystery.

Shannon took the opportunity to start clearing out and packing the space. It would be the second time she'd had to move her equipment. In her next home, the one she'd started to seriously consider, she wanted a studio on-site. One where she could dabble in the occasional portrait if the mood struck. Or a space where she could showcase her new artistic direction, with vast walls just waiting for her to splatter with her work.

The more she thought about the move, in both her home and her work, the greater the chills ran up and down her spine.

From the front door of her office, the alarm chimed, telling her Beverly had arrived.

Shannon stepped from her back room, forced a smile on her face, and went to greet a woman she had no particular need to ever see again.

Wearing black dress pants, a fitted shirt, and a short jacket, Beverly stood in the doorway with her back rod-straight. The thin line of her lips and lifted chin put Shannon on edge.

"Good afternoon, Beverly."

"It's Mrs. Harkin."

Ohhhkay. Guess this isn't a social visit.

Instead of giving the woman what she wanted, Shannon said, "I trust everyone is well?"

Mrs. Harkin took a step into the room and glanced at one of the many boxes Shannon had spread around the space. "Depends on what your definition of *well* is. No one has died, if that's what you mean."

"I wasn't using death as my barometer, but I'm happy to hear it." The woman mimicked Shannon's own mother when she wasn't happy with something. Astute, condescending, and elitist. Hence the demand that Shannon not use her first name. It was the one thing her mother had taught her growing up. *Make people call you by your last name and only gift them with using your first after they've become more than an acquaintance. And employees are to always address you as Miss or Mrs.* Of course, that advice went out the window when Shannon became a Ms. "What can I do for you?" Shannon asked.

Instead of answering, Beverly took a few more steps inside the office, her gaze moving from box to box. "Are you moving your studio?"

"I'm closing it, actually."

She released a short-suffering breath. "I suppose it's hard to stay in business when you sabotage the people you work for."

Now the bitter anger started to make sense. Not that Shannon was going to own any choices Corrie made in Tulum. "I'm not sure what you're referring to."

Beverly snapped her eyes toward Shannon. "You know perfectly well what I'm talking about. You told Corrie she shouldn't get married."

"I did no such—"

"It shouldn't have surprised me, a bitter divorcée like yourself. But to interfere with a young couple so obviously in love. You should be ashamed of yourself."

Shannon found herself tripping over the words *young* and *love*. "Your waxing poetry over Corrie and Victor is ill placed, *Mrs. Harkin*." Shannon put as much sarcasm as she could in the other woman's name. "Corrie voiced to me, twice, that she had second thoughts about getting married. I simply reminded her that she had a choice in the matter. Nothing more, nothing less."

Beverly took a step closer. "What makes you believe she had a choice? The wedding was planned, the guests had arrived, *my* friends were there. Corrie's choice had been made long before flying to that mosquito-infested part of the world."

"Is that what has you so upset? That *your* friends witnessed your daughter's rebellion? It's her life, Beverly. Not yours." How Shannon wished someone had spoken to her parents this way when she was younger. When Angie was still in the picture.

"My daughter's rebellion? Is that what you call it? Corrie has been in tears since she followed your advice and ran away."

Shannon had a hard time believing that.

"Now that she and Victor are speaking again, it's only a matter of time before they patch up this little dip in the road. When they do, you'll be the first to hear that your efforts to break them up were in vain." Beverly tapped the toe of her foot against one of the boxes on the floor. "I hope you don't plan on going into business for yourself again. I'm sure my daughter and Victor will shut you down the second you think of opening shop. And if they don't . . . I will."

Every muscle in Shannon's body tensed. How much of what she was hearing was truth or fabrication?

"Thank you for the warning, Beverly. Now, if you'll excuse me." Shannon indicated the door.

"I'm watching you."

"Is that meant as a threat?"

Beverly lifted one corner of her lips. "If it was a threat, my dear, you'd know it."

And with that, the woman left.

Victor relinquished the keys to his car to the pimple-nosed kid driving the valet at the high-rise condominium complex in downtown Los Angeles.

Through the glass doors, he was told to tell the doorman he was a guest of the Barnums, not that Victor knew Reed and Lori, but those were the names that Liam told Victor to drop.

James, the doorman, escorted him to the elevators and used a special key to buzz Victor to the requested floor.

His palms were sweaty; his heart was more active than normal. Shannon was only a few feet away.

He hesitated at the door, brushed his hands against his jacket, and knocked. He glanced at his watch: 6:53. He was early.

So why was there so much noise behind the door?

He knocked again.

The door swung open to a tall blonde wearing a pencil skirt and blouse. She paused and then broke into a grin. "You must be Victor!"

He offered a single nod. "I am."

Her grin grew. "I'm Lori. Come in." She ushered him through the door.

Inside, several people he didn't know mingled. "Thank you for having me."

"My pleasure. Let me introduce you to . . ."

Victor grazed the room with his eyes and found her.

She wore white. A jumpsuit. Her back was to him as she stood beside a baby grand piano and looked out over the city. The back of the outfit dipped low, giving everyone a glimpse of her slender waistline, hips, and Tulum tan. Her hair was up in a messy bun, and her long, sleek neck had him sucking in a breath.

Since when did necks turn him on?

She was laughing at something someone next to her was saying when her animated features slowly turned his way.

Her playful grin faded and surprise took over.

Voices in the room faded with her smile. They didn't really, but Victor tuned out whatever Lori was saying and just stared.

Good Lord, she was stunning. Poised and elegant.

She said something briefly to whomever it was she was talking to and started walking his way.

". . . my husband, Reed."

Victor heard part of what Lori said as the man at her side reached out to shake Victor's hand.

"I'm sorry . . . what was your name again?"

"Reed," he said, a slight laugh on his lips.

Victor gripped the man's palm. "Right."

Shannon stepped up beside them, the scent of her perfume made sweeter by the woman wearing it. "Victor. What a surprise."

He turned to her, wanted to kiss her hello, and settled with leaning in and placing his lips on the side of her face. "You're gorgeous," he whispered in her ear.

"What are you doing here?" she whispered in his.

"Victor! You came." Avery swept in, dressed in hot pink with a skirt that didn't reach her knees. It matched her blonde hair and bubbly personality.

Shannon stepped back. "I see."

He greeted Avery much the same way he did Shannon. "You look much better than the last time we saw each other."

"Don't remind me." She turned to the man standing next to her. He had to be twice her size, bulky, but not from too many burgers, probably hard work or maybe a few too many hours at the gym. Hard to tell with the dress coat he wore. "This is my husband, Liam."

They shook hands. "You're the one who called me." Victor made sure he said it loud enough for Shannon to catch.

"I am. So glad you could make it."

Avery flashed her teeth with a cheeky grin. "Look who's here, Shannon."

"I can see that. You should have told me you invited him."

Avery squished her smile. "Oh, hell, no. It's much more fun this way."

Those who stood close enough to hear her words started to laugh.

Shannon turned to him. "Then *you* should have told me."

Victor shrugged. "It's only day fifty-six, and you gave me direct instructions to avoid calling you. I'm doing my best to stay within the parameters of our agreement."

Shannon narrowed her smiling eyes.

"You're counting the days?" Avery asked, laughing.

Victor pointed at Shannon. "She started it."

"Oh, God, that's rich."

Reed caught his attention. "What are you drinking, Victor?"

⟋⟍

He cleaned up really well.

And what was he wearing? Every time Victor was close by, the scent of the man lingered in her brain like a fog over the shoreline. She couldn't get enough.

Avery pulled Victor away from Shannon and walked him over to Trina and Wade for introductions.

Lori fell back. "You didn't tell me how good-looking he was."

"You didn't ask."

"Are you really counting the days?"

"He just had a huge breakup. We agreed on three months to give him time to process." But apparently those three months were going to include phone calls, texting, and cocktail parties. And visits from his ex future mother-in-law. She'd forgotten about that until that moment.

Was Victor speaking with Corrie?

She supposed that was normal, but how much talking, and what was being said?

He was there, so that spoke for something . . . right? Or Victor could be a complete player like her ex-husband and keep his cards close to his chest.

The doorbell rang, and Lori left her side to answer it.

Voices had her turning around.

Shannon greeted the couple with kisses and hugs. "I didn't realize you were coming."

Sam and Blake Harrison had become her friends when Shannon signed the contract to marry Paul. Petite with red, curly long hair and a low, raspy voice that men loved, Sam hugged her hard. "I wouldn't miss this for anything."

Shannon questioned her with a look, then words. "You knew Victor was coming."

Sam didn't pretend to deny it. "Where is he?"

"You know everyone else in the room, so I doubt I have to point him out."

Sam did the once-over, found him, and said, "Very cute."

Shannon rolled her eyes and hugged Sam's husband. "Hello, Blake."

"Hey, Shannon. It's been a long time." He kissed her cheek. "And I didn't know about any man. I was told to get dressed and drive."

"This is all a bit premature. We're not even dating."

"Yet," Lori said. "Fifty-six days, according to Victor."

Sam tossed all that hair back with a laugh. "I like the man already." She grabbed Shannon's arm and pulled her toward Victor. "Introduce me."

Chapter Twenty-Two

"... she hopped up from my lap and then proceeded to blame me."

Like clockwork, Shannon jumped in to clarify and embellish the story of their meeting the second he finished his sentence.

"I've known you all of a month, and that is the second time I've heard you tell that story. Each time it gets a little worse." Shannon glanced at her gathering of friends, some sitting, some standing, all of them glued to what she had to say. "He stretched out and I couldn't get to my seat."

"You could have just woken him up," Reed suggested.

"I would have stepped over, too," Trina said.

Victor watched Shannon's expressions as her friends weighed in on the conversation.

"Before Liam, I would have purposely fallen in your lap." Avery's confession had everyone laughing.

"When I asked Shannon her name, she addressed herself as *annoyed*. So every time I saw her in the next couple of days, I thought of her as Miss Annoyed."

"I can beat that. I called you Mr. Phone and Mr. Clueless."

Wade patted Victor on the back, lifted his drink toward his wife, Trina. "Don't feel so bad, Victor. Trina flat-out turned me away the first time we met. She took one look at me and was like, 'Oh, no, Cowboy. This is not gonna happen.'"

"I did not say that."

"No, you said, 'Wade Thomas who?'"

Trina turned to Victor. "I didn't listen to country music. I didn't know who he was."

Wade and Trina were undoubtedly the most famous couple in the room. Multiplatinum country western singer Wade Thomas was one of the biggest in the industry. And Trina . . . well, she owned an exceptionally large part of an oil company inherited from her late husband's estate.

"Sam turned me down," Blake chimed in.

"True story. But I wised up," Sam told the room. "Who doesn't want to be royalty?"

While everyone laughed, Victor shook his head.

Lori helped out his confusion. "Blake is an actual titled British duke."

"What?"

"I'm not responsible for my parents," Blake told him. "But the title does come with a few perks, so I've kept it."

"I thought you said you were in shipping," Victor said.

"I am. And a few other things I've added on over the years. The dukedom was something I was born in. That is nothing more than a title and land in England. The actual business part of being a duke went away a long time ago."

"Owning retail property in England is a business, hon," Sam corrected her husband.

He waved her off. "It doesn't count if you have someone else managing it."

"It counts," Trina chimed in. "I get calls every week about the property Alice left me—"

Victor tuned out of what everyone was saying to watch Shannon. Her long legs were crossed at the ankles, a glass of white wine dangled from her fingertips. Surrounded by her friends and watching her watch everyone else had him thinking about something Avery had said back in Tulum.

Something about Shannon being the quiet, reserved one. Up until now, Victor thought that was a joke. Shannon had been anything but silent since they met.

Yet here she was, listening to everyone tell their stories with very little to say about herself. He wanted to know more . . . How did she meet all the personalities in the room? And there were some pretty big personalities there. Money . . . lots of it. More than he had, that was for sure. Victor had met people through the years whose income dwarfed his, but seldom was it at an intimate gathering of friends. Then again, he wasn't sure the last time he'd gathered with friends like this. The wedding, he supposed. But his buddies from school didn't measure up financially, which always meant that Victor was paying the bill. He'd gotten tired of it and slowly pushed people aside. Which meant he spent a lot of time working and not a lot of time living.

Shannon must have felt his stare. Her eyes lifted to meet his.

His gut warmed with her soft smile.

". . . you'll have to come, Victor."

His attention was pulled back into the conversation by Trina addressing him.

"Of course." He had no idea what he'd just agreed to.

Someone on his left laughed.

Shannon snickered and sipped her wine.

"Okay, Trina, Wade. You gathered us all together tonight for a reason." Lori shifted the conversation, which forced Victor into paying attention.

"We wanted to congratulate Avery and Liam." Trina smiled.

Liam put his arm over his wife's shoulders.

"And meet Victor."

Yeah, he'd sensed that the second he walked through the door.

Wade walked behind his wife, a silly smile on his face, wrapped her in his arms, and rested his chin on her shoulder. He placed one open palm on her belly. "And one other *little, tiny* thing," he said.

The women in the room screeched.

"I knew it!" Avery tore loose of Liam's arm and stood.

Lori reached Trina first. "Congratulations."

Shannon set her wine aside, moisture gathering in her eyes. Victor's gaze followed her as she crossed the room to hug her friend.

Victor stood aside and watched a steady stream of handshakes.

Through the mix of hurried questions and excitement, he heard words of due dates and diapers.

And he watched Shannon. The happiness in her eyes shined, but there was a hint of sadness there, too.

He took the opportunity of the room swimming with multiple conversations to move to her side.

"It looks like you'll have a couple of baby showers to plan this year."

Shannon smiled with a nod. "Yes, it does."

He looked at her, paused. "Do you want children?"

His question resulted in her blinking silently several times. "One day," she said quietly.

Here she was again, the observer. Victor couldn't help but wonder if it was a shell, a way of protecting herself from the elements around her. If the room was any indication, she was the last of her friends to be single, or divorced and unmarried, in any event. Clearly Victor was asked to join the party as a test of some sort. The protective nature of Shannon's friends was evident in the questions they asked him, the way they made him feel welcome and yet didn't put on fake airs. They were weighing him like a father did a daughter's date on prom night.

He liked it.

"Do you think I passed the test?" he asked close to Shannon's ear.

It took her a few seconds to understand what he was asking. The question chased the sadness from her eyes. "Were they that obvious?"

He touched her elbow, felt her tremble, and led her to a quieter part of the room by the window. "Your friends care about you. I think that says a lot about them and you."

"What does it say?" she asked.

He leaned against the window, reluctantly removed his hand from her arm. "This whole party. Inviting me and not telling you . . . they want to make sure I'm worthy." *That I'm not out to hurt you.*

"They're protective."

"You deserve their protection."

"You barely know me."

He smiled. "I'm going to change that."

Her mouth opened and closed without words.

The need to hold her, kiss her, wrap his arms around her until she stopped trembling . . . or maybe until she trembled more. His palms itched to leave with her.

An eruption of laughter flowed toward them.

Shannon glanced away from him, stepped closer.

"Would you like to leave?" Shannon asked.

Victor did a double take.

Her jaw was tight, her smile forced.

The protective hair on the back of his neck stood on end.

"Please," she said. "If we leave together, they won't question my exit."

He took her hand in his, found it cold and clammy.

Victor looked in her eyes as she blinked away the emotions surging to the surface.

He pulled her toward their hosts. Lori broke off the conversation with Trina and Wade when they approached. Her eyes shifted between the two of them, hesitated on Shannon, and then focused on him.

"It looks like I'm being given a coffee date two months early," Victor announced. He glanced toward Shannon to see if she wanted to add anything.

He saw her swallow . . . hard. Her hand gripped his.

"And we thought it would give everyone a chance to talk about us after we leave," he added.

Lori grinned and hugged Shannon.

After the shortest round of farewells Victor could remember, he and Shannon stood in the elevator in silence. Her shoulders started to shake.

Victor placed his arm around her and pulled her close. He had no idea what had spurred the sorrow pouring from her, but he was thankful he was there to catch it.

He handed the concierge his valet ticket and escorted Shannon outside to the fresh air.

She tilted her head back and drew in a long breath.

Victor turned her toward him and placed his hands on the sides of her face.

Her dark eyes glistened, her lips attempted to smile.

"You don't have to fake it with me," he told her.

His words seemed to prompt a small gasp from her lips. He wanted to fix her, whatever it was that was making her unhappy. He settled for brushing away the tears that had fallen from her eyes.

"I'm sorry," she started.

He placed one of his thumbs over her lips to stop her. The flash of lights from a passing car drew her eyes across the street.

Shannon's expression shifted, her eyes narrowed.

Victor glanced over his shoulder and realized that what he thought were passing cars were actually two men holding long-lens cameras pointed in their direction.

"What the . . ."

"Paparazzi," she said in explanation.

She stiffened, her head tilted higher.

"They're not here for me," he said aloud. Only the flash of their cameras kept buzzing the night air.

"I doubt they're here for me either. I'm just a bonus."

The valet drove up in his car, and Victor hastily helped Shannon inside. By the time he had tipped the driver and slid behind the wheel, Shannon was talking on her phone. "Let Wade and Trina know the cameras have arrived." She paused, looked out the window as they drove away. "Only a couple. No, I'm fine . . . I love you, too." She hung up.

Victor sped away from the lights. "That was a first," he said as he switched lanes.

"I'm sorry in advance." Her soft words cut through him. "Although I doubt they care much about me any longer."

"You mean you've dealt with them before?"

She regarded him from the passenger seat. "Are you suggesting that you didn't google my name at one point or another?"

Okay, he was guilty of that. "Well . . ."

"Where do you think those pictures came from? Some were from the press hired by my ex-husband, but the majority were circulated by the opportunistic photographer looking for gossip."

"They didn't find any on you."

She stared out the window. "That didn't stop them from trying, or making up what would sell newspapers."

The more she talked, the less sadness he felt surging off her.

He kept her talking.

"This was my first. What was yours?" He knew, on some level, he was inviting conversation about her life with the former governor. He welcomed it. He wanted to know this beautiful, poised . . . sad woman sitting beside him.

"It was choreographed," she told him. "Shortly after we announced our involvement. I walked out of our engagement dinner to the flash of a dozen cameras. He leaned in, twisted my ear. 'Smile . . . you'll get used to it.'" She sighed. "I smiled, froze . . ."

Victor glanced over, watched her staring out the window.

"I'm just now waking up."

Victor reached out his free hand and placed it on her arm.

She offered a soft smile.

"You think they were there for your friends Trina and Wade?"

"Undoubtedly. When Trina visits on her own, the cameras are harder to find. When Wade is here, there is a pretty good chance someone is hiding in the bushes."

Victor turned off the freeway and kept heading west.

"That can't be easy." He couldn't imagine his life under a microscope.

"It takes a strong disposition, and someone without secrets."

He hadn't thought of that angle.

"Do you have any?" she asked out of the blue.

"Secrets?"

"Yeah." She watched from the corner of her eye.

He thought of the question and searched his mental database. Page after blank page came up.

"Never mind. You don't have to answer that." Shannon's voice deflated.

He raised a hand in the air. "No, no . . ." He paused. "Damn, I'm boring," he finally said.

He heard a small laugh from her side of the car. "Everyone has something."

No . . . high school didn't count, college . . . he studied, he worked, did the typical things kids did who were actually trying to finish school in four years. Then decided four years was too long and left after two. Nothing newsworthy. His business was clean. *Really boring.*

Shannon shifted in her seat, waiting.

"There was that time in the Bolivian jail with that little cartel situation . . ." He lifted a hand from the steering wheel. "But the name change and plastic surgery seem to have gotten them off my scent."

Shannon's shoulders started to shake until finally her laughter broke.

He turned into his driveway lined with palm trees and parked in front of his garage doors.

"Where are we?" Shannon asked.

Victor had driven on autopilot. Not really considering the moment when he pulled up to his house.

"My home," he told her. "But I'm not expecting anything. Let's have a nightcap, talk about my drug selling days, and count the stars in the sky."

If she was nervous, she didn't show it. "We should introduce your friends to my ex bookie . . . I bet they'd get along."

And she pushed out of the car.

Chapter Twenty-Three

Her cell phone was ringing.

Shannon reached out toward the phone jack on her nightstand and found her hand colliding with a lamp.

Her eyes blinked open. Sun from the corner of the room invaded her senses.

The bed was softer, the sheets didn't feel right, and her phone kept ringing.

Victor's.

The memory of crashing in Victor's spare room late in the night surfaced. Her hand landed on her phone. "Hello?"

"Someone is sleeping in." Avery's voice shook some of the cobwebs from her brain.

Shannon swung her feet over the edge of the bed, looked down at herself. She wore an oversize T-shirt that didn't belong to her. "Good morning," Shannon said to her friend. "What time is it?"

"After nine."

Shannon looked around the room to find a clock . . . didn't see one.

"I need some coffee," she said more to herself than Avery.

"I won't keep you. I'm just checking to make sure you're okay."

She wiggled her toes on the carpet covering the dark wooden floors of the room. "I'm fine."

"You left pretty abruptly last night."

"Victor convinced me to sneak away." She offered a tiny white lie to keep the questions at bay.

She heard footsteps from outside the room and then a knock at her door. "Shannon?" Victor called through the wood.

"Just a minute," she said, covering the phone with her hand in an attempt to keep Avery from knowing she was talking with someone.

It didn't work. "Oh my God, he's with you."

"It's not what you think."

"I need to hear all about this."

Shannon didn't believe for a second she'd escape the dozen questions her friend would ask.

"It was late, we'd both had another drink. I slept over. Nothing happened."

Avery laughed. "That isn't a good enough explanation. But I'll let you go for now."

"I'll call you this afternoon."

"Okay. But before you hang up, I wanted to give you a heads-up."

Shannon stood and stretched. "About what?"

"You and Victor made the tabloids last night. A small shot on the front page leading to a full-page spread on the tenth."

Any dust in Shannon's head blew away with the news. "Whatever could they possibly say about me on a full page?"

"It's never flattering."

"Did they photoshop thirty pounds on me and say I was suicidal?" Which had happened a year after the split with Paul.

"No. But I wanted to warn you if you hadn't seen it. And since you're obviously still with Victor . . ."

"Got it." She knew the drill. "I'll call you later."

They said their goodbyes, and Shannon tossed her cell phone on the bed.

In the bathroom, she found a bathrobe and made use of the brush and the extra toothbrush on the counter. She considered putting her jumpsuit on from the night before but couldn't bring herself to start her day without coffee.

One last glance in the mirror . . . no makeup, sleep in the corners of her eyes, a borrowed shirt and bathrobe. This was the-day-after Shannon. If Victor didn't like this look, they had no business spending serious time together. With a shrug, she padded, barefoot, out of her room and toward Victor's kitchen.

He wore jeans. His back was to her when she entered the room, his hands busy pulling cups from a cupboard.

"Is that coffee?" she asked to get his attention.

He turned, his jaw slacked slightly, and his eyes did a slow crawl down her frame.

Shannon shifted her feet under his microscope.

"I might not wash that bathrobe."

She took his words as a compliment and grinned. Her morning look must not have offended him. "Good morning."

He shook his head with a slight groan, turned back to his task. "Coffee with sugar, right?"

"How did you know?"

He poured her a cup. "Every morning on the beach you were huddled over a cup, reading."

"I'll take the coffee, but I'm fresh out of reading material." She took the cup he offered and doctored it with the sugar he had sitting out.

"Did you sleep well?"

"I did. You?"

He sighed. "Do I offer the lie or tell the truth?"

She leaned against the counter, brought the cup to her lips. "Is this like the game of truth or dare?" The java splashed against her tongue, waking her fully.

"Knowing you were across the hall kept me up until three."

She lowered her cup. "I should have gone home."

"No, no, no . . . I wouldn't have slept at all, then."

She doubted that. She sipped her coffee again. "This is really good."

"You've found my hidden talent."

"Making coffee?"

"We all have one thing." He led her out of the kitchen and into his informal dining room. There was a newspaper spread out on the table, evidence that he'd been sitting there for a while.

"How long have you been up?"

"Since six thirty."

"That's not a lot of sleep."

They sat opposite each other, and Victor brushed the paper away. "My internal clock wakes me with the sun. It's a curse."

"It makes you productive." She set her cup down, glanced at the paper. "About last night . . ."

"Yes?"

"Avery called this morning. It appears the paparazzi found something worthy of their magazines last night when you and I walked outside."

He picked up his cup, shrugged. "Like I said, I have nothing to hide. Besides, they won't know who I am."

Shannon shook her head. "They will know your name, your business, and your net worth, if they think it will sell papers. They're not called gossip magazines for nothing."

Victor reached over, placed a hand over hers. "Don't spend one more minute worrying about me."

"I'm not worried, just warning you. We should come up with a statement we both stick to if we're cornered by the media." At least that's how she'd approached them in the past. Scripted lines delivered and repeated to avoid the unfortunate slip of the truth.

Victor drank his coffee and regarded her with a tilt of his head. "What kind of statement do you suggest?"

She hadn't thought about that. Shannon leaned back in her chair and processed the situation aloud. "We need to stay as close to the truth as possible. We met in Tulum."

"That's easy."

She continued. "They will find out about our connection and about Corrie running off."

"I can't imagine they'd care about that."

She looked at him as if he were new. "Your bride runs away and you're seen with the photographer barely a month later. They'll conclude there was something between us either before or during the wedding." As that picture developed in her head, the nastiness that the media would paint started to appear. "They've been looking for something nasty on me for years. It can go a couple of ways. You'll be a cheating bastard who got caught, or I'll be the woman who lured you away. Neither are very flattering."

"Or the truth."

"Truth isn't what they're after."

Victor shrugged. "I can handle it."

"I've found that, so long as there is little fuel, the story just drops. Especially if something new comes around to take its place. It helps that you're not famous and I'm no longer in the public eye because of my ex."

He sat forward. "So we tell them we met in Tulum."

"They'll ask if we have a romantic relationship. Sex sells papers."

He grinned. "And how should we answer that?"

Shannon traced the edge of her coffee cup with her index finger. "Maybe that we're exploring our options."

"Are we?" He flashed his teeth with his smile. "Exploring our options?"

"I'm wearing your T-shirt and drinking coffee in your home. I think we're exploring something."

His gaze drank her in, and his silence had her heartbeat working overtime. "Fifty-five days is too long," he said under his breath.

"Victor—"

"I have dreamt of your lips, of your touch . . . of you every day since we've met. I want to explore."

Her face started to heat. "I don't know how to explore, Victor. I haven't had a casual relationship since before I was married," she confessed.

"Who said anything about casual?"

"You just jumped out of a—"

"Relationship," he finished for her. "I know. But it wasn't right. I can see that now." He reached over and took her hand in his once again. "I met with Corrie last week. You know what I discovered?"

Did she want to hear this? "What?"

"That we were never right for each other. Her immaturity is the tip of the mountain of everything that was wrong about us. I wanted the next step in my life, and somehow thought I could just order up that bride and everything would be fine."

A chord struck in her spine. The fact that she was once the "ordered bride" wasn't lost on her.

"I leaped into that relationship without thinking."

"You're jumping again," she argued.

"No. I'm thinking."

"I'm not sure you're thinking with the right side of your brain," she said.

He grinned. "Admittedly. But it's more than that. Or at least I think it's more than that. It needs exploring to find out."

"Fifty-five days—"

"Is too long."

Her hand started to shake ever so slightly. Fear? Excitement? She couldn't name the emotion to save her life. "The timing is off."

"Why are you so against this? You're attracted. Don't try and deny it."

She removed her hand from under his, pushed back from the table. "I'm an adult," she said more to herself than him. "I don't need to deny anything." *I'm not ready.* As the words popped into her head, her body called her a liar.

"What's the worst thing that can happen?" he asked.

I fall in love. You destroy me. The words ran through her head like a ticker tape on the evening news. None of which she could repeat without revealing too much. So she picked the words that would scare any man away. "I'll get pregnant."

Chapter Twenty-Four

The vulnerability on her face, the fear in her eyes. Where was the strong, confident woman he'd met on the airplane, the force of nature embodied by a woman he thought he knew?

She stood after dropping what he was sure she thought was an epiphany to him, but in fact was old knowledge.

He joined her when she turned her back; the bathrobe he'd placed in the guest room dwarfed her frame. He placed a hand on her shoulder, was surprised she didn't jump.

Victor realized, on some level, that he was acting a little bit like a high school senior pressuring his prom date to get naked. He wouldn't, of course. But he did want to push Shannon out of her comfort zone and make her at least consider the possibility.

"Shannon, look at me."

She didn't.

He ducked closer, made it impossible for her to look the other way.

With a heavy sigh, she leveled her eyes with his.

"Pregnancy is always a risk—" he said.

"I will. It isn't a question of risk. I stopped all forms of birth control months ago. One slip, one tear . . ."

He knew the answer to his question before the words formed in his head but wanted to hear it from her first. "Why?"

She studied the floor, looked up. "I'll be thirty-five next month."

"And you want a child."

She didn't look at him when she nodded. "It's why I was in Tulum . . . I mean, outside of your wedding." She rolled her eyes. "Your nonwedding."

"You were meeting somebody?"

A quick shake of her head dashed away that thought. "No. Not somebody . . . just any . . . I shouldn't be telling you this." She turned.

He placed a hand on her arm. Kept her from walking in the opposite direction. "You had a plan."

"A loose plan."

"I didn't fall into it."

She looked at him as if he were crazy. "No, you didn't. You crushed it. Not that I had found someone, but you were there and reminding me that maybe there was—" She stopped short, her thoughts unspoken.

"You're a beautiful woman, I can't imagine you haven't been given plenty of opportunities."

Her eyes narrowed. "Less than you would think."

"What do your friends think about this plan?"

She hesitated, so he talked over her thoughts. "And to be clear, you went to Tulum to have sex with someone you didn't know for the purpose of having a child."

He waited for her to deny him. Her expression gave her away.

"Avery hated the idea."

He smiled. "I always knew I liked her."

Some of the stress, anxiety, or whatever it was on Shannon's face faded with his comment. "It didn't happen."

"You met me."

"And we didn't have sex."

"We could have," he said. "You didn't let us." Because he wasn't a stranger. Because he brought something to her life that made her revise her plan. The more he thought about what her motivation was for not having sex with him, the bigger his smile became.

"You do realize that all of my friends would have advised me to *not* have this conversation with you."

Victor stepped forward, brushed a hair from her face, and tucked it behind her ear.

She sucked in a breath.

Such a simple touch, and yet she responded in a way that few did. "And what are your thoughts on this conversation?" he asked.

Her gaze met his and paused. "It's liberating, I suppose. Honesty. I'm not used to it."

"Paul wasn't honest with you," he deducted.

Her gaze lowered. "I wasn't honest with him."

That, he wasn't expecting.

He lifted her chin. "One day, I want you to tell me what you weren't honest with him about." Victor stepped closer. "But today, I want to relish in the fact that you are honest with me." And he lowered his lips to hers.

She was timid, maybe a little shocked . . . but she didn't move away.

Victor closed his eyes and pulled in her scent as he drew her close. Her full lips parted. For air? Invitation? He didn't know, but he took advantage of the opening and deepened their kiss. He tasted coffee and mint and Shannon. His mornings would never be the same after such an intoxicating combination.

The timid tip of her tongue met his and shot all the blood from his head south to his groin. Shannon reached around his waist. He felt her nails through the fabric of his shirt. He stepped closer, pulled her body flush with his. The outline of his erection pressed against the softness of her belly and wept to be closer.

He fanned his fingers through her hair, tilted her head back, and worshiped her with open-mouth kisses that left her gasping.

"This . . . this . . ."

He kissed her words away and finally moved to her jaw and the lobe of her delicate ear.

"Oh, Victor."

Her pelvis pushed against him, so he nibbled her ear again.

She responded with a soft moan.

He wanted this woman more than he needed his next breath. "Let me make love to you," he whispered.

Tight fingers spread against his back as he kissed the column of her neck. "The risk . . ."

He'd take the risk. But he told her what she needed to hear. "There are more ways to make love to you without taking risks." He reached for the belt of the robe and gave it one tug.

Her eyes, half open with desire, met his. He could see her weighing her choices and questioned her resolve as she took a small step back. Shannon reached for the sides of the bathrobe and slowly pulled it off her shoulders.

Victor smiled, his body firing in all directions, praising the prize he was about to receive.

"This is a bad idea," she said as the robe slid to the floor.

His T-shirt hung on her, filled out in all the right places, and stopped at the tops of her thighs. Long legs, legs he wanted to worship with his tongue, reached to her painted, bare toes. "A really good bad idea," he countered.

Victor reached for her hand and drew her down the hall to the room where she'd spent the night.

He turned her into his arms the moment they crossed the threshold and kissed away any doubt she had.

Something inside of her clicked. He didn't hear it, but he sensed it. Her lips traveled over his with renewed energy and need. Her hands roamed the span of his back and down over his ass.

His cock jumped in his pants. If he didn't get control now, he would embarrass himself before she could take him in her hand, her mouth. And that was how he was going to make love to her. With kisses and strokes of his tongue. It was as if the thought evoked some kind of pheromone from her skin, because it tasted sweeter when he kissed her neck and pulled the T-shirt aside and licked her shoulder.

"You smell so good," she told him. She nuzzled his neck, took a deep breath. "On the plane I thought it was cologne. But it was you." Teeth grazed his chin.

"I thought you were sick," he teased. "Had I known you were trying to smell me, I'd have leaned over and let you."

Shannon tugged at the edges of his shirt.

His hands rode down her back and then traveled up her shirt. Slender curves and smooth skin had him closing his eyes and imagining what he'd find when he removed the shirt from her back. His thumbs traced the outline of her breasts and ran over the pert nipples. Would they be pink, or dusty mauve? Tan, or a darker brown?

She pushed into his palms and he lowered his head to kiss them through the cotton of the shirt.

"Yes, please," she said.

Her body responded with tight restraint. She pushed forward, head back.

He sucked in one nipple, through the cloth, and caught her when her knees buckled. Shannon was a ripe berry ready for harvest. He teased and nibbled. Let her pull the shirt from her shoulders.

His breath caught.

Victor had seen her frame through the moonlight over Tulum, but never did he imagine just how majestic it would be to hold and touch. "You're exquisite."

A soft, almost doubtful laugh made him tilt her chin and force her eyes to meet his. He didn't repeat his words, he simply kissed her. And when she went pliant in his arms again, he felt his own knees give way and moved her to the bed.

He guided her back, felt her knee slide up his leg as he lowered her. Her dark hair spread over the pillow. He'd imagined this moment the first time she started singing to him at the bar in Tulum. There were fifty ways to leave the one you were with, to be with the one you wanted.

"Touch me," she pleaded.

Victor lowered his lips to the hollow of her neck and farther, until he found and captured one dusky nipple between his teeth.

She surged, all of her. Welcoming, asking.

He answered with the spread of his hand over her ribs and down her slim waist until he met the elastic of her underwear. Slow fingers searched.

So wet. How was it possible she was so ready?

Victor had made love to many women in his life. He'd be lying if he said he hadn't enjoyed nearly every one. The first time, with fumbling fingers and a climax that only satisfied him . . . to the women that pretended and called out long before their breath had a chance to be snatched away. But this woman, Shannon. His fingers found her again . . . she jumped, so he repeated the motion.

"Yes."

Her single word of approval had his lips grazing her skin as he moved down her body, pulling her panties away from her legs until they sat on one of her ankles.

Everything about her was intoxicating . . . the scent, the taste . . . he moved lower and replaced his fingers with his lips. *Tease.*

He did . . . with his lips, his breath . . . his tongue.

Her hips surged forward and his pelvis pushed against the bed between her legs. The need to bury into her was as carnal as it comes, but he held back and made love to her in a way that left them both in need of something more. He settled between her legs and felt his heart singing when she placed a hand on the back of his head to hold him exactly where she needed him.

The muttered words that he couldn't decipher kept him going. He listened to the rate of her breath, the way she held it and pressed her hips forward.

Almost there . . . she was almost there.

Shannon cried out. The taste of her fueled every cell in his body.

She squirmed, pulling at his hair. "I can't take it anymore . . ."

This was where he would have made her climax again, taking her . . .

"Good Lord," she sighed, her body lax on the bed.

He looked up at the perfection of her body, past her thin stomach, over peaks of her nipples, and watched her smiling.

"You're not even undressed," she pointed out.

No. And he wasn't going to get that way either.

"That was beautiful." He dropped a kiss on the inside of her thigh. Told his body to behave and go back into the cave.

"You didn't . . . I mean—"

He crawled beside her on the bed and lay on his side. Somewhere he'd managed to kick off his shoes, and his shirt was open. "Next time, I will."

Shannon placed a lazy hand on his waist and traced the side of his rib cage. "Let me take care of you."

He stopped her hand, cursed his resolve to let her be the one who left satisfied while he was kept wanting.

"Stopping now will probably rank up there as the most unselfish thing I've ever done in my life. Hopefully it will erase some of the asshole you thought I was."

Her smile and chuckle ended with a shiver.

Victor reached over and pulled up the edge of the blanket and covered his view.

A damn shame that was.

"Can I tell you something?" she asked.

"As long as you don't say you faked that."

Her hand paused the soft petting thing she was doing. Shannon pinned him with a hard stare.

"You don't really think—"

He placed a finger over her lips. "No. I don't. Your cry made me feel like a god, so please don't crush me now."

There was her smile again. She relaxed and started moving her fingers. "I was going to say . . . I haven't done this in a very long time. I thought maybe my body forgot how."

"How to have an orgasm?"

She nodded.

"Not even with yourself?"

"Well . . ."

Victor wanted to swallow her coy smile. He propped his head on his arm. "I have something to tell you."

"Oh?"

"Promise you won't hold it against me?"

She sat up, her hair falling over her shoulder. "That sounds like it's something I might hold against you."

He closed his eyes, shrugged his shoulders. "If you don't want to know—"

She pushed on his chest. "Victor."

"Promise."

"Fine."

Fine for a woman was never fine, but he was taking all kinds of risks with her. "My room in Tulum was directly across from yours."

He opened one eye, then the other, and saw her processing the information.

"The moon was very bright, and it seemed the stories of the sea and mermaids coming to life—"

"You watched us." Her jaw dropped, but the amusement in her eyes let him know she wasn't upset.

"I watched you. I'm pretty sure Avery was there, but I wasn't interested in her."

"You're a voyeur."

He touched the tip of her nose. "And you're an exhibitionist."

Shannon leaned back. "I guess that makes us even, then."

"I think it's a perfect combination."

She sank into the crook of his shoulder, her nose to his chest. "How did we end up here?"

He shook his head, closed his eyes. "I don't know. But I don't want it to end."

Chapter Twenty-Five

Shannon walked the vast loft space with her mental checklist of what she wanted. Gary, the real estate agent she'd chosen for her new adventure, was highly regarded in his field, stood a half a foot shorter than she did, and used words like *darling* or *sweetheart* when he addressed her.

"I know you don't want a dark space, but try and look past the brick walls and just take in all that natural light, darling." Gary crossed to one of three arched windows that ran the length of the fifteen-foot ceilings. "You can cover the walls, or maybe just two of them."

Shannon attempted to ignore the dust that had accumulated in the space since the previous tenants had been evicted.

Gary opened a set of blinds that hid some of the light and pushed open the double windows to let the air in. "And smell that fresh salt air. Isn't it perfect? The view is to die for."

Shannon walked to the window and smiled. This wasn't anywhere near where she'd set roots down before. Santa Monica was a completely new and unexpected shift in her world. Just like Victor. Yet the more she considered the idea of jumping with both feet into a new direction with her photography, the clearer the thoughts became.

"All of this can go." Gary waved his hands in the air regarding the partition walls put up by the previous tenant. "There is nineteen hundred square feet down here, and if you'll follow me, I'll show you the best part."

Shannon followed Gary across the room, her sensible heels making clicking noises as she went.

He pointed out a kitchen space that needed a good update before leading her to a stairway. Up the stairs she found a bedroom, flooded with light from outside, where the view just got better.

"Seven hundred square feet of bedroom space for you, Shannon. Even if you decide to buy something somewhere else, you can always use this space to crash after you've had one too many or want to find a new lover in town."

She grinned, ran her hand down the curtains that weren't all that bad. "Do you hide your lovers from each other, Gary?"

"Men are much more jealous than women, so yes."

She already knew about Gary's sexual orientation but found it refreshing to have someone she barely knew talk so openly about it.

"I'm not so sure. Women can be vicious."

He waved her off, started toward the back of the bedroom to what she assumed was a bathroom. "Women scratch, men use their fists." He paused. "Well, some, anyway."

It was a bathroom, light gray slate and clean lines.

"A man must own this space."

"Yes. But tasteful, don't you think?"

She considered it with a tilt of her head. These kinds of decisions never came easy.

"It would take some renovations."

Gary seemed to like her comment—his cheeky smile grew. "I know plenty of contractors."

Shannon shook her head. She'd ask Liam for that advice. Avery's husband was a contractor, and if he couldn't do it, he would steer her in the direction of someone that could.

"I don't know."

"It's a lease option to buy, darling. The owners moved out of California ten years ago and they're tired of owning rental property. You try it on for size and see how it fits, or make them an offer."

Having an out felt safe.

Did she want safe?

What was safe doing for her?

"But let me caution you. If you renovate and make it exactly as you want it, the property will be worth more, and there is no guarantee the owners will accept the offer you could give now."

He'd already presented her with leasing and ballpark purchasing numbers. All of which were within her budget. While she wouldn't have to sell her home, she'd already made the decision to do so. That financial move would make her cash rich and real estate poor. Not something her financial manager would approve of.

Her phone rang. Victor's name lit up her screen. Butterflies jolted within her chest, and the memory of his scent pushed away the stale air in the room.

It rang again.

"I'm going to take this," she told Gary.

"Of course. I'll meet you downstairs."

She clicked on his call. "Good morning."

"Mmmmm," was his greeting. "Say that again."

She bit her smile. "Good morning."

"That's sexy. It would be better if you were in my arms and we were just waking up, but I'll take what I can get."

It was Tuesday. Only two days since she'd seen him after waking up in his home and discovering she had a working vagina. True to his word, he hadn't pressured her to have intercourse. They spent an insane amount of time talking, and an even more insane amount of time kissing and touching. It was almost as if she were back in high school and more was forbidden. Victor had been right, it did somehow erase several letters from the word *asshole* that she'd labeled him as when they met.

"Shouldn't you be working?" she teased.

"I am. Where are you?"

"In Santa Monica, looking at loft space."

"That was fast."

She'd told him about her desire to switch directions over breakfast and the possibility of selling her home. He'd listened, but she wasn't sure how much of what she said he'd actually heard.

"I'm just looking. I'm not good at these decisions."

"Is this business space or living space?"

"Both . . . I think. Or it could be if I wanted it." Although it wouldn't work for a family, it did work for a single woman.

"My office isn't far away. Have lunch with me and tell me about it."

Her first instinct was to tell him no. Go back to the countdown of days. Again the word *safe* flashed in her head.

"What's the address?"

"Let's meet at a restaurant."

"You don't want your employees to see me?"

Victor laughed. "My employees know all about you. I've found no less than three copies of the magazine we managed to show up in scattered all over the break room, lobby, and boardroom. My receptionist has had to ask two pop feature writers to leave today. If you come here, my guess is they'll snag more photographs and make up more lies."

The article had been packed with mistruths. The biggest one being that Victor and Shannon had met before the doomed wedding in Tulum. So far the paper had painted Victor the villain and Corrie and Shannon the innocent victims. Sadly, it made Shannon sound like a weak woman being taken advantage of. She was surprised to hear that the media was knocking on Victor's door. There wasn't a story worth telling there. Still, she knew better than to test fate.

"What restaurant?"

~9~

He picked something quiet and private. A small Italian place that smelled of garlic and carbs. Victor was waiting for her when she walked through the door. He greeted her with a kiss to the cheek and a knowing squeeze to her waist.

Itchy, burning excitement at the sight of him ignited with his touch.

"Beautiful," he whispered in her ear before encouraging her to tuck into the booth.

"Had I known we were having lunch in such a nice place, I would have dressed differently."

He scooted in beside her, placed his palm on her thigh under the table. "Don't ever feel like you need to dress up for me."

"You want me to dress up for someone else?"

He squeezed her thigh. "No!"

His single word was said a little too quickly, and with more force than she'd expected.

"I was teasing."

He blinked at her, patted her thigh he'd just grabbed. "I knew that."

Shannon leaned forward, tilted her lips toward his. He seemed surprised but didn't disappoint her. The kiss was brief, like that of a kiss on a scratch in an effort to mend.

That seemed to do the trick.

"I can't stop thinking about you," he told her. "I'm hoping the promise of more lunches, and maybe a few hours this weekend, will give my mind time to get back to work."

"What happened to waiting three months?"

"Screw that. We're renegotiating that deal."

"Oh, are we?"

"My business won't survive two more months."

"But—"

He lifted two fingers to her lips, silencing her. "Tell me about this loft you were looking at."

And just like that, their negotiations were over. By the time lunch ended, she'd agreed to go to dinner with him on the weekend, a place where she could dress up and he could practice his *charming swagger* . . . his words. He promised to pick her up and have her home by a reasonable hour unless she insisted otherwise or had an allergic reaction to her clothing and needed his assistance in getting out of it. To tide him over until Saturday, he told her he wanted to see the loft she was considering, so they made another midweek lunch date.

They ended their impulsive date with a kiss by her car and a promise for more.

As she drove home, her heart was doing somersaults. She cautioned herself, reminded her heart that Victor might be rebounding, even if he continually told her he wasn't.

Timing was everything, and in his case, it was off by a few months. Shannon couldn't bring herself to stop.

Even if that was the smart thing to do.

⁕

"What did I do to deserve this unexpected happy hour visit?" Victor asked his brother the following evening.

Justin had called earlier in the day and wouldn't take no for an answer. He wouldn't elaborate as to why either.

"Can't I ask to go out for drinks with my little brother on occasion?"

"You can, but you never do."

Justin picked up his beer. "Correction, I don't any longer. I used to all the time, but you continually turned me down."

"I usually work late."

Justin took a drink. "But you said yes today."

Victor leaned one elbow on the bar he'd picked, not far from his office but closer to the neighborhood his brother called home. "I've been working on finding more time for my personal relationships."

Justin smiled. "Mom told me you were coming over a week from Sunday for a family dinner. Is that part of your soul searching?"

"You could say that."

His brother drank from his beer. "Does this have anything to do with Shannon?"

Victor hesitated. "How do you know about Shannon?"

Instead of answering, Justin said, "I'm shocked at how many people I know read gossip magazines."

He should have known. "Don't believe everything you read."

"So there isn't anything between you two?"

"I didn't say that."

"Then there is."

Victor took a drink, set his beer down. "Shannon and I are dating."

Justin shook his head. "You don't waste any time, do you?"

"It just happened. We were trying to wait a respectable amount of time—"

"That sounds like something a woman would come up with," Justin interrupted.

Victor considered the couple they'd met in Tulum and Avery's take on the time frame of rebound relationships. "Shannon needed assurance that I wasn't using her to get over Corrie."

"Are you?"

Okay, that hurt. "No. Why would you think—"

"Because it's only been eight weeks."

"Seven."

"You're counting?" Justin asked.

"No. Shannon is. I don't care if it was yesterday or last year. Corrie was a mistake. Any feelings I had for her are long gone, if they were ever there at all."

Justin set his beer aside and fixed his eyes on Victor's. "Then I need to tell you something."

"I'm listening."

"The day I left Tulum I told Shannon that if I wasn't dating Deirdre, I would have asked her out."

Victor's forearms tensed. "What did Shannon say?"

"That I was the man of her dreams and she wished she could change my mind," Justin said, deadpan.

Victor's jaw started to ache.

"Damn, you're easy." Justin broke into a grin. "Stand down, Vic. She politely told me she wasn't interested."

Victor released the breath he was holding. "Asshole."

Justin started to laugh.

Victor slapped his brother's back a little too hard. "Payback's a bitch."

Chapter Twenty-Six

"I need to change our plans for Saturday," Victor told her as they walked around the loft.

They'd only been there five minutes, and her excitement over meeting Victor was swept away by his words. "Oh."

"I said change, not cancel," he clarified as he dropped an arm on her shoulder as if it belonged there.

"Clarify, please."

He walked her past Gary, who stood in the middle of the room watching them, and over to one of the three massive windows.

"I completely forgot about a charity fundraiser that I sponsor every year. I'd like you to come with me. It's a dinner thing, kinda fancy. I'd skip out of it if I hadn't purchased a table and already seated it with some of my biggest clients and their spouses. Not going would be—"

Shannon stopped him. "I get it. You don't have to explain. But are you sure you want to bring me? People will talk."

"I absolutely want you to go so people *do* talk."

"Great comeback," Gary said from where he stood several feet away.

Victor looked up, smiled at the agent.

"Sorry. Eavesdropping. It's a weakness."

"Say you'll go," Victor said. "Get dressed up for me."

His words reminded her of the conversation they'd had earlier in the week. "What time?"

Once they'd ironed out the plan, Gary drew their attention back to the room.

Victor walked around the space, asking questions and pointing out options. "You could drywall over the brick, but that might feel too modern. Or how about one of those plaster jobs with texture and color, maybe even leave some of the brick exposed like you'd see in Italy on a three-hundred-year-old building."

Shannon stared up at the wall in question and the shape of it started to come into focus. "That's a really good idea."

"Brilliant," Gary added.

She nodded several times. "What about the bedroom space upstairs?"

"You said you didn't like modern."

"Not particularly."

"Then gut the bathroom. Start over with it. I'd suggest you wait to sell your house until after, if you can swing it. Give you time to make this exactly the way you want it."

Gary pointed to Victor. "I like this guy."

Shannon rolled her eyes. "I'm not sure if I could live here."

Victor turned in a circle. "Who said you had to? You said you needed a change. Is this a big enough change, or are you wanting more?"

"I want something that is all me." Not a byproduct of her marriage to Paul, or something she fulfilled because society, or in Shannon's case, her parents, asked it of her.

Victor lifted both hands. "If this isn't it, we keep looking."

"We?" She picked out one word.

"You keep looking, and I keep offering my opinion and support," he clarified.

"What do you think about *this* place?"

He regarded her for a second and then turned to Gary. "Can you excuse us for a few minutes?"

"Of course. I'll meet you outside when you're done."

Once they were alone, Victor turned to Shannon and placed both hands on her hips. "What's stopping you?"

"I'm just not sure—" The thought of change was exciting and new, but the reality of it made her skin itch with uncertainty.

"You said open space, this can open up. You wanted an ocean view. I'm not sure they get a whole lot better."

"It is a pretty great view."

"But?"

She dug deeper and tried to find the reason she was hesitating. "It's the perfect place for a single person." Which she was, but didn't really want to be.

Understanding filled Victor's eyes. "But not a family."

She sighed, lowered her chin.

He brought it back up with two fingers. "Are you pregnant?" he asked.

"No," she denied instantly. "We haven't . . . I haven't—"

"Is owning this going to stop you from getting pregnant?"

"Of course not."

He paused as if waiting for her to add something else.

All she could think of was this was not the conversation she wanted to have with him, although Avery, Lori, and Trina would all be asking the same thing.

"Since you and I have this honesty thing going on, something that makes me a little itchy, I'm not going to lie . . . let me spell this out to you the way I see it." He turned her around to look at the room and wrapped his arms around her from behind.

She relaxed in his embrace and rested the back of her head against his shoulder. It felt way too good, and way too safe, to stand like they were.

"You and I met, which I'm guessing from what you've told me, had you putting your getting-pregnant-by-a-stranger plans on hold. Am I right so far?"

"Yes," she murmured, glad she wasn't looking into Victor's eyes with her confession.

"Phew. That's a good thing. I haven't punched a guy since junior high and don't mind the thought of never doing that again."

She giggled.

"Based on the fact that you haven't jumped me and that you told me about those baby plans, I'm going to go out on a limb here and say that you're not trying to trick me into being your baby daddy."

"I would never—" She started to pull away and turn toward him.

He stopped her by holding her tighter, resting his chin on her shoulder, and kissing her cheek. "Shhh, I know you wouldn't." He paused. "Personally, and probably selfishly, I like the thought of you buying this place or a different one with the same layout. It gives you time to find your new pace in life and us time to get to know each other better."

Her mind raced and caught up with his. "You know, when a man tells you exactly what you want to hear, it's probably bullshit."

He hugged her tighter. "I'm a pretty good negotiator. Even better when I know the motivation of the person I'm negotiating with. Which in this case is you. I promised I wouldn't play you, and that's not what I'm doing." He sighed. "This is not the kind of place to raise a family."

"It isn't."

"Which is why you're hesitating."

She stayed silent.

He placed his lips close to her ear. "You're looking at this place as if you're abandoning the idea of being a mother. And I look at this place as if you're considering that I might just be the father."

Shannon twisted in his arms, backed up, and stared him in the eye.

He stared back.

Dumbstruck. There really wasn't another word to describe how rooted in silence she became with his observation. Maybe because the picture he painted made her realize that was exactly what buying this place meant.

"Most men would be running away if they thought that were true," she finally uttered.

He reduced the space between them and placed a hand on her cheek. "You underestimate yourself."

Her heart was racing. "Victor—"

"Shh . . . I need to do something." He licked his lips and lowered them to hers.

Damn if she didn't melt, right there in a somewhat dingy room occupied by more dust than light, and her world tilted.

An hour later she was writing up an offer and submitting it to the owners of the loft.

~

Shannon had been to dozens of events like the one Victor had invited her to. From charities to fundraisers, the players may change names, but their motivations were always the same.

Most of the charity dinners were filled with wealthy people who needed the personal and business tax write-offs the events offered. Because they were filled with millionaires dressed in five-thousand-dollar suits or dripping in jewelry, the typical businessman or -woman used the event to make new contacts, schmooze old clients, or otherwise increase their bottom line.

Shannon didn't think Victor's event, or motivation, would be any different.

She picked her dress carefully. Something she hadn't been seen in with Paul, although many of those dresses had been donated shortly after the divorce. She did have a few she pulled out if she thought

Paul might be at the event she was attending. Each one of them had a memory of him attached to it. She pushed past several and removed two that she'd purchased while on one of the many First Wives weekends in the past year.

"Conservative? Or lots of skin?" she asked herself aloud.

She approached the full-length mirror wearing only her panties and held each dress up to her frame. The black dress was safer, with a low back that said sexy and a front that said sophisticated.

Then there was the copper sequins with a neckline that plunged so low in the front it would require a little tape to keep her from exposing herself to the room. She thought about Victor's observation about her being an exhibitionist and him being a voyeur.

The black went back in the closet, and Shannon sat down at her vanity and started to work on her hair. Messy bun, nothing tight and uppity. Free. She went a little heavier on her eyeliner and added those pointy ends that Avery did so well. She slid on a pair of nude strappy Jimmy Choos before stepping into her dress. It took a little yoga to zip up the back, but not as much as usual, since the back was nearly as provocative as the front.

A little tape here and a little tape there.

She turned in a circle, ran a hand over her stomach.

There were perks to her slender frame, and wearing dresses like this one, where the straight lines hugged only the right parts and accentuated her breasts, was one of them.

She finished with a pair of diamond cut curtain earrings that flowed from her ears nearly as much as the dress flowed at her heels. A simple diamond bangle bracelet. No necklace. Eyes would be on her. And if a man's gaze lingered longer than expected, it wouldn't be because he was admiring her jewelry.

She could nearly feel the heat of Victor's gaze already.

Her small clutch was filled with the necessities. Lipstick, powder, her ID, cell phone, a little bit of cash, and a condom.

She grinned at the last item and snapped her purse closed.

Her doorbell rang and she checked the time.

Five minutes early.

She smiled and grabbed her coat. There was no way she was going to reveal this dress to Victor until they arrived at the event.

Her heels clicked along the tile floor on her way to the door. Shannon tied her belt on the long coat, squared her shoulders, and smiled.

Victor was in a tux. Clean-shaven, his thick, dark hair combed back. She drank him in.

He looked past her eyes to her hair and the bottom of the coat where her dress peeked through. "Why do I get the feeling this is going to be a very long night?"

"Because you're wise that way?"

He growled and stepped closer for a kiss. "You're beautiful."

His lips met hers, soft, simple. "I like the tux."

"I haven't met a woman who didn't." He winked. "Are you ready?"

Shannon reached around the door and locked it, then remembered the need for a key and retrieved one from her kitchen. She tucked it into her purse, saw the condom, and wondered if she would need it before the end of the night.

Victor placed a hand on the small of her back and led her to the waiting limo outside.

"Someone went all out."

"I only do a couple of these a year. What's the point of having money if you don't enjoy it once in a while?"

She thought of the three-thousand-dollar gown she was wearing and said, "I completely agree."

Because of the infamous LA traffic, it took them nearly an hour to drive to the venue.

Victor poured champagne in the back of the limo and told her about the event.

"They call it Global Task Force. GTF for short. It's been around for a while but started to get its legs when recycling became a fashion."

"I didn't realize tossing my plastic in the right color barrel was fashion."

"For a lot of people, it is. They do a pretty good job of bringing awareness to smaller cities that haven't adopted the idea of recycling on a bigger scale. They have events like this one, where computer companies meet with guys like me who make a profit from removing the usable parts and melting down those that aren't."

"I thought you were in scrap metal."

"I am. I'm just using that as an example."

"Got it. So who am I going to meet tonight?"

He topped off her champagne and smiled. "Some of my oldest clients, like I told you before. Good people. I think you'll like them."

Shannon narrowed her eyes. "Most of these events are all about posturing for power."

"There will be a fair amount of that, but not from me. My accountant told me years ago to pick a couple of charities I could honestly give money to at events like this. My lawyer added that I shouldn't get heavily involved in the slight chance the charity ended up in scandal."

"That's actually really smart."

Victor leaned back. "And the food is usually pretty decent."

She laughed. "It's all about the food."

"And the company," he added. His warm eyes held hers.

"There's probably going to be cameras?"

He nodded. "I thought of that." He lifted his glass to hers. "We're exploring our options, right?"

She drank to that.

Limousines and fancy cars lined up. Thankfully, there wasn't a mob of photographers . . . just a couple that seemed to be there only for the charity.

Victor stepped out of the limo first and offered his hand as she exited the car.

They walked in together, her hand tucked in the crook of his arm. The event was held at a dining hall of a country club that overlooked the Pacific Ocean.

The closer Shannon walked to the coat check, the more her nerves battled her stomach.

Victor shrugged out of his coat and handed it to the young man standing by.

Shannon waited until Victor was done before turning her back to him for his help.

She undid the belt and Victor peeled away her coat.

His gaze heated her back.

The kid in coat check dropped his jaw.

Victor stepped around her. His gaze sizzled and the air snapped all around them. "Whoa."

Shannon decided, right there and then, that she liked rendering this man speechless.

"Oh, boy, am I in trouble."

She faked innocence. "Is something wrong?"

Victor wordlessly shook his head.

"Sir?" The kid waiting to take her jacket called Victor's attention.

"Here," Victor said, thrusting her coat at him.

Shannon looked over Victor's shoulder. "Thank you."

"You—you're welcome," the kid stuttered.

Victor collected himself and placed a possessive hand on her back. "I'm burning that coat," he whispered in her ear.

"I like that coat."

"Are you trying to kill me?" His flirty tone and words kept her smiling.

"Is your cardiovascular health that weak?"

Heads turned as they made their way into the outer reception room. Waiters dressed in black-and-white uniforms were serving wine and champagne, and soft music played in the background.

"It's not my cardiovascular health I'm worried about. It's the other men that are bound to capture your attention. I have a feeling I'm not going to be able to go to the bathroom for fear of someone hitting on you."

Victor took two glasses of bubbly from a passing waiter and handed her one.

"They can try, but I came here with you and I'm leaving with you."

"Amen for that."

"Victor?" A voice from behind had them both turning around.

"We were starting to wonder if you were coming."

It was Shannon's turn for shell shock.

In front of them was Justin, standing next to a gorgeous petite redhead with big brown eyes. Beside them was a couple Shannon least expected.

Victor's parents.

She shivered, suddenly very aware of how little she wore and how bad impressions were everything.

Chapter Twenty-Seven

Victor had to nudge Shannon twice to get her feet to move.

"I'm going to kill you," Shannon whispered from the side of her mouth before they reached his parents.

Victor shook his brother's hand. "Justin, you remember Shannon."

"How could I forget the woman who pegged you for an asshole before she knew your name."

Justin's words broke some of the ice. He leaned in and kissed her cheek. "Wonderful to see you again. This is my girlfriend, Deirdre. Hon, this is Shannon."

She extended a hand. "Lovely to meet you. I've heard all about you."

"I'm a little afraid of what that might imply."

"Nothing bad, I assure you," Deirdre said.

Victor placed a hand back on the base of Shannon's spine and directed her to his parents. "I'm not sure if you were ever properly introduced. This is my mom, Renee, and my father, Scott."

Renee shook Shannon's hand first. "We spoke briefly at the . . . in Tulum." *When posing for the preceremony pictures.*

"I remember."

Renee looked Shannon up and down. "Might I say, that is a stunning dress."

Shannon placed a nervous hand over the exposed skin between her breasts. "Victor failed to tell me you were all going to be here, or I might have worn something a little less . . ." She searched for the right words.

"I'm not sure that's possible," Victor said, teasing.

She wanted to stomp on his foot. "A little more conservative," Shannon said between her teeth.

"Good heavens, why?" Renee asked. "If I could wear that, you bet I would."

Both Victor and Justin looked at their mother.

"No," Justin said first.

Victor shook his head.

Scott kissed his wife's cheek. "Only for me, hon."

Victor's dad shook her hand, placed a second one over hers. "I'm glad Victor brought you. You add class to my son's arm."

Heat warmed her face. "Thank you for your kind words."

Victor squeezed her waist. "Now that we're done with that, I need to find a real drink. I have a feeling I'm going to need it to fend off the men in the room," he told his family.

"There's an idea I can endorse," Justin said, leading the way to the bar.

Shannon took the opportunity to whisper in Victor's ear. "Oldest client, huh?"

He shrugged. "Not a lie. I learned to buy and sell scraps starting with my father. He gave me my first loan."

She held him back a few steps, looked down at her dress. "This dress is practically glued in place. If anything pops out, you had better tell me."

His eyes traveled down, he wiggled his eyebrows.

She slapped his arm. "Victor."

"I will."

"Promise."

"I promise."

They started walking again. He leaned close. "Is it bad that I want something to pop out?"

"Victor!" she warned between clenched teeth.

"Okay, that's bad. Got it."

His parents . . . good God, his parents. "You could have told me your parents were coming."

"I somehow think me asking you to a family dinner this early would have ended up being a no go."

"You'd have been right."

"Then this worked out."

"For you."

He brought her hand up to his, kissed the back of it. "For both of us. You'll see."

For his sake, she hoped he was right. Or that condom was going to remain in its wrapper for a very long time.

⌒୭

Victor was keenly aware of the men watching his date. He couldn't blame them. He'd been in several states of arousal ever since she revealed her dress at the door. Good thing she didn't do it at her house, or he might have skipped the event altogether.

Now he had no choice but to stay by her side and move in anytime he saw someone stepping in too close. And when the photographer came around, Victor was right there to smile for the camera. For the event page of the charity website, they were told. Of course, once they were public, there was no telling where the images would end up.

He was okay with that.

Victor didn't want to hide this thing they were exploring any longer. Even if it appeared that he was the asshole in the saga that was him and Corrie. He didn't care.

He introduced Shannon to a dozen acquaintances and a couple of business associates he'd dealt with over the years.

Only once did his "almost bride" get brought up.

"I heard you got married, introduce me to your beautiful wife."

He hesitated, but Shannon jumped right in. "Victor left the wife at home and brought me instead," she told Sebastian Crane, a once a year acquaintance Victor never spoke with outside of this event.

Justin chimed in once Sebastian regained his equilibrium. Explained that the marriage had never happened.

Victor took the opportunity to steer Shannon away.

Not that he'd expected any different, but the welcome Shannon received from his parents, and Shannon's genuine interest in getting to know Deirdre, was icing on the cake.

No one pulled him aside to tell him she was too young, too naive, or too anything. All he caught in reaction to Shannon was the occasional man releasing a breath after she walked by.

Her dress was killing him. He couldn't help but wish something would pop out so he could touch it and pop it back in.

Thankfully, the night would end with dancing, which he intended to use to his full advantage by holding her close.

"You do realize you're staring," she told him through the second course of their dinner.

He leaned over, whispered, "You wore that so I would."

She didn't deny him. Instead she placed a hand on his lap and continued to make conversation with his family at the table.

The dinner took forever, followed by the longest speech in existence . . . *green energy, save the world, we can make a difference* . . . blah, blah, blah.

The music started and Victor almost applauded.

Instead he scooted his chair back and reached for Shannon's hand. "I've been waiting all night for this."

He was pretty sure his father laughed. He knew for sure his brother made a snarky comment.

It was a charity event, not a frat party, so the music was slow and the dancing was cheek to cheek.

Victor wrapped an arm around her and held her close, his lips right by her ear. "Thank you," he said.

She kept to his lead, smooth on her feet. Nothing like when they tried their hands at salsa. "What for?"

"For being here with me. For wearing that dress."

"You're welcome."

He turned her around, glanced over at their table. His brother had pulled his girl onto the dance floor, and the two of them were talking and glancing their way on occasion. "I think my family likes you."

"I like them, too. They're very down-to-earth."

"Is that a surprise?"

"You haven't met mine. They've gotten better, but . . ."

Victor squeezed her hand. "I'm pretty good with parents."

Shannon laughed. "I know. You would have thought Beverly was the one getting married."

Just the mention of his ex almost mother-in-law left a bad taste in his mouth. "That woman was a little crazy."

Shannon was quick to agree. "Understatement. My mother is enti-tled, not nuts."

"I'll make a note of it."

They danced for a while before Shannon asked, "Why wasn't Deirdre at the wedding?"

He made that long story as short as he could. "She and Corrie didn't get along. Instead of making it hard on Justin, Deirdre bowed out."

"Smart. I like her even more now."

Shannon rested her head on his shoulder, and Victor pulled her even closer. His fingers ran along the back of her dress and touched her exposed skin.

His body responded, and instead of letting his thoughts go wherever erotic place they wanted to, Victor tamped down his libido to save him from being the one that *popped out* for everyone to see.

Shannon sucked in a deep breath and hummed. "How much longer do we have to stay?" she asked.

"Are you tired?"

"No. I want to get you alone so I can take advantage of you."

Victor growled.

∾

The chill in the air as they waited for their car to be brought around didn't dampen her hormones.

Victor was as quiet as she was, their hands clasped together.

Once in the back of the limo, Victor lifted the shield between the driver and the back seat before reaching for her and lifting her onto his lap.

His lips were molten hot, his fingers spreading heat wherever they touched. "You taste as good as you look," he told her between wet, open kisses.

Shannon took the liberty of spreading her hand over his chest and down his side. "I feel like a teenager on prom night." She traced his erection through his slacks.

He stopped her hand. "If you keep doing that, we're going to act like those teenagers in the back of this car."

"That sounds sinful and exciting."

He squeezed the hand he held. "I don't want our first time back here. I want to lay you down—"

"Pin me down," she requested with a nibble to his ear.

Her words had him pressing her palm into his groin. "Good God, yes. Pin you down."

She kissed his chin, ran her teeth along his neck. It felt so right taking liberties with him. Perfect in every way.

"I want you alone, where I can peel you out of that dress like I've been fantasizing about ever since you took off that damn coat." He reached into her coat, caught one nipple with his thumb, and continued to flick its tight bud. "I'm going to make these raw. And every time you see me, you're going to get hard, just like this, with the memories of how I kissed them."

She squirmed. "I brought a condom."

He kissed her hard before setting her aside. "I brought three."

The next thirty minutes were the longest in Shannon's life.

Thankfully, the traffic home wasn't nearly as bad as it was on the way out.

Victor handed the driver several bills and walked her up the path to her front door.

They made it through the door . . . barely.

Victor stopped her two feet inside and took the coat from her shoulders. "This dress is lethal."

"Remind me to wear it often."

His hands slid down her bare arms before his fingers traced her curves on the way back up. He kissed her shoulder and ran one finger on the inside of her dress. He caught the tape and gave it a little tug.

It stung, but her body heated with anticipation.

"Stupid tape."

He kissed away the sting, his tongue dancing on the edge of her breast. "Lovely," he said, sliding his teeth toward her nipple before taking it into his mouth.

The pathway between her breasts to the apex of her legs made her weak. "Don't stop tonight," she pleaded. "I want you inside of me. All of you." Because the question of pregnancy had been brought up before, she assured him the best she could that it wouldn't happen. "The timing is off for a baby. We'll use the condom."

He directed his kiss to her lips and silenced her. "I trust you, Shannon."

She nodded and pulled at where his shirt tucked into his pants. She reached for him, found his skin warm.

Victor pulled his tie from his neck, unbuttoned the first few snaps, and then impatiently pulled the dress shirt over his head.

She'd seen this, covered in salt water in the ocean of the Yucatán. Now it was her turn to taste. So she did, while standing in the foyer of her home. Victor toed off his shoes, holding on to the wall while she dropped one kiss after the other on his chest.

Her hands slid lower.

Victor pushed his pelvis into her palm.

His hands moved around to the back of her dress and pulled down the zipper. With his teeth, he slid one arm out of the dress, and the other just fell away.

With a mountain of fabric pooled at her ankles, Shannon stood before him in lace panties and high heels. Instead of feeling naked, she felt liberated. It helped that Victor's eyes swam with passion.

She took his hand, stepped out of the dress on the floor, and walked him to her bedroom.

He stopped her before she could turn around once they stood by her bed. His hands reached around her from behind, his palms cupped both breasts. "You're perfect," he whispered.

Am I? She felt that way with him talking the way he was, with his touch.

One of his hands moved lower, touching her through the only fabric covering her. "So ready," he told her.

"I am."

The room was dark, only the moon outside cast light into the space.

She felt Victor undoing his belt, his hand pinning her in place with slow, rhythmic motions that made it hard to stand.

"You like that?" he asked, one finger tracing inside her panties and coming away wet.

"Yes," she murmured.

"Do you trust me?" he asked. A flick of his finger over her clit kept her from talking.

She nodded.

He dropped his pants to the floor.

He nudged her onto the bed, facedown. "Lean over here for me."

Slowly she bent at her waist, her feet still in her fancy shoes, her bottom in the air.

She felt exposed, excited.

Victor stood behind her, she could feel him pushing against her underwear. His erection so close, but not there.

She pushed against him and he dropped a kiss between her shoulder blades. "You're so damn beautiful, Shannon."

Her hands clenched the bedding on both sides of her body. He might not be pinning her, but she didn't have a lot of room to move and touch. No, Victor was doing that for the two of them.

He slid his cock past her opening and over the tiny bundle of nerves that made her crazy, and then repeated the motion, all through the cotton of her panties.

"Please," she said when he'd worked her up but hadn't filled what she needed.

He didn't seem to be in a hurry, so Shannon reached between her legs and caught him with her hand. Victor dropped his head to her back before moving away briefly. She heard the wrapper of the condom, and when he came back, he moved her panties to the side but didn't take them off. She lifted up for him, and he took her.

At first, her body didn't know what to think. So full, so thick . . . so damn good.

"I'm a dead man," he said from behind before he started to move.

CATHERINE BYBEE

She loved it, this feeling of being possessed by him, of having him guide her hips to meet his and the feel of his energy.

Victor took one hand and reached around, found her sex, and worked it with every stroke.

She was close, right on the edge, and Victor slipped out.

Shannon wanted to weep.

He turned her around, pulled the panties off her legs, and climbed back up. "I want to watch you come."

He kissed her then, entered her a second time, and kept the motion until there was nowhere else to go. When she reached her peak, Victor caught her cries with his lips and followed with one of his own.

They lay there for several seconds, catching their breaths.

"So good," she said over and over.

"So very good," he said with a kiss.

Chapter Twenty-Eight

Shannon sat at her computer with a four-way video chat connecting her, Avery, Lori, and Trina.

"Someone is looking awfully relaxed," Avery said once they were all connected. "Anything you want to share, Shannon?"

"Am I that obvious?"

All three of her friends nodded.

"Give it up," Trina said.

Shannon couldn't help but smile. "It all still works," she happily reported. "I forgot how great sex feels."

Avery shook a fist in the air. "Go, Victor."

"It helps that he's adventurous and spontaneous . . . and able."

Lori rested her chin on her hand. "This I wanna hear."

And they did . . . in vivid color. For the first time since they'd started this club, Shannon had something to share. All the joy of sharing skidded to a halt when she told them she'd confessed about wanting a baby.

"What?" Avery yelled. "And he didn't run away?"

"Crazy, right?" Shannon asked.

"Unreal," Lori added.

"Not normal," Trina said.

"I don't get it either. We've used condoms . . . lots of them, I'm happy to report."

"Condoms break." Avery patted her barely there baby bump. "I'm here to tell you."

"I know. Which is why I've scheduled an appointment with my doctor in two weeks. I'm going back on the pill." She'd made the decision after the first night with Victor.

"Whoa . . . hold up a minute. Are you giving up the baby making plans?" Lori asked.

"I'm dating someone I really like. I don't think baby making is right at this point. Practicing making babies is a better goal for now, don't you think?"

All three of them sat in silence.

Avery was the first to talk. "Great idea."

Shannon wasn't shocked. "You never liked the idea."

Avery agreed with a shake of her head. "Not for a minute."

"Victor is making me think there might be other options," Shannon told them.

Trina sighed. "And if he isn't Mr. Right? How are you going to deal with that?"

The question had silently surfaced many times. "I will deal with it. Victor has made me realize how much I was missing in life." Not that she wanted to think about life without him, but she had considered the possibility that he might not stick.

"He better not be screwing with you," Avery declared.

"I honestly don't think he knows what he's doing with me any more than I know what I'm doing with him."

"I'll kick his ass if he is," Avery declared.

A pregnant Avery kicking ass . . . this, Shannon wanted to see.

"I'll let him know."

She told them about the loft, which would be closing escrow in two weeks. The fastest real estate transaction ever in light of the fact it was empty and she was able to secure a loan quickly.

"Oh my God. I almost forgot to tell you guys!" Trina exclaimed.

"What?" Lori asked.

"My mother-in-law is moving out."

That was big news. Vicki lived on the compound that was Wade and Trina's ranch in Texas. She lived in a guesthouse but had been a continual pain in Trina's butt since they met.

"That's huge. Is it the baby? Did Wade tell her to leave?"

"It's the boyfriend," Trina told them. "She started dating a guy she met on Cowboys Only."

"Is that like Tinder?" Avery asked.

"Yeah," Trina laughed. "She didn't admit that, of course, but when he insisted on meeting her son and daughter-in-law, Judah let that information slip."

"His name is Judah?"

Trina nodded. "Very religious. I think he's given Vicki a 'come to Jesus' moment. He's a widower, has two grown kids and a granddaughter. Anyway, between him being in her life and Wade buying her a place that isn't right under our noses, Vicki is moving out." She shook her fists in the air in celebration.

"That's the best news ever."

"Tell me about it. It's amazing what happens once someone is finally getting laid," Trina said.

Shannon raised her hand. "I can attest to that."

The four of them laughed and planned their next First Wives meeting, which was to take place in Texas. They had originally planned for something down in New Orleans, but with two of the four of them pregnant, they decided to keep it in the comfort of one of their homes. And it was Shannon's, Lori's, and Avery's turn to travel.

"So, Shannon, how is Victor handling the media coverage?"

"I think he kinda likes it." Pictures of the two of them at the charity event were snagged from the GTF website and splashed on the cover of one of the most popular gossip magazines. Then two others picked up the information and ran with it on consecutive days. "The only reason I think it's become a thing is because Paul announced his run for Congress."

"That was my thought," Lori said. "It will all blow over soon. It always does."

"That dress was spectacular," Trina told her. "Daring for you."

Shannon sat back and grinned. "Hey, I sunbathe in the nude these days. I'm evolving."

That brought a chorus of cheers and a new direction of conversation.

An hour after they finished their video chat, a call came through from an unknown caller. Shannon nearly let it go to voice mail before answering.

"Hello?"

"You raging bitch!"

Shocked silent, Shannon waited for some clue as to who was on the phone.

She didn't need to wait long.

"You were screwing him all the time, weren't you?" A woman, could have been Corrie, but didn't sound like the soft, careful girl she'd met all those months ago.

"Who is this?" Shannon asked, her guard up.

"You told me to leave him, that he didn't deserve me. All so you could snag your claws into him."

Yup, it was Corrie. "That is not what happened," Shannon said, trying to calm her down.

"Right under my nose. I feel so stupid. Which is exactly what you wanted, isn't it? Now Victor won't take my calls. You're on the cover of those magazines with my fiancé when it should be me."

"Corrie, calm down."

"Don't you fucking tell me to calm down. You've ruined my life. I'm the 'blonde bimbo that was cast aside to make way for royalty.'" Corrie was quoting the article. The only way Shannon knew that was because Samantha Harrison had texted the quote and said, "Welcome to the monarchy." They'd laughed about it.

"You and I both know that is not what happened. You walked out on him. We were all there."

"You told me to."

"I did no such thing." This conversation was going nowhere.

"Yes, you did!" Corrie was screaming now.

Shannon pulled the phone away from her ear. "I'm hanging up, Corrie."

"Don't you fucking dare. I'm not finished—"

Click!

Shannon stared at her cell phone, wasn't surprised when it immediately rang again. *Unknown caller.*

She let it go to voice mail.

❧

Victor dropped the latest magazine with an article about Shannon on his desk. This time the images were mainly of her behind the camera as she took pictures of him at his doomed wedding.

Someone at the rehearsal dinner caught the two of them in the background of a selfie when Shannon had poured her drink all over him. It was out of focus and grainy, but it was definitely him with Shannon's hands on his chest. She'd been attempting to apologize. The memory of the moment brought a smile to his face. She'd really hated him at that time.

Okay, maybe *hate* wasn't the right word.

Irritated.

Which he deserved.

Only this picture accompanied an article with direct quotes from Corrie, according to the reporter, about Shannon stealing her man.

There was a picture of Corrie in her wedding gown, an image he'd never seen, probably taken by one of her friends.

It was the ugliest article to date. While it didn't touch Victor, he couldn't help but wonder what it was doing to Shannon.

Every time he brought up the media, she waved it off. "I'm not a Kardashian. This will all blow over. Trust me. I'm used to it."

Yeah, well . . . she might be used to it, but he wasn't.

A knock on his office door had him putting the magazine aside.

Stephanie walked in with the daily agenda. Her gaze skidded past the magazine on his desk before she set the folder she carried right on top of it.

They went over his schedule, and she brought his attention to a summit meeting he normally attended in Asia the following week. "I've already booked the flights and hotels."

"How many nights?"

"I have you flying into Beijing Sunday and leaving the following Saturday, per normal. Did you need me to change it?"

He shook his head. As much as he wanted to shorten the trip, he knew he couldn't. With the new ban on plastic recycling imports going into China, his presence and keeping his finger on the pulse of the scrap metal industry in the country were imperative to his company, for all the employees that worked for him and depended on their paychecks to feed their families.

"Okay, I've scheduled our interpreter to meet you at the airport. All the files and articles that will be brought up are in there." She pointed to the folder on his desk. "All translated and highlighted."

"Perfect," he told her.

She stood to leave and hesitated.

"Anything else?" he asked.

She glanced at his desk. "That one was mean-spirited."

He looked at the garbage magazine under his mountain of work. "All lies."

260

Stephanie nodded. "That's what I thought."

"I'm guessing the staff has been up on their reading."

"Hard not to when your private boss's personal life is splattered on the front page."

"Don't believe a word of it," he told her. "Shannon is nothing like what these people say."

With a timid smile, Stephanie left his office.

He tapped a pen against his desk in thought. He had an eleven o'clock board meeting to discuss China.

Lunch would have to be quick, maybe a sandwich at the café across the street.

"Acknowledge the elephant in the room."

His decision made, he picked up his phone.

Shannon's voice made him smile.

"Hey, sexy. Do you have plans for lunch?"

Chapter Twenty-Nine

Victor heard her laughter when he opened the door from the board meeting.

"This one is my favorite," he heard Shannon say when he rounded the corner. His executive staff followed him down the hall that led to their row of offices.

She half sat, half leaned on Stephanie's desk, pointing at an open magazine. She wore a dress that went past her knees with a kitten heel that looked like she was working in the office instead of visiting.

He'd hinted that he needed her help dispelling some of the office rumors and would she mind coming by so they could go to lunch together. Obviously she didn't need any more coaching than that.

She caught sight of him and stood. "There you are," she said as she crossed to his side.

He caught her kiss on his cheek and placed a hand on her waist.

"You're early," he told her.

"No, you're late," she teased.

He looked at his watch. Two minutes past twelve.

"Now you're just being picky."

She smiled and turned her attention to the audience standing beside him. "Stating facts, hon." She reached out her hand to Andrew, standing at his side. "I'm Shannon."

Victor jumped in to make the introductions. He could tell by the expressions of his staff that she'd charmed them all with a smile. To seal the unity, she turned to a stack of articles on Stephanie's desk and handed it to Andrew. "I brought some fun reading material for the water cooler. I especially like the one about how my anorexia is back in full force after Victor and I met."

Laughter, and lots of it, filled the hall.

She turned to him. "Since you said you had to have a quick lunch, I brought some from that deli you mentioned. I thought we could eat in your office, if that's okay with you."

"Great idea."

Shannon turned to his staff. "Lovely meeting all of you. Sorry I took some of your lunch time away."

Victor pushed her toward the open doors of his office and closed them inside.

He turned to her the second they were alone and removed her lipstick the best way he knew how.

"We are not doing this in your office," she said five minutes later, when it became obvious that he had every intention of *doing this* on his desk, against the wall . . . in his office chair . . . the couch.

"Give me one good reason why not." He bit her ear.

"Because you asked me to come to make a good impression with your employees, not become the heroine of your own *Fifty Shades of Grey* novel."

She made him laugh. "I missed that one."

Shannon pushed him away, slightly. "You should pick it up. It's very . . . inspiring."

Yeah, so he'd heard. "Maybe I will."

She wiggled her eyebrows. "I'll look forward to it."

With reluctance, he put some space between them, took the sack holding their lunch, and moved to the sofa. She sat beside him and helped him spread out their meal.

"Your office is bigger than I pictured. Your staff seemed very nice."

He opened the wrapper on a sandwich, smelled tuna, and handed it to her. "Everyone does their job."

"Are there happy hours with the boss?" she asked.

"No. I haven't made time for that."

She shrugged. "Any reason why?"

"I never felt the need." He took a bite of his ham and cheese.

She picked up her tuna, nibbled. "You know, having a good relationship with some of your key staff outside of the office will help dispel anything they might find on the front page of the papers. Not that I think all of this is going to continue, but it might be something to consider."

Victor nodded. "Except that up until a couple of months ago, before I met a certain someone, I was labeled an *asshole*."

Shannon grinned. "Yeah, but Justin called you a *loveable asshole*."

Victor wiped his mouth. "I'll have to thank him for that half-ass compliment."

"Just a suggestion."

He thought about the article he'd read about her and her relationship with the household staff at the governor's mansion. "I'll see what I can do."

He took another bite of his sandwich, and she kept talking. "So, uhm . . . I got a call from Corrie the other day."

Victor stopped midbite. "Why is she calling you?"

"I'm sure it will blow over."

"What did she say, Shannon?"

She set her lunch aside, a polite smile spread on her lips. "It was ugly. There was yelling and name-calling. From her side, not mine. She blamed me for your split, accused us of sleeping together before the wedding. It's obvious she's reading the papers."

He set his sandwich down, his appetite faded. "I'll call her."

"Which is what she wants, Victor. The whole thing smacks of something young girls do when they think someone has taken their prom date away."

He couldn't help but wince.

Shannon reached a hand out. "I'm sorry. She isn't *that* young, but she said things she knew for a fact weren't the truth and said it with such conviction it's like she believes her own lie. I thought you had the right to know. And since she has obviously decided she likes the pages of the gossip magazines, I'm sure she's not done yet."

"She has no right to slander you."

Shannon placed a hand to her chest. "I can take care of me."

He leaned over and kissed her briefly. "I'll take care of it."

And when they finished their lunch, and his staff started funneling back into the office, Victor made a nasty call of his own.

Shannon rolled over and placed her head on Victor's bare chest. "I can't believe you're leaving tomorrow." They'd gotten in the habit of spending every other evening together, if only for a few hours. They'd have dinner and make love, or make love and have dinner. Sometimes food wasn't necessary at all.

"It's only a week."

She sighed. "I know. I can handle it."

His chest rumbled with laughter. "I'd take you with me, but I would never get anything done."

"I couldn't go, anyway. Escrow is closing, and I need to be here for the walk-through. Besides, I'm excited to clean the new place up."

"You can hire that done, you know."

"I like the work. Makes it more mine."

"Scrubbing floors makes it more yours?" he asked.

She looked up at him, enjoyed the way he stroked her back when they were like this, talking after they'd taken complete advantage of each other's naked bodies.

"I might even try my hand at some of the construction."

He lifted her fingers to his lips, kissed them. "If I thought you were doing that out of financial need, I'd hire the crew for you."

"It isn't about money."

"I know." He smiled at her. "Do you realize that you're the only woman I have dated that I didn't worry about being after my bank account?"

"That's sad."

"True."

"Still sad." The irony that the reason he didn't worry about her being after his money was because she was living on Paul's smacked her in the ear. She wanted to bring it up but thought it was probably a conversation that needed to wait a little longer in their relationship. If they ever did start talking about forever, revealing that she and Paul had an arrangement from the start was something she would have to do.

"Can I ask you something personal?"

"I'm naked and on top of you." She rubbed her bare leg against his as if emphasizing the point. "Ask away."

"Does Paul pay you alimony?"

Okay . . . apparently they were on the same plane of thought.

"No," she answered honestly.

"Oh, good."

"Why is that good?" she asked.

He squeezed her close, pushed back the hair falling into her face. "Because I don't want another man taking care of you in any way."

"Very bohemian of you."

"What can I say? You bring it out in me."

Her eyes narrowed. "You do realize that the money I do have is because of the prenuptial we signed before we were married."

"I can handle that. I wouldn't imagine a wealthy man not taking care of an ex-wife to a certain point."

"But a monthly check is hard to look past?"

He grinned. "Work with me here. I'm new in this world."

She placed her hand under her chin. "What world is that?"

"The one where I'm channeling my caveman ancestors because the woman in my arms makes me think beyond myself."

There he went, making her melt again. "You know, when a man tells you exactly what you want to hear—"

"It's probably bullshit," he finished for her.

She laughed, and before she stopped, he'd changed positions with her, pinning her shoulders against her mattress. "Tell me if you think this feels like bullshit."

And when he was finished with her, any doubts she had floated out the windows with her passionate cry.

Shannon drove him to the airport because she could and he wanted her to. His return flight would drop him off in the early morning hours, so he insisted that he would call her once he was less than comatose with jet lag.

Instead of driving home, she found herself at Lori's door with a bottle of wine.

She lifted the bottle of Chianti as she walked inside. "You're the only drinking friend I have right now. And I need to drink."

"Happy drinking or sad drinking?" Lori asked for clarification.

"Both. Victor had to go to China for a week."

Lori led her inside and straight to the kitchen. Her high-rise con-dominium was only a couple of floors below Avery and Liam's, but the two of them were at his parents' for a Sunday dinner.

"Where is Reed?"

"Out on an *assignment*."

"How very secret service that sounded."

"Yeah, I don't know all the details, but Blake asked for extra security at one of his meetings."

"On a Sunday?"

"It's at a golf course," Lori explained.

"Ahh."

Lori popped the cork and splashed wine into two glasses.

"So, China?"

"Yeah."

The wine left a smoky aftertaste on her tongue.

"You're falling for him."

Shannon sighed. "I think I already fell."

She shared several details with Lori over takeout and Chianti, and they both laughed and sighed at all the parts that girls loved.

Lori invited her to a party that Friday to distract her. Reed was working, and it would help her out, or so Lori told Shannon. She jumped on it, not wanting to be alone.

Funny how for years she'd spent much of her time in solitude, and now, after Victor, she didn't want that life any longer.

With their plans made, Shannon said goodbye and made her way home.

Fall was making its way into Southern California, which meant some days were the hottest they'd see all year, but the nights were often cool.

She pulled into her garage and closed the door behind her. Inside the house, she switched on the lights and rubbed her arms.

She kicked off her shoes, leaving them by the door leading into the garage. The house was unusually cold, so she immediately went to her thermostat and turned on the heater.

She heard the ducts working and smelled the summer dust being burned out of the system. She considered another glass of wine by her fireplace. Maybe curl up to a good book.

A breeze tickled the hair on her arms when she moved into her living room to turn on her gas fireplace. The curtains on one side of the room blew inward. She didn't remember leaving a window open. But that explained the artic temps inside.

She moved to the window to close it and something sharp cut the bottom of her foot.

"Ouch," she cried out, looking down.

The carpet covering her tile floor was covered in glass. The foot she'd unknowingly stepped into the glass started to bleed.

Shannon stepped back on impulse, into another shard with her other heel. From there, she hobbled on the uncut parts of both feet until she sat on her sofa. Both of her feet were bleeding, the right had a decent shard sticking out of the arch. She removed the glass with her fingertips, wincing at the pain. She needed to cover it quickly or ruin the rug she stood on.

On tiptoes, she carefully made her way into the kitchen, where she grabbed the paper towels to sop up the mess.

Shannon paused and looked into the living room. Her midcentury home had many of the original windows from when it was built, hence why there were shards of glass instead of chunks that didn't cause as much damage when stepped on. That thought was followed with a more obvious one.

How had the window broken in the first place?

Wadding the paper towels on her feet, she slid back into her shoes, ignoring the pain it caused, and walked back into her living room. She pushed back the curtain to see a hole with lots of jagged pieces sticking out.

Her first thought was a ball . . . maybe the neighborhood kids had been playing outside during the day.

She turned a full circle, searching the room for what she was sure would be a white leather ball hiding under a chair or table.

It wasn't.

Instead of an innocent ball, she found one of the decorative rocks from her front yard resting against the wall in the back of the room.

Someone had broken the window on purpose.

She looked at the hole again. It was too small for someone to have crawled through.

But that didn't stop Shannon from looking around the house.

Satisfied that no one was inside and that nothing had been taken, Shannon returned to her living room and considered her options. Instead of the police, where a report would be filed, a squad car would show up at her door, and the media would return, Shannon called Lori.

"You made it home?" Lori said when she answered.

"I did. To an unwelcome surprise. Is Reed home yet?"

"He just walked in the door. Is everything all right?"

She glanced at her foot, knew she'd need a couple of stitches before the night was over.

"Not really."

⌒

"Definitely not an accident," Reed declared after doing a complete search inside and outside her house.

Lori sat next to Shannon on the couch, her arm over her shoulders. Now that the adrenaline was starting to drop, the pain in her foot was getting worse.

"I didn't think so."

"A side window suggests whoever did this was hiding from the street view. Your neighbor's house doesn't have a direct line of sight. And you've obviously stopped setting your alarm when you leave."

Shannon had been lax on the security system in the past year. That would change after this.

"Who would do this?" Lori asked.

Only one name came to her head. "Corrie."

"Victor's ex?"

Shannon nodded. "She's left me several messages, all pretty angry that Victor and I are together."

"Threatening?"

"Not directly. Just bitchy. Reminded me of high school."

"You can file a police report," Reed suggested.

"And add fuel to the tabloids? No. She's a scorned woman, barely an adult. She's searching for attention, and I don't want to give it to her."

"She broke a window," Lori reminded her.

"I bet that's the last of it. This is a cowardly adolescent act."

"Don't underestimate her because of her age," Reed said. "Younger people have done worse."

Shannon heard the wisdom in Reed's words. "If I file a report, and they bring her in for questioning, then what? She gets attention and seeks more? How likely is this vandalism going to be linked to her outside of an eyewitness?"

Reed was once a detective before he went into private security. He knew the system better than anyone.

"Not likely."

"Did you keep the messages on your phone?" Lori asked.

"No." She held up a hand before Lori could continue. "I will from here on out."

"Good. All of them."

Reed removed his cell phone from his pocket and started snapping pictures of the room. "In case we need them later," he told her.

Shannon removed the pressure she was giving to the bottom of her right foot and peeked under the paper towel.

Lori saw it and stood. "Okay, that's it. We're going to the hospital. Honey . . . can you?"

Reed turned to them, saw the problem, and moved to scoop Shannon up in his arms.

"I can manage."

Reed didn't listen. "I'm sure you can."

He walked her out to her garage and into the passenger seat of her car. Lori followed with her purse and house keys.

"I'll stay here until one of my guys can come with some plywood and close this up. I'll meet you," he told his wife.

They kissed and Lori slid behind the wheel.

As they backed out of the driveway, Shannon turned to her friend. "Thank you for doing this."

"You don't have to thank us."

"I know."

"You do have to promise me something," Lori said as she turned the corner.

"What?"

"Anything else, from a doormat kicked out of place or a heavy breather on the phone, you tell us."

"I will."

"Does Victor know about Corrie's phone calls?"

Shannon watched the lights going by. "I told him about the first one. He called her and told her to let it go."

"She didn't."

"No, she got him to talk to her, which is what she wanted."

"And you didn't tell him about the other calls?"

"No. And I don't want him hearing about this until after he's home. Which is another reason I didn't want to call the police."

"Fine. I get it. But anything more serious, and he's brought up to date on everything."

"You sound like your husband."

"No." Lori turned into the ER parking lot. "He sounds a lot like me."

Chapter Thirty

Shannon wore flats and a long dress to hide them when she joined Lori Friday evening.

The rest of the week was free of broken windows or a need to go to the hospital. She'd had a couple of brief conversations with Victor, brief mainly because of the time difference and his work schedule. But when they couldn't talk, they sent flirty texts to say they were thinking about each other.

The tabloids seemed to have moved on to bigger stories, and Corrie was MIA.

Shannon's theory about letting it all blow over was working out.

Unlike the charity event Shannon had attended with Victor, this was a formal cocktail party for a lot of Lori's lawyer-type friends, set up as a fundraiser for one of her colleagues who was moving into the political arena.

It was the kind of event that Shannon knew well and Reed avoided if he could.

She and Lori mingled with the crowd, listened intently to the rhetoric, and spoke in hushed tones when no one was listening.

Shannon felt the weight of men staring at her and often had to thank them politely for their offers of seeing them socially and then promptly tell them she was involved.

"Where were all these men last year?" Shannon whispered to Lori at the midpoint of the event.

"Here. But you weren't putting out the *available* vibe."

"I'm not available."

Lori glanced over the heads of the people standing around them. "More than you were last year."

There was some truth to that.

Lori's smile dropped and her eyes narrowed in across the room. "What the . . . ?"

Shannon felt her skin warm, and she turned to find the source of the heat.

Paul.

"Did you know he was coming?"

"Of course not."

Shannon lifted her chin, felt a familiar and unwelcome lump in her throat at the sight of him. Tall and charismatic. The man parted the sea of people by just walking past.

"I can head him off," Lori offered.

"Don't be ridiculous. He's in the past. We're both adults."

Lori didn't seem convinced. "He's staring at you."

Shannon looked away. "I can see that."

Lori moved in front of Shannon, blocking his path. "He's a rabbit hole not worth following."

"I know that."

And that was all the time they had to talk before Paul stepped up beside Lori, his warm eyes settling on Shannon.

"What a wonderful surprise to find you here," Paul said directly to her.

Lori turned toward him and smiled. "Thanks, Paul. But I'm married now."

He winked at Lori and kissed her cheek. "Hello, Lori. How have you been?"

There was never any real bad blood between the two of them. Although Shannon knew Lori's loyalty lay directly in Shannon's court.

"I'm fine. I see you're still working the room just by being in it."

His eyes found Shannon again. "A blessing and a curse, I'm afraid."

"I don't see the curse," Lori told him.

"It's hard to find who your true friends are when people put you on a pedestal."

Okay, he was definitely speaking directly to Shannon.

He leaned forward, kissed Shannon's cheek. "Hello, Shannon."

"Hello, Paul. You look well." A little too well, if she was being honest with herself.

"And you're glowing."

"I would give credit to the new man in her life," Lori said quickly.

Paul stood back, tilted his head. "So I've heard."

"I didn't realize you read the gossip columns," Shannon said.

"My staff does."

Right . . . his staff. The people who orchestrated many of the images she'd found of herself on the front pages of the tabloids when they were married. The disappearance of her anonymity came with the paycheck. She'd been willing to sign up for it until her heart became involved. That's when she realized the price for being married to Paul was much too steep. "Right," Shannon said with a sigh.

Paul took a step forward, spoke to Lori out of the side of his mouth. "Would you give us a few minutes alone?"

Lori seemed surprised by the question and looked to Shannon for her approval.

"I'm fine," she assured her friend.

Lori's mouth moved into a tight line. "Behave," she scolded Paul before walking away.

Paul took Shannon's elbow and led her away from the crowd. "Should I know what I did to deserve her disapproval?"

She waited until they'd found a quiet corner before calmly removing her arm from his fingertips. "I doubt you're that naive."

His smile used to devastate her. Especially when he looked at her as he did now, soft and smoldering. "How is it you become more beautiful every time I see you?"

She felt her guard go up. "We're not doing this, Paul."

"Doing what?"

"The thing where you make me believe I mean something to you when I don't. We don't have to fake it anymore."

He shook his head. "You've always meant something to me."

She kept her tone even, a smile on her face for anyone who may be watching. "Yes, a means to an end."

"That was mutual."

She swallowed. "In the beginning."

She could see his breathing picking up, did her best to keep hers even and unaffected.

"I should never have let you go," he said quietly. "Biggest mistake of my life."

Three years ago, she would have told him that she never left and he could get her back. But not now.

"It isn't your fault that you didn't love me." She choked on the word *love*.

"Of course I loved you."

She looked into his eyes. Was he that well practiced at telling lies that he could tell her what she always wanted to hear and make her believe him?

"If that were true, you wouldn't have let me go. Our divorce would never have happened."

He lowered his voice. "That was our contract. What you wanted."

Shannon turned her body to try and hide her reaction from anyone watching. "You know better than anyone that is *not* what I wanted. You made love to me the night before you handed me the divorce papers." Just thinking about it made her angry. At the time, all she had been was hurt.

"That was wrong of me."

"It was criminal."

"I'm sorry, Shannon." He reached a hand out, placed it on her arm. "I want another chance."

Why was he saying these things to her now? "I have someone in my life."

"You're not married."

"He's important to me." And he was, much more than the memories she'd held on to of her life with Paul.

"What if I fight for you now?"

She smiled and took a step back. "Your opportunity to win that fight is long gone."

"I don't believe that. I see how you look at me."

She'd have to work on that. If in fact she looked at him with any longing whatsoever. She lifted her chin, calmed her speeding pulse. "Spend your energy and fight. Go ahead. Maybe it will do you some good to learn that you can't have some things back once you've kissed them goodbye." Her words were a challenge, one she was pretty sure he wouldn't take her up on. Paul never groveled. For good measure, she leaned in briefly and lowered her voice. "Goodbye, Paul."

He stopped her with a soft touch to the side of her face. "I'm not giving up."

She flinched and then stopped herself. A wounded ex-wife was what he expected. So she let her lips split into a smile and calmly walked away.

"That looked intense," Lori said once Shannon was back at her side.

"Yeah, well, looks can be deceiving." She glanced around the room, no longer wanting to be there. "You know that when a man tells you exactly what you want to hear . . . it's probably bullshit."

"I think I told you that."

"You did."

Lori motioned for the door. "Do you want to leave?"

"Absolutely."

⤳

When The Cat's Away!

That was the headline, and once again Shannon found herself on the front page of several magazines, from obvious gossip columns to political satire on the pages of the local newspaper.

This smacked of a setup.

She wanted to call Paul out, give him a piece of her mind. She hadn't seen the photographers at the event but should have smelled them the second Paul moved her to a private corner.

In all the years since her divorce, she'd never truly gotten angry with the man, but that ended the moment her e-mail flooded with Google alerts with her name in the search engine.

"Is he that big of an asshole?" Avery asked when she called early in the morning.

"I didn't used to think so."

"Is there a chance he doesn't know anything about the photographers?"

"Slim to none. He needs people to think he's trying to mend things with me. Righting his past so he can get re-elected. I bet his rating goes up in the polls by the end of the week."

"Asshole," Avery said under her breath. "Has Victor seen these yet?"

"I doubt it. He's flying back today, probably in the air right now." She glanced at a clock and tried to calculate the time he said he was leaving to the current time in China . . . it all jumbled in her head.

"Some of those pictures look really convincing. If I didn't know you, I'd think the tabloids got this one right."

"They didn't. I told him goodbye and I meant it. Finally."

"Lori told me he said he was going to fight for you."

Shannon glanced around her kitchen. "I don't see bouquets of flowers or half a dozen messages of his love flooding in."

"Delete the messages and throw away the flowers."

"That's my intention." Not that she thought they were coming.

Only a couple of hours later, she would have lost the bet.

A dozen red roses arrived at her door with a simple note.

I miss you.

It wasn't signed.

Angry that he would even try, Shannon marched out to the full trash bin in her driveway, put the flowers on top of the pile, and went about her day.

~9~

After a twelve-hour flight, made longer because of delays both leaving China and arriving in Los Angeles, Victor felt like the walking dead. Much as he wanted to surprise Shannon with a midnight call, he fell into bed after a much-needed shower and didn't wake until ten the next day.

When he did, there was a stack of magazines and newspapers on his doorstep. They were tied in a big purple bow with a handwritten note.

She doesn't love you!

Victor spread the papers on his dining room table and looked at the pictures.

He had to be missing something.

Shannon and her ex-husband looked as if they were rekindling a flame.

Something didn't feel right. He looked at his calls and didn't see her number in the log.

A message from his brother saying "Call me" caught his attention.

"Hey, Vic," Justin said, picking up on the second ring.

"Is everything okay?"

"I was about to ask you the same thing."

Victor could hear the busy noise of a machine shop in the background.

"I flew in last night." He glanced at the tabloid on his table, closed his eyes, and shook his head.

"I thought as much. Hold on . . ."

Victor heard the noise in the background start to fade and then go away altogether. "I couldn't hear you."

"That's better."

"I wanted to see how you were doing."

Victor scratched his head. "I'm fine."

"And Shannon? Are you guys okay?"

Okay, none of this was in Justin's normal conversation. "I think we're fine." He thought of the papers, purposely put space between him and the images of Shannon and her ex.

"I'm not one to pry, but Mom called me, said she saw Shannon in a newspaper at the grocery store. Have you seen it?"

The reason for the call cleared in his head. He sighed. "Yeah." He picked up the handwritten note that was left with the papers. *She doesn't love you.* "I don't know what's going on. I haven't talked to Shannon yet."

Justin paused. "Are you going to be okay?"

"You think the papers are telling the truth?"

"I think you jumped in really fast after Corrie."

Victor ran his hand through his hair, suddenly more nervous than he had been before calling his brother back. "It's probably bullshit."

"And if it isn't?"

His heart fell into the pit of his stomach with the thought. "She and her ex were a long time ago."

"Looks like they saw each other while you were in China. At a political fundraiser. That couldn't have been an accident."

No denying that.

"Listen," Justin said. "I don't want to add to your stress, I just wanted to tell you I'm here if you wanna talk, or get drunk, or whatever. Twice in one year is a lot for anyone."

"Yeah . . . okay." This was not happening again.

"Love you, bro."

"Yeah. Love you, too." He hung up.

Instead of picking up the phone and calling Shannon, he dressed and went straight to her house.

He pounded on her door and called her name. When she didn't answer, he glanced through the front window.

Nothing.

His palms started to sweat.

Oh, who was he kidding? His heart rate had soared the second he'd seen the pictures, elevated even more with Justin's phone call, and now might need some serious drugs to find a normal pace.

He started to dial her number before he noticed the trash at the end of her driveway.

The roses he'd sent her sat on top of the garbage.

His step faltered.

Something inside of him started to chisel away and break.

This was not okay. Not again. Not with Shannon. Was he so easy to leave, to forget?

He finished dialing her number.

"You've reached Shannon, please leave a message and I'll get back to you."

Hearing her voice made his heart shatter.

He didn't bother with a message.

He wished now he'd put her on Friend Finder so he knew exactly where she was. Only the thought hadn't occurred to him.

It was Sunday morning . . . afternoon. He'd forgotten to set his watch to the current time. The last time they spoke she was excited about the loft, so that's where he headed.

Victor tried to calm down, talk the caveman off the ledge. He was still half-dead from flying and cautioned himself against jumping to conclusions. But damn if he was going to ignore the pictures he'd found. Maybe Justin was right. Maybe he was jumping too fast with Shannon. What if she wasn't over her ex?

His stomach wanted to erupt.

Worse, his heart started to break.

If she was walking away, she'd have to do so face-to-face. No running away! Not this time.

He violated several speeding laws in his haste to drive to her loft and even parked in a red zone when he couldn't get into the tenant garage.

He heard music from inside before he knocked on the door.

When she didn't answer, he let himself in.

Shannon was on her hands and knees, her arms reaching out in front of her as she worked a worn spot of the floor with a sponge. The simplicity of what she was doing was lost with the feeling that his world was changing with every breath.

"Hello," he said from behind.

She jumped, turned his way, and dropped her head. "God, you scared the hell out of me."

She was beautiful, even with dirt smudged on her forehead. "Sorry. You didn't answer the door."

It took her a second to get to her feet. She turned to him, took one step, and then froze. "What's wrong?"

What's wrong? She couldn't be that clueless. "You don't know?"

She blew out a breath. "Hold on." She moved to the blaring radio and turned it off.

The room plunged into silence.

Shannon looked at him again. Paused. Anything that looked like a smile fell from her face. "You read the papers."

He nodded. "Yeah. *All* of them."

She started to smile and stopped. "You believe 'em." She wasn't asking a question.

"Tell me they're wrong."

"Of course they're wrong. How could you think for a minute they weren't?"

He pulled the picture that was the most convincing out from the inside pocket of his jacket. "Explain this."

She took the picture from his fingers, handed it back. "Explain what, Victor? That a photographer took a picture, out of context, wrote a bunch of lies, and splattered it everywhere? Is that what you need to hear?"

He ticked off the facts that couldn't be denied. "You went to a political fundraiser."

"Lori asked me to go. Reed hates those things."

"Where Paul was going."

"I didn't know he was on the guest list." She placed both hands on her hips. "As if I need to explain this to you."

He looked at the photo again, winced at how intimate it appeared. "He's touching your face, Shannon. Is that photoshopped?"

She turned her back to him, her chest rising and falling rapidly. "I was telling him goodbye, Victor."

He ran his hands through his hair. "I thought you did that years ago."

"Divorce doesn't always mean you stop caring for someone. He needed to hear it again."

Victor stood back. "You still love the man."

"*Loved* . . . past tense. But if you need me to spell that out for you, maybe I was wrong about us."

"All this posturing about me taking time to get over Corrie, and it was you needing time to get over Paul."

Shannon turned in a circle, put space between them. "This is a ridiculous argument."

"I went to your house."

"So?" She was pissed. How was she the one upset when it was him getting screwed?

"You threw away my flowers."

Her jaw dropped. "I thought they were from him."

It was Victor's turn to pace the room. "He's sending you flowers?"

Her hands flew in the air. "You went through my trash?"

"They were on top of your trash."

She walked past him and to the front door. "Enough. Get out. You either trust me or you don't. And obviously, you don't."

Some of his fire started to turn to smoke. "Shannon . . ."

She shook her head vehemently. "No. Go. I can't." She opened the door wide and pushed him through.

When he had to back up to keep the door from slamming in his face, he realized his mistake.

He knocked, heard the click of a lock sliding into place followed by her music being turned on and the volume placed on high.

Shit!

Chapter Thirty-One

Shannon paced the loft, clearly heard Victor trying to talk to her through the door. How could he believe anything the papers said?

When it was obvious that he'd left, she slid down the wall and stared at the bucket and sponge that had occupied her morning.

She'd seriously miscalculated the man, and all for what? She'd promised herself years ago to never let a man make her cry again, and here she was, sitting in the middle of her brand-new loft with tears running down her cheeks.

Runaway emotions were the worst.

Her phone rang.

She glanced at the screen, expecting to see Victor's image pop up. She'd taken a few snapshots during their time in Tulum and had attached one to his number . . . only it wasn't him.

She picked up the call. "What do you want, Paul?"

"Hello, beautiful."

She scrambled to her feet, turned off the music. "Stop. You have no right to call me that anymore."

"I want to take you to dinner . . . so we can talk."

"No. Paul, stop. Okay. Just stop."

"You saw the papers."

"Of course I saw the papers. Everyone saw the papers. Which is what you wanted, isn't it?"

The fact he didn't immediately deny her accusation told her what she wanted to know.

"I want you back."

The teeth in the back of her mouth started to strain under the pressure of her clenched jaw. "You *need* me back. It isn't the same as want, so be honest with yourself. Your campaign manager is probably waiting for your call to tell him I'm on the hook."

"You weren't like this when we were married, Shannon. Victor Brooks isn't good for you."

Hearing Victor's name roll off Paul's tongue was like ice on a bad tooth. "You know nothing about Victor."

"He's a garbage man, Shannon. Takes trash from others and sells it abroad. You deserve better."

"How dare you."

"I'm sorry. That was out of line. You belong in cocktail parties and diamonds, the life we had together."

"Had, Paul. And it was all a facade."

"You wanted it to last," he pointed out.

"At one time, yes. But we've been over this. I'm finally over you. And if you think selling pictures to the tabloids was the way to win me back, you'd be wrong. All it did was point out the kind of man you are. You used me to get what you wanted the first time. I won't fall for it a second time."

"You signed the Alliance contract just like me. Who is the one pretending now?"

"I said goodbye last night. I meant it."

She heard him take a breath. "Fine." His voice changed. "What will it take?"

She pinched her brows together. "What do you mean?"

"Six million was your price the last time. How much do you want now? Double?"

The knot in her throat stuck.

"Fifteen?" he asked. "Name your price."

"You make me sick."

"Will twenty million make you less ill?"

"Fuck you, Paul." Any feelings she'd had for the man disappeared with his proposition.

She hung up.

Her phone immediately rang again. This time it was her mother.

"Good Lord, now what?"

Drying her eyes with the back of her hand, she faced her mother's call because ignoring it would bring twice the pain. "Hello."

"Shannon, honey, how are you?"

Shannon, honey, was always a bad sign. "I'm fine, Mom. What's up?"

"I'm calling to make sure we're still on for your birthday dinner."

Birthday dinner? Good God, she'd been so busy and preoccupied with the loft, Victor . . . the stitches that still pained her with every step, she'd forgotten about her birthday the next day.

"I don't know, can we postpone that?"

"I'm not sure how one can postpone their birthdays. If I knew how, I would have years ago."

Shannon tried to keep the tears from falling. "I'm having a bad week."

"I can help make it better. Paul called and asked if he could join us."

Shannon bounced back. "He what? When?"

"He called a couple of hours ago. I saw the paper, honey. I can't tell you how hopeful your father and I are about a possible reunion. Why didn't you tell me?"

"Mom . . . there is no reunion."

"Paul made it sound as if there was."

"Paul is full of shit."

"Shannon!" her mother scolded her.

"No, Mom. Cancel the dinner. I won't be there. If Paul calls, tell him to revisit our last conversation."

"Honey, please."

"Mom . . . listen to me carefully. I love you. I love Dad. Thank you for wanting to celebrate my birthday with me, but not this year. I have other plans." Like slipping away to sulk in peace.

"I'm so disappointed."

"I am, too." And she hung up.

Pent up energy had her scrubbing the floor harder. Calls came through, but she didn't answer any of them. Victor, Lori, Avery . . . even Trina.

She got the feeling that if she didn't leave the loft soon, they would all descend upon her like locusts. In the bathroom, she washed her face and swept her hair back into a ponytail. Dark glasses, in case some camera-toting asshole was outside trying to capture more pictures.

In her car, her phone rang again.

Unknown caller.

"Hello!" Her greeting was an accusation. When no one started talking, Shannon's anger spiked again. Paul would say something. "Hello?"

Nothing.

There was only one person she knew young enough to be the heavy breather on the phone. "I know who this is. You aren't fooling anyone, Corrie. Why don't you try growing up?" Shannon disconnected the call.

It rang again.

She punched the answer button, felt her heart slamming against her chest. "Grow the fuck up!"

"Whoa . . . whoa . . . Shannon?"

Familiar voice . . . not Corrie. "Who is this?"

"It's Angie."

Shannon rested her head against the steering wheel and blew out a breath. "Oh, Angie, I'm sorry."

"Phew . . . hello, big sister. This is Shannon, right?"

"It is. I'm sorry. I'm having a really crappy day."

"Apparently. I don't think I've ever heard an f-bomb fly out of your mouth."

They didn't come often. "Today is that kind of day."

"That sucks, and on your birthday."

"That's tomorrow . . . apparently." She really had forgotten.

"Oh, yeah. I guess I should have figured that out. I got your message last month and started feeling guilty for ignoring it."

That was nice to hear. "Why did you?"

"Selfish reasons. But I don't want to add to your bad day. I wanted to call and wish you a happy birthday and tell you I love you."

Okay . . . tears were starting to fall again.

This was getting ridiculous. "I love you, sis. I miss the hell out of you."

"You should come visit me sometime. With all those millions, it isn't like you can't afford a ticket."

Which was true. "I have to know where you are before I book a plane ticket."

"I'm in Barcelona. I thought you knew."

"Barcelona? I thought you were teaching English for the Peace Corps somewhere remote."

Angie laughed. "That was, like, five years ago."

"Mom said . . ."

"Mom says a lot of things. I've been in Barcelona for three years. Still teaching English, but not to indigenous people. I could only volunteer for so long before I realized I needed to make my own income."

"We have so much to catch up on." She thought of Victor, Paul . . . her new friends and new direction in life.

Victor.

"Are you serious about me visiting?" Shannon asked as she switched the engine over in her car.

"Of course."

"How does tomorrow sound?"

"Are you serious?"

"Great, what's your address?"

"You're for real?"

"I told you I was having a bad day. You just made it better. Give me your address, Angie. If you can't clear your schedule, that's fine. I just need to get away, and seeing you sounds exactly like what I need right now."

Three hours later, Shannon was boarding a plane with clothes she'd shoved in a bag to avoid lingering at her house and being cornered by anyone.

She sent a group text to her friends.

> I'm not pulling an Avery . . . or a Trina . . . Okay, maybe I am. I'm going to visit my sister. I will text the location later. Wouldn't want the freaking media hacking my messages and following me. And Lori, tell Paul to back off. Remind him of what he signed way back when. I need to clear my head. Love you all, Shannon.

And she turned her phone off. Which was how it would stay until she wanted to pop back up on the radar. Between Friend Finder apps and her supersleuthy friends, Shannon was bound to find someone on the other end of the plane ride aside from her sister.

Lori found Shannon's text the second she was out of the courtroom and walking to her car. Before she could read it all, Avery was calling. "What the hell?"

"Did you talk to her?"

"No. Did you?"

"No." She picked up her pace, opened her car door, and tossed her briefcase into the passenger seat.

"Isn't her sister in Africa or something?"

"Or something. Has Trina heard from her?"

"No, Trina called me," Avery said.

Lori turned the car over, looked out her rearview mirror. "I'm calling Paul, you try Victor. Something must have gone down."

"I'm on it."

Avery hung up.

Before Lori called Paul, she contacted her husband.

"Hey, honey, how was court?" Reed asked before she had a chance to say hi.

"I need you to find Shannon's sister."

"Excuse me?"

"Angie . . . Redding, I think. I don't believe she ever married. She was in the Peace Corps last time I heard anything about her."

Reed cleared his throat. "Do you want to tell me what this is all about?"

"Yes, later."

"Can't you just ask Shannon?"

Lori rolled her eyes, pulled out of the parking space. "If only it was that easy."

She hung up before Reed asked more questions and then dialed the number she had for Paul. For five minutes she was given the runaround before he finally got on the line.

"Hello, Lori."

"What did you do?"

"Excuse me?"

"Don't play coy with me, Paul. You said or did something to Shannon. Fess up."

He was silent.

Lori waited and gripped the steering wheel to keep her mouth from opening and screaming at the man.

"I asked her to come back."

"And when she told you no?" *Please, please, Shannon, tell me you said no.*

"I offered her another contract."

It was a very good thing Lori was at a stoplight. "I'm going to play lawyer here for a minute . . . Are you listening, Paul?"

He was silent.

"Your contract specifically stated that any continuation or changes or anything in regard to Alliance has got to go through us first. You're in direct violation just bringing the subject up without consulting us first. Do you understand that? Or have you forgotten everything you learned in law school?"

"Yes, Counselor."

Good! The man could understand basic English.

"Now that we have that out of the way . . . Are you that big of a moron?"

The light turned green, and she shifted her car around a slow driver and hit the gas. "I understood you were a player when you signed on to Alliance, the risks were spelled out to Shannon, but you changed the rules when you filled her with hope that you were both more than temporary—"

Paul started to interrupt.

Lori didn't let him. "You didn't love her, fine. But you knew damn well she loved you, and you worked that for all it was worth. Now that Shannon is finally over you, you try and drag her back? That makes you a special kind of douchebag, Paul."

"I'm glad you're being diplomatic about this, Lori."

"Oh, I'm not being diplomatic. I'm being a friend who is pissed off."

"Fine. Now that your tantrum is out of the way—"

"My tantrum hasn't even started."

"I want to hire Alliance again."

She laughed. "Not in this lifetime."

"One good reason why . . . and don't say *Shannon*."

Lori sucked in a breath. "Alliance as you knew it no longer exists. In fact, it was someone searching for the truth behind your marriage to Shannon that helped shape our new business model. If you remember right, you and I had a conversation about this two years ago." The fact that Lori's now husband, Reed, was the private investigator searching for dirt on Paul's hands was left unsaid. "Having you as a client a second time would be entirely too risky."

"I forgot all about that," Paul said with a sigh. Maybe she was finally getting through to him.

"Why don't you find a wife the old-fashioned way? Leave Shannon and Alliance out of it."

"I'll consider your advice."

"Good. You do that."

"I never meant to hurt her, Lori."

She wanted to believe him. "If that's true, then leave her alone now."

"I'll let you extend my apologies, then."

"I'll do that. Goodbye, Paul."

"What did you do?"

Victor stood behind his desk when Stephanie escorted Avery into his office the next morning.

"Hello, Avery."

Stephanie ducked out of the room, but if Victor was laying bets, he'd place one on her standing close to the door to overhear the conversation.

"I swear to God, Victor, if I find out you were playing her, I will kick your ass."

The term Wade used for Avery, *the blonde pit bull*, flashed in his head.

He looked at the small baby bump that was just starting to pop out.

Pregnant blonde pit bull.

He decided the desk between them was probably a good thing.

"We had a fight. I'll make it up to her." He was giving her some space since she wouldn't take his phone calls.

Avery took a step forward, placed both hands on his desk. "And how do you plan on doing that when she's left the country?"

Victor was vaguely aware he was staring. "She what?"

"Africa, or Brazil . . . someplace that probably doesn't have running water. What did you do?"

His head was racing. "Slow down. What are you talking about?"

"She went to her sister's . . . who is some tree-hugging do-gooder living in a hut somewhere. Does that sound like something Shannon would be good at?"

He started to answer and Avery cut him off. "No. She isn't. She's fragile and delicate and needs protection. And you did something, so give it up. What was it?"

The emotional roller coaster that was Avery standing in front of him was something that needed a careful hand.

"I believed the newspapers."

"You . . . you what?"

"About her ex-husband."

Avery gasped. "Paul orchestrated the whole thing. How could you be so stupid?"

Yeah, he'd asked himself that question for the past twenty-four hours. "Jet lag?"

Avery tossed her hands in the air. "Great! That's just great. Shannon finally breaks her sexual sabbatical for a man who doesn't trust her any farther than he can throw her."

He'd ask about the sabbatical later, right now he wanted to know more about Africa. "She's in Africa?"

"I don't know where she is. No one knows where she is. She ran off. Do you know how unlike Shannon that is? Me, yes . . . Trina, check. We're the runners. Shannon is the rock. She never runs. She thinks and considers her options in quiet silence. Until you." Avery blew out a breath and rubbed her stomach.

Victor suddenly felt the pull of his protective male sex. "Avery, please calm down."

She snapped her head his way.

He warded her off with a display of his palms. "This can't be good for your baby. I know you're upset, I get it. I'll fix it. I promise I will. But if something happens to you, Shannon is never going to give me the chance."

Avery took a couple of steps, turned, and sat in the chair.

He waited for her to take a few breaths before he sat opposite her and spoke as calmly as he could.

"How can we find out where Shannon's sister lives?"

"Reed is working on it." Avery opened her eyes, which sparkled with unshed tears. He hated to see a woman cry. "Did you know that today is Shannon's birthday?"

Victor frowned. "No." That was something he should have known.

Avery nodded. "What a mess she must be. Between last week, the papers . . . you . . . her birthday."

Victor stopped trying to pick apart the fact that he didn't realize today was Shannon's birthday and analyzed Avery's words. "What was last week?"

"Corrie vandalizing her house. A late night visit to the ER . . . ," Avery said as if he should have known what she was talking about.

"Whoa, back up. Corrie did what?"

"She wasn't positive it was Corrie, but yeah, she was pretty sure."

It was Victor's turn to feel his blood pressure rise. "Can you start at the beginning? I don't know anything about this."

When Avery completed the tale of rocks, windows, and stitches, Victor turned hard. No wonder Shannon was so upset and unreasonable when he'd asked her for an explanation. Here she was, trying to save his worries by keeping the situation away from him while he was away on work and unable to do anything about it, and here he was . . . not trusting her.

Such an asshole.

"She was even going back on the pill for you. Do you know that?" Avery was in tears now. "For over a year she's been talking about how much she wants a baby, and then you come along and she's like, 'No, can't risk an accident and him running away.'" Avery looked at her stomach. "I told her it wasn't all that. Emotions all over the place, the need to pee all the time. And the morning sickness. Such a mess."

"Did you drive here?" he asked.

She grabbed a tissue from his desk, blew her nose with a nod.

He pulled his cell phone from his pocket and dialed Liam's number. "Let me get you a ride home."

As soon as Liam tucked his wife into his car, Victor called Reed.

Chapter Thirty-Two

Shannon pushed her toes into the sand of the Mediterranean waters. Her sister sat by her side, a blanket covering their shoulders. She'd forgotten how alike the two of them were. Angie had put on a few pounds and her hair was shorter than Shannon remembered, but she was the same.

When Shannon arrived in Spain, she crashed on Angie's couch for six hours. Now it was dusk, her birthday almost a memory, and the two of them watched the sunset.

Shannon explained the past few months of her life and Angie listened.

"Why did you marry Paul?" Angie finally asked when Shannon had run out of words.

She studied her pink toes, realized she was in need of a pedicure. "Money," she finally revealed.

Angie blew out a breath.

"Freedom, a way out from under Mom and Dad."

Angie looked away.

"Don't look so shocked. It wasn't a lot different from what you did."

"How can you say that?" Angie asked.

"You ran away, found a cause . . . to escape them. Tell me I'm wrong and I'll believe you."

Angie shrugged but didn't deny her.

"I wasn't that brave. I finished college with a major they approved of and set out to follow the photographer dreams I'd envisioned while in school. Maybe I would have found success if I was also a journalist or spent my summers as an intern for the paper. But I didn't, and the back room studio I started barely put food on my plate. Mom and Dad refused to help, and I'm not afraid to say that when it comes to my life skills and living on next to nothing, I'm ill prepared."

"So you sold out." For once, Angie didn't sound as if she were accusing her of a deadly sin. More like acceptance.

"I did. I sought after a solution that would give me the financial freedom I needed at the same time I would make Mom and Dad proud. The difference was, I knew my marriage would end in divorce."

Angie pulled away, stared at her. "You played him?"

Shannon shook her head. "God, no. I don't think I would even know how to do that. It was an arrangement. His idea, actually. Two years, a quiet divorce . . . I got the money, and with a wife at his side, Paul won the seat as governor."

Angie shoved her shoulder with her own. "Holy cow, Shannon. That's brilliant."

"Yeah, but then I went and fell in love with the bastard. Not so brilliant. I've spent the first half of my thirties pining for a man I can't have, and now that I find one I can, he doesn't trust me."

"Does Victor know about your marriage with Paul? The truth about it, I mean?"

"Not completely. I've hinted. I've been open with him about everything else. The details of why Paul and I married are irrelevant."

"If Victor thinks you're still in love with your ex, then your previous husband would be a pretty big obstacle."

"I told him it was over. I meant that. And Victor chose to listen to the lies of the newspapers instead of coming to me first. He doesn't trust

me, Angie." And where were they if there wasn't trust? On different sides
of the planet, that's where.

Angie leaned her head against Shannon's shoulder. "Don't you
think you might be overreacting just a little?"

"Have you ever been in love?" Shannon asked.

"Yeah."

"And when it ended, how did you feel?"

"Like my world was over."

"Exactly."

They sat in silence for a little while. "The world is still here, you
know."

Shannon leaned against her sister. "I know. But I'm going to ignore
it for a little while. Don't worry, I won't take up residency on your
couch forever. I need to adjust my lens and make things come into
focus again."

Angie nudged her. "Will a stupid amount of tequila help?"

Shannon laughed. "Maybe not a stupid amount, but I think a
couple of shots might be in order."

Angie pushed to her feet and reached out for Shannon to follow.
"I know the perfect place where birthday shots are always on the
house."

"Tequila . . . I have a feeling this might not end well."

Angie laughed. "I'll take care of you. I owe you."

Shannon brushed sand off her butt once she stood. "How do you
figure that?"

"Mom and Dad picked on you when I ran off. You took on the
burden of pleasing them, and I skipped that altogether."

"You were the rebel, I was the peacemaker. It's just how we're wired."

Angie shook her head. "No, I acted like a child and you acted like
the adult. I'm not sure either of us were right, but there is no changing
it now."

Shannon hugged her sister. "Lead the way to my birthday shots, little sister."

They turned toward the path that would take them back to Angie's apartment and stopped.

A woman stood leaning against the wall that divided the beach access from the parking lot above.

She wore a wide-brimmed hat, a long coat, boots, and dark sunglasses.

Sasha.

"Do you know her?" Angie asked.

Shannon nodded. "Yeah. I do. Can you give me a few minutes?"

Her sister moved to the path leading home and stood by, waiting.

"That didn't take long," Shannon said to Sasha, a woman who worked alongside Reed in matters of security and finding people.

"You weren't trying hard to hide." Her thick accent, a mix of Russian and German, cut as much as her stare.

"It's silly that they sent you."

"*They* didn't. Trina is pregnant and upset. So I came." Sasha was Trina's sister-in-law from her first husband. And even though the woman pretended she couldn't care less about everyone around her, it was obvious by her actions that she was a walking contradiction.

Guilt rolled in Shannon's stomach. "I didn't think—"

"No. You didn't." She pushed off the wall. "Call her, or I will."

Shannon turned to her sister, and when she looked back, Sasha was walking away.

Before they hit the bar, Shannon called each of her friends individually, told them she was in Spain and that she was fine.

No, she didn't want to talk about it.

Yes, she was about to get drunk with her sister.

And when she learned that Victor was looking for her, she asked that they keep her location to themselves for now. She needed to figure out where the man fit in her life, *if* he fit in her life.

Victor sat in Shannon's living room, his knee bouncing as he glared at the boarded up window.

It was two in the morning.

He wasn't leaving until he talked to her. Logically, he knew she wasn't coming home that night, but that didn't stop him taking up space in her home.

And if Corrie returned to do something stupid a second time, he'd catch her in the act.

Besides, he'd told Reed where to find him once he found out where Shannon had run off to.

Such an idiot.

His phone rang. The sound startled him.

"Reed?" he asked, recognizing the number.

"You're still there?"

"What kind of question is that? Yes, I'm still here. Have you heard anything?"

"She's fine, Victor."

He released a long breath. "Where is she?"

Reed hesitated. "In a civilized place, doing civilized things."

The answer pissed Victor off. "What the hell does that mean?"

"It means she's not in a hut contracting malaria."

"Elaborate."

"Dude, I like my balls where they are. My wife and I have an understanding."

"And I respect that. Now tell me where she is."

"Victor . . ."

"We're talking about the woman I love. I made her angry and she ran off. Do you know how it feels to be shut out?" He was yelling. "I know it's my fault, but I can't make it right without seeing her."

For a second Victor thought maybe Reed hung up the phone.

"Her sister's name is Angie Redding. Barcelona, Spain. You didn't hear it from me."

Victor smiled, grabbed his coat. "I owe you."

"If I'm singing soprano the next time I see you, you'll know why."

Victor hung up the phone and headed toward the airport.

~~

"Shannon?"

Angie called her from the front of the apartment. When Shannon walked around the corner from the kitchen, she noticed her sister leaning with one hand against the frame of the front door, staring into the hall.

Shannon walked up beside her and looked over her shoulder.

"Does this one belong to you?"

Victor was fast asleep, his head propped up against the corner of an adjacent apartment, his tie gone, his suit looking like he'd been sleeping in it for days.

"Yeah," Shannon said.

"Let me guess, Victor?"

One of her friends had ratted her out.

Or maybe it was Sasha.

That was more likely.

Shannon turned back to the room.

"It's kinda sweet that he flew all this way."

She turned around, watched his even breathing a few minutes longer.

"Are you just going to leave him there?" Angie asked.

"I'm considering it."

"Does he speak Spanish?"

"I don't think so."

Angie motioned toward apartment number 305. "Mrs. Hernandez always comes out around nine to walk her dog. Dogs barking and a woman screaming in Spanish is quite the sight to wake up to."

"Might be worth it."

Angie started to shut the door. "Your call."

"Wait."

Angie grinned.

She wasn't up to this. Their morning had been a little slow, taking into account the amount of drinking they'd done the night before. Angie had reminded her that she was only thirty-five and had a whole life to find the right man. By the end of the night, Shannon was promising to return to Spain every year to listen to her wiser, younger sister.

Right now Shannon needed to deal with the one passed out in the hall.

Using her right foot, Shannon nudged Victor's shoe twice.

He didn't budge.

She pushed it again.

Nothing.

His chest rose and fell. So, not dead.

Just kinda dead to the world.

She pushed the side of his leg, the second time a little harder, and she called his name. "Victor."

He jumped as if the hounds of hell were waking him from death. "Shannon!" He called her name before his eyes came into focus.

Victor scurried to his feet and wiped his lips with the back of his hand. He looked between the two of them. "You didn't tell me you were twins."

"We're not," Angie told him. "I'm a year and a half younger."

They both moved away from the doorway.

Angie looked at her. "I'll be in the kitchen. Yell if you need me."

Shannon gave her sister a smile, thankful she was there.

Victor stumbled through the door, running a hand through his hair. The five o'clock shadow on his face looked a little more like a full weekend of stubble. "Can I use the bathroom?" he asked.

Shannon motioned for the door where the washroom was and used the time he was in there to collect her thoughts.

Let him say his piece and then move him on his way.

He returned from the bathroom looking like he'd run a wet comb through his hair. His eyes were a little more focused, and some of the color had returned to his face.

"Thank you for not turning me away," he said once he took the seat opposite her.

"I considered it."

He paused, picked his words carefully, from what she could tell.

"I screwed up."

"Yeah, you did."

"I'm sorry. I could tell you I had been up for hours, that my emotions were shot, wondering what would happen if the tabloids told the truth . . . but all that would be making an excuse when I really don't have one."

Shannon felt some of her anger dissipating with his words.

"I trust you, I do. I know I didn't show that with how I reacted, but believe me, I do."

"A trusting man wouldn't have behaved that way."

"It's Paul I don't trust. I know I'm not the biggest catch out there. That your ex shares your past, and that you might just want him back."

"I don't want him." With all certainty, Shannon knew her life with Paul was over and not worth repeating.

"I know that now. I do. Please hear me out. I realized, with all my time alone circling the globe the last few days, that your single status since your divorce means that the break between you and him really hurt you. The fact that you made it clear that you weren't a person I could play and get away with it . . . your defensiveness when we first met . . . all of that fueled my head, and my imagination ran with it. I told you I was going caveman. I'm not proud of it, but I can't seem to stop myself when it comes to you."

"Even the caveman needs to trust when he's out hunting, Victor."

"I have never been a jealous person. Not with Corrie, not with anyone. Until you. The thought of you leaving scared the crap out of me. And then you did it. This has been the longest three days of my life."

She could relate to that.

"I love you, Shannon. And I will do *anything* to make it up to you."

Hearing him utter that four-letter word was music to her ears. She cautioned herself. "When a man tells you what you want to hear . . ."

"I'm not giving you a line." He leaned forward, rested his arms on his knees. "When Corrie left me standing alone like a groom on top of a cake, all I could think of was . . . *well, that's over*. I didn't chase her down and force her to hear me. But I'm here, Shannon, and I'm going to force you to hear me. I love you! I want you in my life, my world . . . my arms. I'm going to make mistakes and screw up, but I hope you care enough about me to find forgiveness and a second chance. I've been an asshole all my life, and sometimes I fall back on those habits. I need you to ground me."

He reached out and took her hand in his.

She searched his eyes and found them welled with unshed tears.

A lump that had formed in her throat sat like a rock in a stream that air needed to flow around. Her breath sounded like a choking engine. "Letting you in has been the most daring thing I've done in five years. You have the power to devastate me."

He took both her hands, squeezed them hard. "I won't. With God as my witness, I will never be that man. I can't stop you from walking away, but it won't be my back you see leaving." He leaned forward, rested his head on their joined hands.

Shannon's hands started to shake, the decision to risk pain for the love he offered or go on living in the world alone . . .

She removed one of her hands from his and placed her palm on the side of Victor's face.

Slowly he looked up at her. "The problem with loving someone is that even if you walk away, the love is still there."

"Don't walk away."

A single tear fell from her eye. "I love you."

He captured her hand against his face, pushed into it, and closed his eyes. "Say that again."

"I love you, Victor."

He opened his eyes, took her face in his hands, and brought her lips over to his. Their kiss was salty with her tears and sweet with their hearts.

He broke their kiss to pull her into his arms; his steel embrace locked her in the moment.

"Don't ever leave me," he whispered.

"Always give me a reason to stay."

He stood, taking her to her feet with him. "I'm going to give you my name, my life, my family. I'm going to give you all the babies you want. I'm going to shackle you with all the reasons I can."

Shannon shook her head, placed a finger over his lips. "All I need is your love."

"You already have that."

The world shifted and fell into place. "We're doing this."

He nodded. "If you ask me, it's already done."

And he kissed her one more time.

Epilogue

One Year Later

The playroom in Shannon and Victor's new home took up the entire basement.

Playpens were set up and being used as cribs for Lilliana—or Lilly, as Wade and Trina called their eight-month-old daughter—and Max, Avery and Liam's nine-month-old son.

Some of Shannon's recent photographs peppered the walls of the room.

Lori half sat, half lay on the plush sofa, her belly propped up on a pillow.

"How is that sciatica?" Trina asked as she handed her a wineglass full of milk.

"Great if I don't lay on my right side. I swear these kids are killing me already, and they're not even out yet. Good thing there are two of them, because I'm not doing this again." Lori and Reed had visited a fertility clinic when their attempts to get pregnant without it failed.

"That's what you say now," Trina said. "You'll change your mind."

Lori massaged her right hip and flexed her leg. "I don't think so."

Shannon eased herself into the rocking chair Trina had just left after feeding Lilly and putting her down for a nap. Simon, her unborn son, kicked a rib before he started dancing on her bladder. "Victor and I are waiting a year and then doing it again. Back-to-back . . . all the diapers at once."

Avery tipped her wineglass in the air. "I can drink to that."

Shannon toasted with sparkling water, regretted it when she realized she would have to vacate her comfortable seat to use the bathroom . . . again. "I just realized that the last time I had alcohol was at my wedding." A small ceremony that had taken place during their First Wives meeting at Trina and Wade's ranch in Texas. With two of her best friends heavy in their pregnancies, Lori stood beside Shannon, and Justin took his place beside Victor.

The memory of Victor's face when she'd walked around the corner and up the small path to exchange vows with her husband was etched in her brain forever.

They both cried, which got Trina and Avery going, and before you knew it there were sniffles rising up like a chorus from those who watched.

Angie had flown in with the promise of returning after Simon was born.

Paul announced an engagement shortly after the papers grew bored with Shannon and Victor. His future wife was young. Not Corrie young, but at least a decade separated them in age. Shannon couldn't help but wonder if he'd found another woman to fake forever with. She was just exceptionally happy that person was no longer her.

And Corrie, she got a visit from Reed with a list of crimes he would see she was charged with if she approached Shannon again. Seems that was all it took, because Corrie stopped coming around.

"That's what happens when you get pregnant on your honeymoon."

Shannon shifted positions in an effort to get comfortable. The task was useless this close to her delivery date. She gave up and stood. "I have to pee again."

Trina and Avery laughed.

"I don't miss that," Avery said.

Shannon left them alone with their conversation about Kegel exercises.

"Okay, Simon . . ." Shannon spoke to her son once they were alone. "I need you to give Mom a little break." A pull along her back told her that was wishful thinking. When she stood from the toilet and looked down, she realized her blissful night of relaxing would have to wait.

She blew out a breath and looked at herself in the mirror. She used the brush to pull her hair back, tied it in a loose knot, and applied a little lip gloss.

"Let's do this," she said to herself with a smile.

She emerged from the bathroom and walked past her friends to the stairs.

"Going somewhere?" Lori asked as she walked by.

"My water just broke."

Avery jumped to her feet.

Lori set her glass down and rolled off the couch.

Trina was already up the stairs.

"You have hours, you know that, right?" Avery asked after giving her a hug.

"Yeah, but I'm older than you, and the doctor wanted me at the hospital if my water broke before labor set in." And from the cramping in her back, she wasn't entirely sure she hadn't been in labor most of the day.

Several sets of feet trampled down the stairs, Victor's leading the pack.

Her husband jumped the last two steps and grasped her arm. "It's time? Really?"

She winced through a cramp, blew out a breath. "Yup . . . pretty sure I didn't just pee my pants."

Wade stood beside them and made a *whoo hoo* sound.

Trina and Avery shushed him and pointed to the sleeping children.

Liam kissed Avery's cheek. "I'm driving."

"I can manage," Victor said as he started the slow ascent up the stairs.

"Oh, no. Liam almost crashed on the way to the hospital with me. Trust me, Victor . . . you just sit in the back seat with Shannon."

"We'll meet you there in a couple of hours," Wade said with a wink. "I'll chill the champagne."

～⑤

Ten hours later, Shannon held Simon to her chest with Victor at her side.

She couldn't stop crying. "Look what we made," she quietly said to her husband.

Victor's big hand brushed back his son's puff of hair, all clean after the nurses returned him from his first bath. "He is one big link in the chain shackling you to me."

They'd made jokes about balls and chains every single step of the way since Barcelona.

"Isn't he beautiful?"

Victor looked up at her. "You're beautiful."

He kissed her tired cheek. "I love you."

"I love you, too."

Simon wiggled in his sleep.

"I think we need to let the masses in so you can get some rest."

Shannon nodded, and Victor left the room, only to return with a parade of their friends. The babies had been left at home with a nanny, since the hospital didn't allow infants other than those just born in the ward.

Simon was passed around and pictures were taken.

Avery was holding Simon and talking in a high-pitched voice. "You and Max are gonna cause lots of trouble, aren't you?"

Wade leaned in and whispered, "And look out for my daughter."

"Max is going to want to date your daughter," Liam said.

"Bite your tongue." Wade was serious.

They laughed.

"No, really . . . that's not funny."

"It's kinda funny," Trina said.

Lori rubbed her stomach. "You never did tell us why you decided on the name Simon."

Victor took Shannon's hand, and they both looked at each other and smiled.

"Because Garfunkel is a lousy first name."

Acknowledgments

The minute I type the words *The End* when finishing a manuscript, I have the pleasure of adding my thanks to the back pages of what will become a novel. With the fact that this is the thirtieth time I've had the pleasure of writing these acknowledgments, I realize they often sound like a repeat. However, thank-yous need to be given, and this is where I do it.

In each stage of the writing process, there are people who take center stage. In the case of this series, it starts with my agent, Jane Dystel. I say it in every book and mean it with all my heart. Thank you for being a cornerstone in my career, and even more for being my friend.

To Maria Gomez, my acquisitions editor at Montlake, and the entire Amazon Publishing team, thank you all so much for making me feel like a queen . . . tiara and all. Cheers to the next five million copies sold.

To Kelli Martin . . . lady, I've said it before and I'll say it again . . . I love you. Your years of working with me on developmental edits have made me a stronger writer. I appreciate all that you do!

Now back to Kayce and Libby. Celebrating my fiftieth birthday on the shores of Tulum started out as a party but ended up deeply rooted in the pages of this book. From salsa dancing, bathing in insect repellant, and drinking mezcal (I don't recommend, dear reader) to flesh-eating fish in the cenotes and bats in water-filled caves, I had the best birthday ever.

However, the absolutely most fantastic part of the entire trip was being there with the two of you. I love you both!

Oh, wait . . . the skinny-dipping in our private pool was kinda badass, too. Except when the staff arrived with a surprise birthday cake and champagne . . . but we'll leave that for another story.

Cheers,

Catherine

About the Author

New York Times, #1 *Wall Street Journal*, and *USA Today* bestselling author Catherine Bybee has written twenty-nine books that collectively have sold more than five million copies and been translated into more than eighteen languages. Raised in Washington State, Bybee moved to Southern California in the hope of becoming a movie star. After growing bored with waiting tables, she returned to school and became a registered nurse, spending most of her career in urban emergency rooms. She now writes full-time and has penned the Not Quite Series, the Weekday Brides Series, the Most Likely To Series, and the First Wives Series. For more information, visit www.catherinebybee.com.